J.B. WILLIAMS

Aarde

Part 1B

Fourth edition

ISBN: 979-8-9895133-5-2

Editing by Stephen Zimmer
Cover art by J.B. Williams

This book was professionally typeset on Reedsy.
Find out more at reedsy.com

Contents

Chapter 1

"Will you stay?"

Those words echo in the darkness. Nesschter's ears are in pain from the sharp ringing by the two gunshots. He gradually opens his eyes and sees he is still kneeling in front of the ditch, alive yet not well.

Gravel crunches beside him, his cuffs are removed, and the chains are thrown in the ditch. A few seconds later, Caro walks in front of Nesschter and holds out his hand.

"Get up. It's time to go," says Caro.

Nesschter hesitantly grabs Caro's hand and is pulled up. He rubs his wrists and looks at the two Avus who nearly killed him. They have holes in their heads, the parched dirt sucking their blood deep beneath the cracked surface.

"Help me dump the bodies so we can get out of here," says Caro.

Nesschter quietly grabs the arms and Caro grab the legs of the deceased Avus and throws them in the ditch. When they are done, Nesschter stares at Tia's corpse, unable to move or speak. He wants to apologize, but the words don't come out. Caro has to drag Nesschter to his vehicle, which is a blocky car with armor plating and the Division 4 logo.

"Snap out of it. I need to get you out of here, and you being a dope isn't helping," says Caro.

"Why are you doing this?" asks Nesschter.

"Balik paid me a pretty payment to make sure you're alive," says Caro.

Nesschter's gut twists into a knot. "Great... You do realize you're a dead bird walking, right?"

"For now. But once I'm off Aarde I'll be a live bird walking. I've already sold my stocks, emptied my accounts to hard cash, and signed my lease over to my ex. She's going to love the house until the bills come in."

Caro pops open the trunk.

"Get in," says Caro.

Nesschter stares at Caro, and the Avus nods to the trunk.

"Get in. I paid the guards off, but I don't want street cameras seeing you next to me," says Caro.

Nesschter reluctantly climbs in, finding his company being a long jacket, a brimmed hat, and a traditional Lupiank tunic, plus a traditional Avus thawb with a beaded belt rolled next to it. Then Caro shuts the trunk, and Nesschter is encased in darkness.

Chapter 2

Nesschter has been in the dark for a while. He hears the gravel road gradually changing to a paved road, and the speed slowing down as Caro reaches bumper to bumper traffic.

The hours' worth of constant stop and go make him queasy, which is made all the worse by thinking of Tia's corpse and wondering if Xajil will go after Ara. Or maybe even Don. Maybe both?

The vehicle reaches a steady speed and keeps going for a little while before it slows to a stop. Next, the trunk pops open and Nesschter is pulled out by a pair of Avus wearing armored vests.

He finds himself in what was once a beautiful building. Crumbling brick and splintering wood frame the space, lit by scattered lanterns. Empty display cases stand among the debris, while faded posters and chaotic graffiti cover the walls beneath a ceiling webbed with cracks and dangling cables.

There are two more Avus standing in front of Nesschter, armed with pistols and wearing vests. Nesschter shrugs off the Avus holding him and Caro walks in front of him.

"Relax, they're with me," says Caro. "I just need some help watching you while I drop off the car."

Nesschter looks past the Division 4 car and sees that it came through a makeshift garage door covering a hole in the wall. The door is being held up by a scrawny Avus that is shaking and muttering as his feet dig into the floor.

He looks further down in another direction and sees more Avus sitting on three ratty couches, eyes glazed, mouths open. They have ice packs taped to their heads, and on a table in the center of the setup are many N–Light pills and stacks of gift cards.

This setup is being watched by a muscular, gray Avus with black and white lines on his face, cybernetic arms, sunglasses, an armored vest, and a rifle.

"What's wrong with them?" asks Nesschter, nodding to the dazed Avus.

"N-Light newbies," says Caro. "Earlier they were bouncing around, reliving their memories, now they're burnt out."

Nesschter stares at the group, and Caro gives Nesschter his thawb and the Lupinak tunic.

"Put your tunic on and hold the thawb for me until I get back from HQ," says Caro.

"How long will you be gone?" asks Nesschter.

"Not long."

"Will you grab Ara? I think Xajil might go after her, too. I also need my watch and knife."

"Don't worry about the secretary. She'll be fine. Xajil doesn't suspect her. As for your stuff... I'll think about it."

Caro gets in the government vehicle and drives off. As soon as he leaves, the scrawny Avus releases the rope with a relieved sigh, and the garage door slams down with a floor shaking thud.

Without the sunlight pouring, the room becomes dim with lantern light flickering and shadows dancing on the broken walls. Nesschter looks at the group of Avus staring at him.

"So, you're Division 4," says one of the guards; an Avus with brown feathers, a light-gray tipped crest, white speckles on his face, and a white beak. He is wearing a light gray broken zipper hoodie and a dark gray shirt underneath

"Formerly. I was recently fired," says Nesschter.

The speckled Avus chuckles, puts his talons on Nesschter's shoulder, and leads him to a bathroom with a broken toilet, a shattered mirror, and a sink with brown goo dripping through its broken pipe.

"It's strange seeing a Lupe in Division 4. Gacaraen Lupes don't exactly get along with the GSAU," says the Avus.

Nesschter grunts.

"And I'll take that," says the Avus while taking Caro's thawb and putting it in a plastic bag. "And you get changed. Hot dogs are on the grill, and we got drinks in the cooler."

Nesschter sighs heavily, goes in the bathroom, and quickly changes. When he is out, he is wearing a green tunic with white Triskelions on the collar and cuffs, and a dark green belt with white Triskelions.

The smell of hot dogs fills his nose, but he isn't hungry. The speckled Avus waves him over, and he goes to an area with various chairs surrounding a huge grill placed under a hole in the roof. Some of the chairs are car seats, some are lawn chairs, others are office chairs.

Nesschter takes an office chair, and the Avus gives him a paper plate with four hot dogs on it. A white female Avus with dulled talons, golden bands around her hazel eyes, a green crest with gold tips, and long white feathers on her head and shoulders approaches the group. She is wearing a sleeveless shirt underneath an armored vest and carrying a shotgun. She sits on the lawn chair next to Nesschter and studies him when she gets her plate of hot dogs.

"What's your name, Lupe?" asks the female Avus.

"Nesschter. You?"

"Rara. That one over there is Gyrij."

The speckled Avus waves with his spatula, and Nessschter returns with a two-fingered wave. Then he looks around and sees a few more Avus, all armed with weapons, taking chairs, drinks, and hot dogs.

"Do all of you work for Balik?" asks Nesschter.

The Avus group laughs and Nesschter frowns.

"We don't work for Balik," says Rara. "We work with him. Our boss is Caro, and he doesn't work for Balik, either. He works with him. They have a partnership. And a good one, too. If it wasn't for Caro giving Balik a heads-up about the crackdowns, then *every* big N-Light dealer in this city would have been relocated and lots of money flushed down."

Gyrij reaches into a cooler and tosses Nesschter a can of soda, gives Rara a can, and sits next to her in a car seat.

"Speaking of relocation... You said you're Division 4," says Gyrij.

"Former," corrects Nesschter.

"Where are people relocated to?"

Nesschter hesitates. "Their graves… There's a mass grave outside of the city. A big ditch, miles long, filled with… bodies…"

Nesschter's voice drifts off as Rara hisses and gives Gyrij a packet of five N-Light pills from her pocket.

"I told you so," says Gyrij.

"How do they hide that?" asks Rara.

Nesschter shrugs. "A fence?"

The group mutters in their avian language and Nesschter looks around the area. It appears to have been an eatery at some point, but now it is mostly empty. The buffets have been gutted and the menus shattered. More ripped and faded posters cover the walls, the windows to the outside are boarded up, and the brick and tile are discolored and crumbling.

"What is this place?" asks Nesschter.

"We're in a museum's cafe," says Rara.

"What's a museum?"

"This place."

Nesschter frowns. "I know, but what was it for."

"Oh… I don't know… Does anybody know?"

Rara looks around, and some Avus shrug or mutter, and then the large Avus with cybernetic arms enters and grabs a handful of hot dogs from the grill.

"A museum was a building that allowed the people to see into the past," he says. "After the GSAU took control, Milo Gailo ordered all museums to be emptied and shut down, and the relics were destroyed. Then there were the libraries. Historical books and their copies were also hunted down and destroyed, and historians were… *persuaded* to alter information. Those that didn't go along with it were relocated."

The cyborg sits on the ground next to Nesschter and holds out his hand.

"By the way, the name is Varil Mevi," he says.

Nesschter shakes his hand. "Nesschter. Nice to meet you. And should I ask how you know what a museum is?"

"I was with the Preservation Force, which was designed to preserve the

GSAU's power by removing problematic elements within the AAHU ranks and within society, which also included Aarde's history. But now you know it as Division 4."

Nesschter looks down. His claw taps the soda can and his eyes dart right to left, as if reading passages from a book. The Avus look at him, and Varil raises a brow.

"Are you okay?" asks Varil.

"I was Division 4, but never heard of the Preservation Force," says Nesschter.

Varil does a double take. "How? That's basic Division 4 history."

"Xajil didn't include that part when he altered my memories."

The Avus stare at Nesschter, dumbfounded, and the former agent eats a hot dog, its skin black and crispy, and the inside lukewarm.

"Hold on, your memory got scrambled?" says Gyrij.

Nesschter nods. "Yeah. I was given N-Light by... a friend after we had an argument. I didn't believe her when she said my memory was altered. After I took N-Light, I realized what Xajil did to me."

Gyrij pulls out a phone. "I'll tell you what, give us her address and description, and I'll have some of my buddies bring her over for safekeeping."

"I would rather get her myself," says Nesschter.

"We can't do that. We have explicit orders to keep you here for the time being," says Varil.

"How long will that be?" asks Nesschter.

"Until Caro says we can let you go," says Varil.

Nesschter narrows his eyes and Rara pats his leg, making him flinch.

"It won't be too bad," says Rara. "My boyfriend will be by shortly with his friends and we'll have fun."

Then a bell rings five times, and Rara leaps up with a grin.

"Speaking of boyfriend!" says Rara.

Rara runs off. Nesschter, Varil and Gyrij follow her to the lobby where the customers lounge under new guards' supervision. The scrawny Avus has opened the garage door, allowing a white van to enter. The garage door slams shut, and the van's side door slides open. A vaguely familiar sunburned human with light brown hair emerges, making Nesschter's ears perk up.

"Baby!" cheers Rara.

"Hey, chica!" says Chester Hartvinn.

He grabs Rara's hips, pulls her in, and pecks her cheeks. She giggles and her long crest bobs and her tail feathers flex. And as this happens, other humans come out with coolers and weapons, and they all pause when they see Nesschter.

"Who's this?" asks Chester.

Nesschter keeps a cool expression, but he is secretly terrified of the group hearing his erratic heartbeats. He recognizes Chester by sight and scent, but he doesn't know if Chester recognizes him. Sure, he was fully masked when they had their last encounter, but still. What if the human recognizes his build? Or his voice? Or his smell?

"That is Nesschter. Caro is having us watch him for a little while," says Rara.

"Oh... Nice to meet you. Name's Chester." He shakes Nesschter's hand and sizes him up. "So, why are you hiding with Caro's crew?"

"Personal reasons."

"Right. Secrecy and stuff. Got it. Anyway, I brought stuff for fun." Chester goes to the van and pulls out... "BOARD GAMES!"

"Heck yeah!" says Gyrij.

Gyrij takes a couple of boxes of board games off Chester's hands, and he leads the group back to the dining area.

"We're going to have so much fun!" says Rara.

But Rara was wrong.

Nesschter did not have fun. In fact, he has realized just how much he hated board games. Each minute the group plays their games is a minute that Nesschter feels like his soul is dissolving. The boredom is unbearable, and the losing streak is as constant as the rising sun. And no game is truer of his hatred and misfortune than Monopoly. If Monopoly was a person, they would have been decked in the schnoz already.

"Looks like someone's going to jail!" says Rara.

Nesschter's eye twitches and his claws extend into his leg as he grips his shoe piece, which is on a "Go to Jail" slot. His hand trembles, his fur bristles with a growl rumbling, and the group stares at him with amusement or worry.

"Whoa, chill, big guy. It's just a game," says Chester.

A game where Nesschter has only one property and five dollars. But Chester is smart enough to not say that part out loud.

Then the bell rings, and Gyrij stands up.

"Let's see who that is," says Gyrij.

The group leaves, and when they enter the lobby, they see a low-riding red car with tinted windows and spinning rims with alternating lights of red, blue, and green in them. The rims slow to a stop, and Caro steps out of the driver's side, still in his uniform.

"Is my thawb clean?" says Caro.

"It's in a bag by the grill," says Gyrij.

"Good." Caro bangs on the roof. "Hey, don't be shy! Get out!"

The passenger door stays shut for a few more seconds, and then Don cautiously steps out but keeps his hand on the door. This brings Chester and the other humans to tilt their heads slightly or mutter words of confusion.

"Don?" says Nesschter. He glares at Caro. "You brought Don but not Ara?"

"Yes," says Caro.

"Nice to see you too, buddy," says Don.

"What about my watch and knife? Did you bring those or leave them behind?" asks Nesschter.

Caro pulls out a taped-up bag and tosses it to Nesschter.

"The cameras saw me taking those. Be grateful that I don't give a crap about any of this junk anymore, or else things would have been very different," says Caro.

Nesschter tears open the bag and finds his knife and pocket watch. The watch is still making its odd ticking, and the knife is just as sharp as last time. With those checked, Nesschter looks at Caro.

"Is Don on your payroll?" asks Nesschter.

"No, but when Xajil finds out that you aren't dead he'll will come after you, and I figured you could use a familiar face for protection," says Caro.

"Balik wants to kill Don, though."

"Just tell him he's your bodyguard."

"You're taking a gamble."

"Maybe, but I won't be on Aarde very long, so I don't care."

During this exchange, Chester approaches Don with heavy steps.

"George?" says Chester.

"Hey, Chess. Long time no see. How have you been?" says Don.

"What happened to you? You disappeared and Balik said you were a rat."

"Uh, yeah. Let's just call that water under the bridge."

"So, you... You son of a-"

Chester yanks out his pistol, but he is quickly disarmed and has a pistol barrel pressed against the side of his head while he is turned to a meat shield. The group jumps up with their weapons aimed at the pair, and Don tilts his weapon to the ceiling.

"I'm not here to fight. I'm only here because Nesschter needs a friend," says Don.

"All of you lower your weapons," says Caro irritably.

After some hesitation, the group lowers their weapons. Don nods and smiles at Nesschter, while easily keeping Chester in a choke hold.

"And you aren't happy to see me. That makes me a little bit upset," says Don. "Though, I admit, I'm not as much eye candy as Ara, so I would be upset too if I was in your position."

"Really?" sneers Nesschter.

"Hey, I'm just saying..."

"You're just saying you're going to let me go," says Chester.

"Sorry, I'm not too comfortable letting you go just yet... By the way, have you finally admitted to being Nesschter Norkit?" says Don.

"Yeah," says Nesschter.

Everyone in the group looks at Nesschter with various levels of shock, and Caro sighs heavily.

"Yes, he's a Norkit. Stop gawking. Nobody is allowed to hurt Don. He's Nesschter's bodyguard. And Don, let go of Chester. There. Done. I don't have time for this garbage," says Caro.

Don looks at the guards, who are keeping their weapons down, and he aims his pistol straight up so they can see him turning on the safety. Then he releases Chester and pats him on the shoulder. Caro shakes his head and walks towards the eatery, and the group follows him.

"Sorry about that, man," says Don while giving him another sympathetic pat on the shoulder.

"Your betrayal hurt more than this," says Chester.

"I know I'm sorry, but..." They enter the room, and Don's eyes snap to the board game on the floor. "Is that Monopoly?"

"Yeah," says Gyrij.

"Can I join?"

"No, we're in the middle of the game," says Chester.

"He can take my place," says Nesschter.

"Cool!" Don sits down and rubs his hands together with a grin. "Which piece is you?"

"The shoe."

Don's smile drops. "Aw man. I don't want to be the shoe. Can I be the battleship?"

"No. I'm the battleship," says Chester.

"Can we trade?" asks Don.

"I'm not trading the battleship for the shoe!"

"I'm the thimble. Want to be the thimble?" asks Rara.

"Babe, don't. He's a Division 4 rat."

"Water under the bridge." Don picks up the shoe and gives it to Rara, and she gives him the thimble. He puts it on his pinkie with a large grin. "Yeah. Thimble~"

Chester glares at Rara. And Nesschter rubs the dove on his watch with his thumb as he watches Caro grab his bag from Gyrij and go to the bathroom. He comes out a few minutes later wearing the thawb, and Nesschter approaches him.

"So now that you got your end taken care of, me and Don will leave and grab Ara. Thank you for your help, but now it is time for us to go," says Nesschter.

"You're not going anywhere," says Caro.

Nesschter's fur bristles. "I can't stay here. I need to get Ara before Xajil gets her."

"She's fine," stresses Caro. "But *you* need to stay here until Balik is done doing what he's going to do. When he's done, he'll get you. That was our agreement. He paid. Now I'm paying Gyrij and Varil to keep you safe until Balik gets you. Now sit down and eat a hot dog!"

"And what's Balik doing?"

Caro sighs irritably, looks at the time on his phone, then looks at Nesschter.

"Long story short, Balik is on the war path because of his house getting firebombed. I don't know the details, but rumor is that he razed Parudasi Fusas and had hundreds of Talos Yeshniv's men executed."

Nesschter's ears droop, and Caro nodded.

"Yeah, he's gone off the deep end. Now I don't know what he's planning, but if I was a betting bird, I'd say he's going to be gunning for Xajil Ojin next," says Caro.

"Xajil won't be an easy target. But we still need to get Ara out of Shio. When Xajil finds out I'm alive, he'll go to her for answers, and he *will* hurt her," says Nesschter.

Caro's crest twitches and Gyrij approaches the three.

"I already offered to send someone to get her, but he wants to go in person," says Gyrij.

"Out of the question. Balik wants Nesschter here until he gets him personally" says Caro.

"How about I go?" suggests Don, still sitting on the floor.

"I will send someone over to grab her," says Caro. "You need to stay here and protect Nesschter. Plus, Nesschter is right. With him being alive, Xajil will look for answers, and you'll be the first person he talks to."

Caro pulls out a phone and slips a counterfeit ID. With the fake ID in, the phone lights up and he dials a number. After a few rings, someone answers, and the two exchange words via clicks, chirps, whistles and squawks. After a minute or two of this, Caro hangs up and looks at Nesschter.

"I'm having some associates pick up Ara to bring her over here. Happy now?" says Caro.

"I have to go with them," says Nesschter.

"Tough shit. You're staying here. Gyrij, Varil, make sure he and Don don't go anywhere."

"And where will you go?" asks Don.

"Off the planet. Maybe I'll go to Oros? Or out in the Furies System. Aarden currency is crap, so I'll be working wherever I land." Caro puts his hands on both of their shoulders. "Good luck. Both of you. And stay put!"

Nesschter exhales and flexes his claws. "Fine... But I want updates on Ara."

Caro looks at Gyrij. "You take care of that. I sent Haso and his guys to get her. I have a ship to catch."

Gyrij gives a thumbs up. "Got it."

"I'll see you guys... whenever."

And with that, Caro leaves, and Nesschter flops in his seat. He hears Caro drive away, and Varil puts more hot dogs on the grill. Rara gives Nesschter another plate of hot dogs and a can of soda. He quietly thanks her and pulls out his pocket watch, closes his eyes, and listens to its ticking.

Ti-Tick. Ti-Tock.

Ti-Tick. Ti-Tock.

Ti-Tick. Ti-Tock.

Chapter 3

Tick. Tick.

Ring. Ring.

Tick. Tick.

Ring. Ring.

Tick. Tick.

Ring. Ring.

Balik sluggishly puts his phone to his ear, his glazed and droopy eyes staring ahead as he holds his open thermos tightly.

"Hello?" says Balik.

"*It's your buddy,*" says Caro. "*I got it done. A few of my friends are helping, but as a word of caution, that guy I told you about is over there.*"

Balik's gaze hardens. "Why?"

"*Your brother is close to him. And he needs a familiar face to balance him out. I'm not saying you should spare the guy, but if you want to take him out, perhaps you should make it look like an accident.*"

Balik sips from his thermos. "Uh huh..."

"*Also, Ara is in Shio.*"

"I don't care."

"*I'm sending some guys to get her. Nesschter wouldn't stop badgering me about her. So, when you're done doing what you're doing, you might see her, too.*"

"Cool."

"*... Are you okay? You sound off.*"

Balik hangs up, takes out the battery, and chucks it behind his shoulder. Then he walks forward in a dazed state and looks at the crates of weapons, ammo, explosives, body armor, and a few spinal shield generators. Barzee worked very fast for their delivery, and Balik is pleased about it, but that is not what is bothering him.

He looks at the tunnel that has been dug beneath his shack. They have been working on it for a while. Balik had hoped to have more time to plan and execute his strategy to perfection, and, in turn, redeem his family name. However, after the devastation from Xajil and Talos, there is no longer any waiting. Xajil must be dealt with, and Shio must burn. There is no time left for the Norkit Family, and they need one last hurrah to go down in history to make up for their failures; and he will be the one to see it done.

A string of lights and braces travel all the way down the tunnel, and Balik can see Jarvis, Khal, and some guards approaching him in the distance. Balik sips from his thermos and strolls forward.

"The digger hit an interesting spot," says Khal.

"Really?" says Balik knowingly.

"It's another tunnel system. This one is not a mine, though. This one is well built, but damaged. It appears to be a bunker network the three of us are familiar with."

"Fire damage?".

"Fire damage, shrapnel, bullets. We've even discovered a lot of burnt bodies," says Khal.

Balik's lips twitch and his hands grip the thermos tight as he closes it.

"Show me," orders Balik.

The guards, Khal, and Jarvis lead Balik down the tunnel, which has more guards and workers moving the stashes of armaments and clearing out the broken rock. When they reach the area in question, Balik sees their large drill machine is sitting idle in the middle of a massive hallway with concrete walls, dead lights, and exposed pipes and wires.

Burn marks cover the concrete and metal doors, and bullet holes and shrapnel scratches pocket the area. He hears chatter down the hall and sees lights moving around. Some go around corners, others go through doors, and some shrink as they continue going forward.

Balik looks at the floor and sees bodies have been placed by the wall. All of them are shriveled with clothes and equipment melted to them, and decades of decay have left their bones cracked and splintered. Most are Lupinak, but there are quite a few humans and Avus skeletons mixed in the lineup. And some of the human skeletal structures show genetic altering, and others have burnt robotic attachments.

Balik's heart races as he looks at the bodies. He can hear their screams and feel the heat blistering his skin. Gunshots. Roaring fire. Crackling electricity. Ticking. All of it is colliding and rolling over each other like filthy water in a storm surge.

Balik takes a sip from his thermos and holds out his hand to Jarvis. Jarvis gives him a flashlight, and he and the group walks down the hallway. As they walk, Balik moves the light in a slow circular pattern, revealing more scorched concrete, warped metal, and broken pipes. The walls have remnants of blue bands, and on the wall is a large symbol with pieces burnt off or discolored. It is a sun behind a tree in full bloom.

"Does this look familiar, Jarvis?" asks Balik.

Jarvis nods and walks ahead to a room with its door on the floor. The hinges have been destroyed, and the wall has crumbled due to a powerful explosion. The rubble was blown far into the room, and Balik follows Jarvis inside while Khal remains outside.

There, they find a destroyed alter and pews torn up from bullets and fire. There is also a choir booth, which has been reduced to a crater and a ring of burnt and splintered wood. Jarvis stares at that spot intently.

Balik shines his light on it, and Jarvis remains motionless, save for a twitch on his finger.

"Are you okay?" asks Balik.

Jarvis leaves, and Balik follows him out, and they face each other while other workers throw down glow sticks or set up lamps.

Did you know the digging path would bring us here? signs Jarvis.

Yes and no. I had a hunch this place was nearby, but I didn't think it was this close to my shack. But this will speed up our schedule, signs Balik.

Jarvis stares at Balik, and a group of Revivalist soldiers approach them.

"Colonel Norkit, sir, the group was wondering... What is this place?" says the lead soldier.

Balik looks at the group, and Jarvis takes a spot next to Khal. Balik sips from his thermos before focusing on the group of young soldiers.

"I'm not surprised you don't recognize this," says Balik, voice hollow. "Most of you missed the war—whatever name they're calling it these days." He gestures at the scorched walls. "These are the Vagsten Tunnels. Gacerae's final stronghold. A labyrinth that once sheltered our people from orbital strikes and moved our troops and supplies unseen beneath enemy lines."

Balik points at one of the faded lines on the wall.

"There were twelve color-coded sections," continues Balik, his voice flat. "We're in Blue. Nesschter's zone. I commanded Red, beneath Vagsten itself." His fingers tighten around the thermos. "Federation's Tunnel Dragons came with flamethrowers. AAHU troops followed. Their orders were simple: leave no survivors."

The soldiers shifted uncomfortably, Jarvis squeezed his hands together, and Balik drank the last of the chicken soup in his thermos.

"The Red Zone was the last to fall, despite our best efforts to defend it..." says Balik. "I barely escaped with a few others, and when that happened... Vagsten fell... When I failed, they took Vagsten and destroyed it."

Khal and Jarvis lowered their heads, and others tried to keep their eyes on Balik, who was barely lit by the flashlight and glow sticks behind him. His eyes are narrowed, and his hands clutch his thermos tight as his pocket watch ticks loudly in the tomb.

"Our moment is coming," says Balik. "And I promise you, when we strike, the Great Society will remember Vagsten."

Chapter 4

Ara's apartment door clicks shut as she enters, the windows automatically tinting and the TV's volume increasing slightly so she hears the unity message being broadcasted. She sits on her bed, Division 4 secretary uniform rumpled, surrounded scattered empty bottles and spilled antidepressants. She kicks off her shoes, peels away her socks, and runs her fingers through her white mane, her green eyes fix vacantly on the floor.

She was expecting to see Nesschter today but didn't. In fact, all day she has been getting weird looks and hearing gossiping whispers. Words were barely said to her all day. She ate alone at lunch, and guards were always watching her, either in person or from the cameras that trailed her movement. She was even followed home by a camera drone.

Now, she feels like the TV is watching her. She started having that feeling ever since Nesschter looked at the TV when she gave him the N-Light, but today the feeling is front and center, clawing at her brain.

Ara lifts her eyes to stare at the TV. Her hands are held tight, and her throat bobs as she swallows a hard lump. She pushes herself off the bed and approaches the TV. It is playing the propaganda loop of a growing city with crystal-like skyscrapers and jagged structures and winding roads.

She stares at the circle in the center of the TV's rim and puts her hand over it. The footage immediately switches to a black screen with white letters in multiple languages, all saying: *'Resident 0132-525-8872-269, Ara Lyra Giovine-Parsen, Remove Camera Block!'*

10

9

8

7

Ara removes her hand and walks backwards, her eyes wide and wet. She falls on her bed, short of breath as tears roll down her cheeks.

She looks at the picture of her and Aiden, slowly grabs it and holds it on her lap as she rubs the frame. Her thumb brushes their faces, and her fingers feel the grooves on the frame's side. The frame is thicker than normal, and a little push on the top pops out an N-Light pill from the bottom.

It falls on her lap, but she doesn't grab it. Instead, her tears patter on the picture frame, as she struggles to remember something about the picture.

All she remembers is blobs, scattered voices, and flickers of joy and sadness. She needs to remember more, but it hurts her brain trying to bring clarity. And now that Nesschter is missing, she is afraid that she lost another light.

Ara's chest and throat tighten thinking about losing another person she loved, and she looks at the TV again. She wants to take N-Light, but the TV has already seen her take it multiple times throughout her stay, and now multiple steps are marching down the hallway. She knows they're coming for her.

The bottom of her door slides open and a small circular vacuum machine slips in and starts vacuuming.

The steps stop outside her door.

Ara holds the picture close to her. The door's magnet locks disengage, and her ears droop when six Avus wearing bullet proof vests enter, armed with electric batons and shotguns slung on their shoulders. Two stay by the door, three remain near the TV, and the lead approaches Ara.

"Ms. Giovine-Parsen?" says the Avus.

Ara nods, and he holds up a badge.

"I am Kwari, officer of the Office of Civilian Observation. We have some questions we need to ask you. Please stand up," says the Avus.

Ara stands up on shaky legs, leading to the N-Light pill falling to the floor. One of the Avus' crest's twitches, and Kwari types something down on a small handheld device. The vacuum robot leaves the apartment.

"Put the picture down and approach slowly. No sudden movements," orders Kwari.

Ara gently sets the picture down and walks towards the group, wringing her hands.

"What kind of questions do you have for me? I can answer them as best as I can, but I probably won't have good answers," says Ara.

She finishes with a nervous smile, but none of the Avus show any signs of sympathy.

"Do you know the whereabouts of Agent Holden Hosenheim?" says the lead Avus.

Ara's eyes flick between the group, among which the three in the back have inched closer.

"I... I... No. Not at all!" says Ara. "We had an argument a day or two ago and I kicked him out of my apartment. I haven't seen him since!"

"We need to find him, and any information you can give us will be great," says the lead Avus.

"What did he do?"

"He assaulted Director Xajil Ojin and was seen on camera murdering four Division 4 agents."

Ara shakes her head. "That doesn't sound right. He loves his job. This must be a sick joke! He wouldn't do that! Let me see those badges!"

The group of Avus hold up their badges, and Ara squints and rubs her chin with her claws extended as she studies the leader's badge.

"Ma'am, retract your claws," says Kwari.

"No. You have to be fake! Who are you really working for?" says Ara.

Kwari draws his electric baton, which prompts the others to do the same. Ara steps back, her ears splayed back and her tail twitching.

"We are Observers under the direct orders of Xajil Ojin to either speak with or apprehend you. Now tell us where Agent Hosenheim is," says Kwari, tapping his baton's trigger to release an arcing display of sparks.

"I already told you, I don't know. Now, get out of my apartment," says Ara heavily.

Kwari hisses. "Where is Agent Hosenheim, you whoring Lupe!"

"Not here! Get out of my apartment!" shouts Ara.

Kwari jabs Ara in the side with the baton. She yelps and stumbles back. Then she bares her teeth with a loud growl and points her claw at the door.

"Get out!" yells Ara.

Kwari swings, and Ara blocks the baton with her arm and punches him in the beak. He staggers back, squawking and clutching his cracked beak.

The other three Avus rush forward and assault her with a barrage of baton strikes that leaves her heart racing, muscles tight, and body burning from the constant surges of electric currents. Ara swipes at the Avus assaulting her and tries biting, but she is quickly overpowered and shoved to the floor.

Her cheek is rubbed again the carpet, white fur on light gray. Kwari keeps her pinned as he jabs his electric baton into her neck while other agents zap her thigh and lower back. Each jolt burns all the way through her nerves to her teeth, making her limbs spasm and her nails scrape the carpet. Sweat glues her uniform to her body, and her breaths are heavy and strained, quivering and whimpering.

"Where's Holden Hosenheim? Where are you hiding him, comforter slut?" sneers Kwari.

"I don't know where he is," gasps Ara. Her breath breaks in a wet cough, spit and snot pooling beneath her. The next baton lights her up and she screams, limbs flailing helplessly as electric fire surges through her veins.

"Your file says you two are very close," snarls Kwari, applying another shock under her jawline so her teeth crash together and her vision briefly fuzzes out. "Tell us where your buddy is!"

"I don't know," pants Ara hoarsely.

"Liar!"

"I'm not lying!" sobs Ara, hands scrabbling at the carpet as they drag her upright by the mane, setting her on her knees. The pain radiates out from her neck, down through her arms, sharp, electric pain seeping into her muscles, melting her thoughts into a blurry mess of confusion.

Kwari jabs his baton Ara's her ribs, making her scream again. The air stinks of ozone and burnt fabric and flesh, and the Observers hold her mane to keep her from doubling over.

"Where is Agent Hosenheim? The file said you two were buddies, you two were good friends. The file saidyou are his childhood sweetheart! So tell us, secretary whore!" shouts Kwari.

Ara grits her teeth, and her reward is another crackle between her thighs, a shock punching up into her gut, making her clench and double over, screaming in agony.

"Search this place! We'll make her cooperate, one way or the other," says Kwari.

The Observers rip open drawers, pop open bottles, and tear apart clothing and other objects for hasty inspections before being tossed away.

One of the Observers plucks Ara's picture frame off the bed, and another rips open her nightstand, upending pill containers so the capsules scatter like beads across the mattress. They snatch one of the white-and-green pills, roll it between hard fingers, and break its coating, revealing the red gel interior.

The Observer sneers and smears the red gel in Ara's mane."Thought she was cute hiding her N-Light."

Kwari grabs the frame and thumbs the release, popping out the hidden N-Light. "Xajil said she was a junkie. Funny how Holden went after two junkies. Must have a thing for damaged goods."

Ara can barely breathe, her vision swimming, fur sticking with sweat. An ice-cold shiver runs up her spine as one of the agents dips his baton beneath her skirt and rubs the inside of her thigh with its two-pronged tip while another holds her up by her throat, his talons pressing against her flesh, waiting to puncture at a moment's notice.

"Where else are you hiding N-Light?" sneers the Observer, his crest bobbing.

His talons tighten on her throat, forcing her chin up as another Observer rips her skirt down the side, baring her white furred thighs and hips, matted with sweat.

Ara watches helplessly, heart racing and face wet with tears as the disguised N-Light pills are crushed under their boots, grinding the gel and powdered coating into the gray carpet, leaving dots that look like fresh blood on the fabric. Each crush makes Ara twitch and whimper, her hear cracking more and more as each path to faint memories is destroyed in front of her.

"You're in a lotta trouble, Lupe. Make it easy on you. Drugs and boyfriend. Go! Speak!" barks Kwari, his broken beak raking the edge of her cheek, hot breath prickling her fur while his baton tip nudges between her legs again and lingers, savoring the tremor in her muscles.

"Fuck you," says Ara, her voice airy and red hot and wet eyes staring ahead.

"Alright then. Search her," orders Kwari.

The Observers swarm Ara. Her muscles twitch helplessly as their taloned hands search everywhere, from under her arms, behind her knees, even between her toes and fingers. They rip the remnants of her skirt away, tug her jacket down to her elbows and tear her blouse open, sending the buttons scattering, exposing her undergarments.

Ara screams and curses and thrashes, but her cries are mocked and her attempts at escape are met with zaps that leave her howling in agony, and her fur burning and muscles aching.

One Observer presses behind her, lifting her tail and raking through her white fur. When she twists, a pair of Observers hold her arms away while another cuts her bra off, exposing her chest in full. Attempts to cover herself are futile and met with laughter and the Avus squawking and chirping in their avian language.

Ara trembles with each ragged breath, tears streaking down her face and her eyes darting around for any way to escape while one of the Observers searches her bra and others search her jacket and torn blouse

Talons pry her mouth open and other hands squeeze and prod every part of her body, searching for hidden N-Light.

Ara wails as they violate her, her body jerking with each new intrusion. Her teeth are tapped and her tongue is pulled up, and her hair is roughly tugged as talons rake her scalp.

"No fake teeth and nothing under the tongue," says one Observer.

"Nothing in her hair or tail," says another Observer.

"So, she isn't hiding N-Light in or on her body, but we know she's hiding the traitor. Alright, *Ms. Ara*, tell us where Holden is, or the inspection will continue," says Kwari.

Ara coughs. "I don't know where he is."

The air smells electric, full of ozone, burnt fur, and sweat. Ara's head swims, muscles spasming beneath the Avus talons, every nerve sparking as one of the Avus keeps the baton pressed just below her ribs, the threat of another jolt making her entire body tremble. No escape, not even enough air in her lungs to cry out again. Their talons dig into her fur, her blouse hanging uselessly and her exposed body being catalogued by the Observers' eyes, hungry, cold, and filled with lust.

Ara's neck is squeezed again, talons barely shy of drawing blood, the pressure making her vision go foggy.

"Talk," order Kwari.

"I don't... I don't know..." pants Ara hoarsely.

She looks past Kwari, at the TV. It is mocking her with the looping unity video, the city's crystalline towers and cheerful people.

Kwari grabs Ara's hair and tugs her head, so they are eye to eye.

"I dare you to lie to me again. Where is Holden Hosenheim?" says Kwari darkly, his crest flicking.

Ara gasps, her heart rattling in her ribs, tears, sweat, and drool dripping from her. She swallows, and with another deep breath, her gaze hardens as she looks at Kwari in the eyes, her battered body reflecting back at her.

"Holden... Is gone... I killed him," says Ara. She smiles, her fangs gleaming in the light and her body trembling at the sight of batons sparking. "And when Nesschter comes for me, he's going to kill all of you."

Kwari leans closer, his broken beak nearly brushing her snout. The two continue staring. Ara's chest is heaving with her heavy breaths, but her pained and defiant smile holds firm. Kwari's crest twitches and he tilts his head side to side. Then he snarls, grabs Ara by her throat and slams her back against the floor, leaving her ears ringing and pushing whimpers from her throat as he leans down, taking up her entire vision.

"Liar," hisses Kwari.

* * *

Across the street from Unity Rise, four Avus huddle in a taxi marked with a "Closed" sign, their bodies stiff. They watch Ara being hauled out of the building, a black bag obscuring her face, her arms bound behind her back, her body limp, and wearing only a large shirt. The large shirt hangs loose and doesn't cover her lower body, revealing the burns and scratches on her matted white fur, with the most consolidated on her flanks and inner thighs. Her feet drag across the pavement, and her exposed fur is wet and unkempt as if she just got out of a shower.

The small crowd outside is forcefully pushed aside by the Observers. They throw Ara into the back of an armored jeep, and the officers excitedly crowd in after Ara. Their van drives off, and the four Avus follow it with their eyes until it is out of sight.

"Well shit," says the driver.

"That sucks," says the front passenger.

"So, who's going to tell Caro about this?" says the first back passenger.

"Caro is going on vacation. We need to tell Gyrij," says the second back passenger.

"How about this… We call after we get lunch," says the driver.

The Avus nod and murmur in agreement.

"Good idea. There's a fast-food joint nearby that has a promo meal deal for that movie. We can get one of those large cups with cool pictures on it!"

"Good call!"

And so they speed off in the opposite direction of the Observers, paying no second thought to Ara's fate.

* * *

"Now boarding Flight A-61. Now boarding Flight A-61," says an announcer over the intercom of the Shio Launch Port.

The launch port is crowded and bustling with activity as various alien species move their way through the crowd, all clamoring in their native tongues while the message repeats in different languages. A tinted window gives the travelers a view of large aircraft parked by boarding tunnels.

While travelers wait for their gate, they can enjoy a meal, gift shops, internet cafes, gyms, or lounges, all of which are advertised with neon lights, moving advertisements, and seductive poses of various couples.

In Caro Naji's case, he already spent his time eating at the Klumsy K's diner and has all his possessions in duffel bags. The Shio Launch Port is the only place in the Connected City where hard cash can be used. This made it easy for Caro Naji to bribe the right people with a mix of cash and N-Light to allow him through the gates without scanning.

Now, with his bags full, his appetite quenched, and his gate called, Caro weaves his way through the crowd. When he reaches his gate, marked with a holographic projection, he sets down his bags and pulls out his ticket.

But as soon as his hands extend to the stewardess, a sharp, electric pain stabs his neck and surges through his body. Caro crumbles to the floor and gasps for air while the crowd yells in fright and retreats.

A pair of Avus Observers quickly cuff him, hoist him to his knees, and put a muzzle on his beak. Then they put a black bag over his head and drag him off, while ordering the crowd to remain back.

When the black bag is removed several minutes later, Caro finds himself in a dim, concrete room with a camera and microphone. He is cuffed to a chair that is bolted to the floor, and standing across from him, behind a table with a folder on it, is Xajil and Darius.

Shit, thinks Caro.

One of the Observers removes the muzzle from Caro's beak and steps aside, and Xajil steps in front of Caro while Darius goes to the side, barely in the prisoner's peripheral vision.

"Where is he?" asks Xajil.

"Who?" asks Caro.

The Observer slams his baton against Caro's hand. Bones snap and Caro howls. Xajil's expression remains neutral, and the Observer moves to the other side while Darius remains silent, stepping further into the darkness.

"Where is he?" repeats Xajil.

"Who's 'he'?" snarls Caro. "I can't tell you if I don't know who 'he' is."

The Observer slams the baton on Caro's other hand, snapping the bone to pieces, with one of his fingers going crooked. Caro howls again and curses, as he stomps the floor and shakes his head.

"Fuck! FFF-uuuck!" Caro seethes and glares at Observer, his bloodshot eyes shining in the light from the tears. "Damn you, you sick fuck!"

Caro glares at Xajil, while his blood dribbles to the floor.

"And damn you below Hell! You twisted fuck! Fucking devil!"

Darius looks at Xajil, and Xajil takes a deep breath and puts his talons on Caro's shoulders.

"Where is he?" says Xajil.

"I don't know who you're talking about!" yells Caro.

The Observer aims his baton at Caro's head, but Xajil holds his hand up, freezing the Observer. Then Xajil takes a deep, long inhale, and exhales slowly as his talons sink into Caro's shoulder, ripping flesh and cracking bone. Caro seethes and twitches violently in his seat as blood seeps down his torso and drips off Xajil's talons.

"Bring them in," says Xajil.

The Observer leaves, and when they return a minute later, they are wheeling in a cart with a small case on it. They open it, and Darius picks up a bag of N-Light pills. Caro's eyes widen, but they quickly shut with him wincing when Xajil digs further in his shoulders.

"I know you were paid in N-Light. The GSAU Banking Services flagged your withdrawal, and the Society Mortgage Company alerted us of your title transfer. And I know you murdered the two Agents that were scheduled to relocate Holden Hosenheim. And now I know you partnered with Balik and told the Revivalists about the raids in Shio. I know Holden is still alive, and I will find him, but it will be easier for all of us if you help me fix this mess," says Xajil.

Caro snickers and shakes his head. "You're just going to relocate me anyway. But... I'll bite. Nesschter Norkit is at your mom's place. I saw him go through the back door."

Xajil tenses and his breathing trembles. His talons sink deeper into Caro's shoulder before abruptly yanking them out. His shaky breathing has a low hiss to it as he grabs Caro's face, smearing his blood on his feathers.

"Let me fix this, Caro. For old time's sake," says Xajil.

Caro laughs painfully, his body trembling as blood pours down his shoulder. "Fix it? Bitch, you're one of the guys that broke everything! Aarde is hell because of you and Gailo and the Asvens and a million other pricks who duped retards like me to go along with your plans!"

Xajil's muscles lock, his breathing getting louder and his crest twitching.

"Should I hit him?" asks the Observer.

"No," says Xajil flatly.

"If you hated the GSAU so much, why wear our uniform?" asks Darius.

"I liked the money, and before you get snarky, I liked the extra money Balik gave me to peddle his drugs. And it was worth it to break the GSAU's experiment! Worth it break. Your. Shit!" says Caro.

Xajil rips his talons away from Caro's face, tearing his cheeks. Caro curses up a storm, banging his feet and broken hands as blood pours from the flaps on his face. Darius swallows and flinches when Xajil yanks the bag of N-Light from him, and he stifles a yelp when Xajil grabs his uniform tie, tugging him hard enough for him to lose his footing.

"We're going to have a long night of sifting through the cameras. Have finest coffee and creamer available," says Xajil.

"Of course," stammers Darius.

Xajil releases him and removes the contents from the folder on the table, not even glancing at Caro as the injured Avus moans and makes garbed curse.

"And put the Observers on alert. They are to move out as soon as we find Agent 505," continues Xajil, now makung a funnel with the folder.

"What about him? And what about Ara Giovine-Parsen?" asks Darius.

Xajil looks at Caro. The injured Avus is trembling, his face and chest drenched in blood, but Caro hand trembles as he raises his middle finger and his shredded face manages a sneer.

"Keep Ara in the cell overnight. As for Caro? He's too broken to fix." Xajil looks at the Observer. "Hold his beak open."

The Observer forces Caro's beak open, ripping more fragile flesh, and Caro thrashes weakly in his seat, cursing and sputtering blood. Xajil calmly approaches Caro and shoves the rolled folder down Caro's throat and pours all the N-Light pills down the tube.

Caro's screams and gags are distorted, and he violently thrashes in his chair, shaking the chains and spraying blood from his shredded cheeks while his eyes dilate. He coughs and sputters, the fingers that aren't broken dig into the chair arms, and soon pink-tinted foam and blood bubbles past the tube and cheek flaps. His eyes become blood red with sweat soaking his body. Then he stops moving, and blood oozes out of his ears and eyes and trickles out of his mouth.

The Observer steps away and Xajil pulls out the tube, straightens the folder out, and returns the contents to it, uncaring of the blood seeping into the parchment. After that, he puts the folder under his arm and looks at Darius.

"You're supposed to be getting coffee ready," says Xajil.

Chapter 5

Nesschter's cheek rests on his fist, and his droopy, dim eyes are on Don, Rara, Chester, and Gyrij playing Monopoly. On his lap is his other hand, holding his pocket watch with the case open and the watch ticking.

While watching the game, he keeps his ears perked for any signs of vehicles approaching, or even waiting for a phone call or text message regarding Ara. But the long wait has left him wound tight, and the ticking minutes only make the tension worse.

The group playing Monopoly are in their own world, ignorant of the smell of mold, hotdogs, and sweat. Oblivious to the putrid water dripping from rusted pipes and the skittering of little bugs. Parts of the museum have also shifted, leading to a random pop or creak here and there. Guards also walk around, chatting lightly, and mules deliver gift cards and pick up the customers, which are black-bagged and hauled away in vans.

Nesschter looks at his watch and sees six hours have already passed. His fingers tighten on his watch, and he rakes his claws through his short, black mane. He breathes heavily through his nose and glances at Gyrij. And, like a magic trick, his phone rings.

Gyrij takes out his phone, and after seeing who it is, he excuses himself and answers. A combination of chirps, squawks, and hisses and clicks follows soon after, and his agitation becomes clearer by the second.

This brings Rara, Chester, and Don to look at Gyrij, but Nesschter keeps his eyes on the decaying wall in front of him. He has a feeling he knows what happened, so he is trying to keep himself calm at this point. A minute later, Gyrij returns and paces in circles a few times before looking at Nesschter.

"They already took her," says Gyrij.

"When?" asks Nesschter.

"They don't know. But when they got to her apartment they saw the bar on her door."

Nesschter takes heavy, deliberate steps to Gyrij. "We were waiting for six hours. What were they doing?"

"That's what I asked, and they said errands."

"What kind of errands?"

"Grocery shopping, and they probably got high."

"Great! I should have gone to get her myself! But because you sent a bunch of idiots, Xajil has Ara!"

Don approaches Nesschter with his hand extended to him. "Hey, relax. We know Xajil has her, so we already have a lead, and we can work from there."

"That's the problem!" snaps Nesschter. "Xajil has her, and that means he will relocate her!"

"He's not going to relocate her. Maybe it's just an eviction?"

"She has N-Light!"

Don stiffens. "Oh..."

"Yeah. Oh," snarls Nesschter. "Xajil has Ara. She has N-Light. Xajil will put a bullet in her head because of it. I have to save her before that happens."

"Not going to happen. Caro ordered us to keep you here until Balik was finished with his project," says Gyrij.

"Caro is retired," says Nesschter.

"Doesn't matter. It was his last order."

"You're going to have to break it."

"I'm not breaking any orders for you."

"Then you're getting punched in the face."

"Is that a threat?"

"It is. Now get out of my way."

"No."

"Move."

"No."

"***Move!***"

Suddenly, Varil grabs Nesschter, turns him around, and there is a moment of confusion and pain caused by a robotic fist to the face. It all ends with Nesschter and Don locked in a room with u-locks around their necks and their hands cuffed, trapping them against poles. Both are bruised, bloodied, and dirtied, and Gyrij, Varil, Chester, and Rara are standing in front of them.

"I don't know why this is hard for you to grasp, but we're getting paid to keep you here until Balik picks you up, so we're going to keep you here," says Gyrij.

Nesschter growls and Gryij narrows his eyes.

"Don't act like that. You brought this upon yourself," says Gyrij.

"Can we rough up Don a bit more?" asks Chester.

"You hit me enough," says Don.

"I want to hit you again," says Chester.

"Leave him for Balik," says Gyrij. "We need to get some shopping done. We still have time before the store closes and there's a special on milk and eggs."

"Supermarket is going to be crowded," says Chester.

"Well, it's the only way we can get milk and eggs for less than two hundred gailos, so we need to hurry." Gyrij points at Nesschter and Don. "You two stay put. We'll bring you some snacks and drinks later."

"You can't just leave us trapped like this. What if we need to use the bathroom?" asks Don.

Varil puts a bucket in between them and then the group leaves, locking the door behind them. Their footsteps fade, and Don sighs heavily and bangs his head against the pole.

"This is getting old," says Nesschter.

"What is?" asks Don.

"Getting captured. Three times... Three times! First Balik, then Xajil, and now Gyrij!"

"Well, my suggestion is to stop getting involved in situations where you are easily mobbed and captured. Especially when I'm next to you. But it seems to me you like the whole bondage thing."

"What are you talking about?"

"I'm just saying you got a little excited about the idea of tying up Ara, and you have a habit of putting yourself in situations that leads to you getting tied up in some capacity."

"Xajil stabbed my hand after he captured me! Why the hell would I like anything that makes that possible!?" says Nesschter.

"You tell me. You're the one with the bindage thing, and you seem to be gravitated towards women that'll hurt you. Like Ara, who bit you, and those hot guards Chairman Asven has. Especially that Aki chick. That's a looker. And you were dumb enough to let her go?"

"I didn't-"

"Don't play dumb with me. I know what tension between exes look like, and those three ladies... Man, you were dumb."

Nesschter huffs irritably. "I didn't dump Aki. She dumped me. Just like Mi and Sakura did. *After* they asked *me* out."

"That's completely backwards."

"Shut up."

"But I think I know what your problem is. You got dumped because you won't let anybody in, and you're all moody because you're snuffing out your inner light and afraid to get close to people. Am I right?"

Nesschter rolls his eyes, and Don smiles.

"You're not a bad-looking guy. You got a nice build, good colors... You just need to loosen up a bit and let the light shine out of you. Smile more... Stuff like that. Them ladies will fall over you, and you won't die alone and miserable and full of regret," says Don.

"Enough," says Nesschter.

"I'm not coming on to you, if that's what you're tense about. I'm just saying if you loosened up a bit you won't be miserable."

"I'll take that into consideration. But before that, we need a way out of here."

"Any ideas?" asks Don.

"No... The cuffs are too tight, the u-lock is almost choking me, and..." Nesschter wiggles his body, which only leaves his throat aching from the u-lock. "The pole is sturdy. Your pole is probably the same."

"It is."

Nesschter sighs irritably and bangs his head against the pole. "I guess we have no choice then... We'll have to wait until Rara comes back, and then you can flirt us out of here."

Don grins. "Nice. I like the way you think. I'm sure they'll be back soon. I mean, how bad can grocery shopping be? If it's like Inner Shio or Iselae City, then it'll be a breeze!"

* * *

Rara groans and leans on the handle of her cart, with Chester and Gyrij flanking her. Their cart is filled with a couple of cartons of six-pack eggs and two quarter-gallons of milk, plus some random snacks, cereals, and synthetic meats. The market is crowded, with customers ranging from humans, to Avus, to Lupinaks, to random aliens from who knows where. The shelves are bare due to people buying products in droves. Some going as far as taking swipes with their arms, to push as much product as they can into their carts.

Camera drones fly overhead, keeping a bird's eye view of the shoppers, and police officers in riot gear stand guard at the double doors leading to the storage room, with more stationed at the front and by the back entrances. They have their riot shields strapped to their arms and their electric batons at rest.

While the people clamor and bicker, employees walk around with reflective, padded vests and hard hats, trying to restock, but hungry hands usually snatch the products off the carts or out of their hands. And during the commotion, an intercom makes a loud, screeching jingle that gets plenty of annoyed reactions.

*"Attention customers! This is Society's Supermarket Management! Today is the last day before gift cards are one hundred percent taxed! And food tax **will** be increased to thirty-three percent!"*

There is an uproar of swears and numerous foreign yells, and some throw boxes or packaged single toilet paper rolls at the intercoms.

"Taxes on selected pharmaceutical products will be increased to thirty-five

percent! Toiletries will be tax increased to forty percent! Baby care products will be tax increased to fifty percent!"

"Oh, come on!" screams a customer.

"This is a mandatory announcement. All tax revenue will go to the renovations of Shio Outer Ring and Shio expansion. The Great Society of the Aarde Union thanks you for being good citizens. Remember, we are all Aarden!"

"**Fuck you!**" yells another customer.

The intercom clicks off, and Rara's group heads to the checkout. It is crowded, it is noisy, and when Rara's group reaches the cashier, the cashier's hand is shaking. He is a shriveled Lupinak with a sheen of sweat, and an Avus wearing a thawb and a Society's Supermarket vest hurries past him.

"Work faster, Lupe! Lots of customers! Last day, last day before people get mad, get really mad!" says the Avus.

Outside, Rara sees an armored vehicle on treads with a water cannon manned and ready to fire. Police cars are in position with officers guiding traffic in and out of the parking lot. She also sees the charging price is 80 gailos a minute; and the charging station has a line of cars around it. The liquid fuel pumps are not any better.

"Your total is five thousand one hundred and twenty gailos," says the cashier.

Rara, Gyrij, and Chester stare at the Lupinak. The Lupinak swallows, and Gyrij sighs heavily and pulls out his ID card.

"We'll have to split the bill," says Gyij.

Rara shakes her head slowly. "This is ridiculous, and it will peck the Core in the neck if they don't fix this! Just you watch!"

* * *

It is late in the afternoon, and the Core is calm. Calming music plays in the towering buildings and shopping plazas. Perfectly paved walkways stretch between steel and glass monoliths and the brick-and-mortar stores. The crowds move with quick steps, all dressed in crisp, colorful suits and extravagant dresses, all masking calmness while working to get their errands done before the nightlife takes over. Nobody pushes, nobody yells. The chaos of the Outer Ring beyond their wall is completely ignored.

Inside Shio's largest mall, the Shio Grand Mall, soft jazz mixes with the glow of blue-white lighting, mirrored walls multiplying the lines of shoppers, each one moving with their expensive products. Among the crowd is Jasnee with Aki, Sakura, Mi, and Garo, keeping a protective bubble around her as she shops.

Everything in the mall is organized. Through the glass, every shelf is filled. No one fights, there is no sweat in the air, only the faint scent of tropical breeze being puffed through concealed nozzles, sizzling food and spices from the food court, and cologne and perfumes from the kiosks.

All around the Core, lines at registers are short. Security drones drone hover overhead, optics quietly scanning faces. Good behavior is rewarded with points and bad behavior is punished with deductions.

Young couples buy takeout, swiping cards, laughing softly at some private joke. The elderly with perfect perms and clothes browse products with their gloves on. Nobody stares, nobody lingers. None of them acknowledge the smoke and noises rising from beyond the Core's wall.

Down on the avenue, restaurants set up their outdoor tables. Waiters deliver fine dishes and drinks.

The movie theater's lobby is full with customers excited to see that one movie made by that one guy. The entrance smells like buttered popcorn and carbonated sugar and other snacks.

All over the Core are inescapable ads displaying products. They are on billboards, walls, windows, elevators. If an eye can see it, there is an ad. They promise unity, progress, new apartments, good schools, and excellent products. In a pillared plaza, a teacher leads her class of tiny, identical uniforms in a song about Aarde's bright future, their hands waving in perfect time, their chaperones beaming at the display.

In the day life of the Core, no one screams. No one fights. Not here. Not in the Core.

But in the center of the Core is Xajil Ojin, standing in the dark War Room, watching the Outer Ring break apart in real time. Watching with him is

Darius and dozens of Avus and humans, each with their own pair of computer monitors, studying various camera feeds and information about tagged protesters.

Little squares and rectangles surround pedestrians and vehicles, trailing them for seconds at a time. The second monitor scans and brings up their ID, which includes last updated physical features, bank account, social points, credit score, and current employment or government benefits.

So far, the crowded streets have been a nightmare to sift through. The Outer Ring is one giant slum of crowded, dirty buildings crumbling under decay and swift building practices post War of Unification. Some are even remnants of ruined buildings with new plaster and brick to plug the holes.

But while Darius and the Avus are scanning, some more than others, Xajil turns his focus on the camera in Ara's apartment. The placement of the TV and the lack of walls in her apartment, as mandated by the Connected Cities Residential Architecture Standardization Code, has allowed them to see much.

Right now, Xajil is watching police sift through her apartment.

Ara's money has also been seized by the state, bringing her bank account to zero. Unfortunately, the treatment from the Observers, the police, and now Division 4 has not convinced her to give up Holden (or Nesschter, as he now calls himself).

"Yeah, this one is definitely being relocated. There's N-Light everywhere," says a Shio police officer.

"Nothing we can do about it. Bag the N-Light and let's get out of here," says another officer.

Xajil takes a dose of anti-anxiety pills and chugs his bottled water. He brings up Ara's profile. Currently, her score is at fifty percent due to resisting questioning and apprehension. But when the information is processed in the system, and with all the N-Light she has in her possession, that will drop down to zero, and then comes the relocation. Unless Xajil stops it.

Xajil scales Ara's profile to half the screen, opens a login window, and enters his information. His file comes up, and after some searching, he brings up an "Immunity Page," and enters Ara's information.

Once her information is submitted, Ara's file switches with "Immunity" in the three main languages stamped across. With that, she will be safe from relocation, but there will still be a process for her to go through, so she will have to remain in their custody for a while longer.

While Xajil contemplates this next part, he returns to the camera feed, minimizes it, and brings up another window. He accesses the old footage from her TV camera and selects the date after the party.

He watches Ara and Nesschter enter, he hears the conversation, the argument, the pleading, the crying, the yelling and hitting. The longer the two fight, the tighter Xajil's talons link, and the heavier his breathing becomes.

When Nesschter is shoved out, Xajil spots Ara slipping the N-Light in his pocket, and after she slams the door, Ara slumps to the floor with her back against it. She remains on the floor, crying. A few minutes later, she sluggishly gets up and goes to her dresser and grabs a bathrobe and pajamas.

Xajil switches the camera feed to the bathroom, which is placed in the corner to give optimal coverage.

When Ara enters the bathroom, Xajil checks the time on his watch, then glances around to see if others are doing their job. They are for the most part, but they are also bored and will probably fall asleep soon.

Xajil's eyes snap back to the camera when Ara turns on the shower. Steam rolls out of the shower tube, and Ara puts her pajamas on top of the toilet and unknowingly faces the camera's direction as she peels off her dress. It falls to the floor, she steps out of it, standing in black-laced undergarments that emphasize her chest and thighs.

Xajil takes a sip from his bottled water as she kicks her dress away, and his focus is on her build: slim and toned with a flat stomach. The white fur is thin in most areas, so he can see the muscles that are fitting for a female, with being prominent, but not large, and her white fur is thickest on her hips, shoulders, and between her breasts, where the fluff travels to her neck.

Xajil's heart races as he watches her strip down. It gets faster when she removes her undergarments and carelessly tosses them aside.

He watches her go in the shower and she slumps in the tube and holds her knees to her chest. He can't see any details, since the fogged glass is covering her, but watching her, Xajil wonders how she would feel under his touch.

He has only ever held Avus females, bedded them, too, and due to Avus' notorious fertility, he got four eggs. He also got divorced four times and has yet to see any of his offspring. But he knows what feathers feel like; he knows the intimate touch of talons, the swaying between firm and gentle of grooming. He knows what Avus muscles feel like in moments of passion and lust.

But how would a Lupinak feel? How would *Ara* feel? Would her fur be soft? Would her muscles tense and relax under him? Would she always be warm? Could she serve as a blanket? A towel? Would her voice next to his ear send a shiver down his spine? Could she burn out the darkness rotting him, as she was so determined to do with the Norkit Brothers? Would she let him have her if there was no one left for her? Could he own her? Would she beg? Or would she snap her jaws and make him fight for it?

He toggles the feed forward. The next set of files is timestamped right during the raid. The six Observers entering, their interrogation after, followed by tearing apart her apartment. Ara remained defiant, which impressed Xajil. Then comes the group violation. Their swarming bodies all over Ara leaves Xajil's breath tight and his heart excited. He even feels his own pulse bumping against his throat as he watches them violate her as one large group, unrelenting, remorseless.

It reminds Xajil of the War of Unification. The female Lupinak were prizes. Avus loved using them until they manage to escape or died.

He never participated, but he always watched. The humans and traitor Avus were sometimes used as prizes, but humans, despite their intelligence, died the fastest while the Avus' lasted a little longer. But Lupinaks proved to be very durable.

And just like Xajil witnessed their durability during the War of Unification as soldiers and prizes, he is now witnessing the same durability in Ara as the Observers have their way with her. As he watches the feed, he can't help but wonder if he'd be able to do the same to Ara when the time comes.

No... Not Ara. Someone else. Erase her painful memories to make her new. Make her his for good.

Flashes of red pop into Xajil's peripheral vision, snapping him out of his trance. He turns off the video and looks at the giant screen, watching red flash across the screen as protesters are highlighted in red boxes.

As he watches the chaos, he stiffly rubs his trembling hands together, trying to push the images of Ara's violation out of his mind to focus on the task at hand. Yet, the more he pushes, the more his heart races, pumping dark desires and jagged guilt through his veins.

While watching the live feed, he sees some rioters ransacking a gift shop, and one of the ransackers leaves with a giant, white wolf plushie, bringing Xajil's crest to bob.

He turns on another feed on his computer, giving him a live recording of Ara in her de-escalation cell. Ara is dressed in an orange jumpsuit, huddled in a corner, her face marked with the scratches, her hair wild, and her eyes bloodshot and weighed down with dark bags.

'Dora will be a nice name for her,' thinks Xajil.

The door to the War Room suddenly opens, and Xajil watches an Avus Division 4 Agent approach him.

"Sir, we have the information room prepped. Do you want us to bring Ara Giovine-Parsen in for questioning?" asks the Agent.

"Is the drug testing done?" asks Xajil.

"Yes sir."

"And?"

"It cooperates with the Observers' reports. She has traces of N-Light. We also did a brain scan and found that one spot on the brain that gets messed up from lots of N-Light usage."

"The hippocampus."

"Yes sir."

Xajil takes a deep breath and flexes his talons and crest. "Keep her in her de-escalation room for another forty-eight hours."

The Agent stiffens. "But sir, if we don't act now, she won't remember anything useful. Especially after two days!"

Xajil glares at him. "Do as I say. Keep her there. Make sure no one else touches her."

The Agent hesitates. "Yes sir."

CHAPTER 5

The Agent leaves, and Xajil goes back to watching the growing protests on the large screen. As time ticks by, his breathing gets heavier, his talons tap together, and he swallows more pills. Then Xajil goes back to Ara's apartment recordings and resumes watching her shower.

Chapter 6

A thunderous gunshot snaps Nesschter out of his trance. He blinks and looks around. Morning light pours through holes in the wall, and Gyrij and Varil enter with heavy steps. They unlock Nesschter's and Don's necks from the poles, remove their cuffs, and pull them up.

"Up and at 'em. Breakfast is almost ready," says Gyrij.

Gyrij and Varil then escort Nesschter and Don to the eating area, where Rara is burning patties on the grill. Other Avus are eating the burnt patties off paper plates. When they see Nesschter and Don, some pause to stare at them for an extended period, but most quickly return to their meal.

"Where's Chester and his group?" asks Nesschter.

"They had to bolt. Work stuff. You know how it is. Imitation meat patties are all you're getting, by the way," says Ara

Nesschter and Don sit on lawn chairs, and Rara comes by a couple of minutes later and gives them paper plates with black and crusty patties. Gyrij gives them bottled water while Varil watches them with a tranquilizer gun in his grip.

"Are you worried we'll try something?" asks Nesschter.

"I know you will," says Varil.

Gyrij sits in an old plane seat. "It's nothing personal, but our orders are to keep you here."

"I know," says Nesschter. "But-"

"You're worried about Ara. I get it. But there's nothing we can do about that. So, we're sitting here until Balik gets you."

Nesschter frowns but quietly eats his breakfast while his pocket watch ticks in his ear. As he and Don eat, the Avus chirp among themselves while Rara hands out more food.

"I find it hard to believe that Balik would work with Avus," says Nesschter.

Varil tilts his head slightly. "Why's that?"

"When I took N-Light, I saw memories of my time fighting the AAHU during the War of Unification. I was with Balik, and he was... losing himself quickly. He really didn't like you or humans. I remember mass graves of Avus and humans, and I remember Balik going from a lighthearted person to... unstable."

Varil nods. "The war changed all of us. I used to have a video channel about models. Then I got drafted by the AAHU and I lost both of my arms in the war. First time was a faulty grenade that blew up in my hand. The second one was to a Lupinak who pounced on me and ripped it off with his teeth and claws."

Don grimaces and Nesschter nods.

"I've lost all interest in models, too," continues Varil. "I've tried to go back, but every new box I bought just collected dust. Even the glue went bad. So I donated the boxes and deleted my channel."

Nesschter scrunches his brow. "Why?"

Varil shrugs. "I guess it was just too painful to hold on to it."

"Do you regret doing it?"

Varil nods. "Yeah."

Gyrij leans forward and Rara sits on a bucket with her plate.

"To get back to what you were saying, Balik works with whoever he needs to in order to ship N-Light into Shio and to other Connected Cities and Towns. Well, Hebediah did, anyway. He started it after the war ended, but Balik took over operations after he died," says Gyrij.

Nesschter almost expected his heart to skip a beat, but it didn't. Hebediah is a name and a face, but he is just a blip in his memories. It's a feeling he does not want since Hebediah is his father, but the love just isn't there, no matter how hard he tries to feel something other than indifference.

"Old age, I'm guessing," says Nesschter.

Rara, Gyrij, and Varil look at Nesschter with various levels of confusion.

"No. He got incinerated with a fire missile not too long ago. Where have you been living?" asks Gyrij.

"The Core," replies Nesschter flatly.

"A whole new world," says Rara with a dreamy sigh. "So, is it as clean as they say it is?"

Nesschter wags his hand side to side. "More or less. Depends on your idea of clean."

"Clean streets, stocked shelves, good housing, and good paying jobs," says Rara.

"You don't have that out here?" says Nesschter.

"Running N-Light is a good paying job," says Gyrij. "But it is also dangerous. I've seen plenty of good Avus killed or arrested or relocated because of it. As for the stocked shelves and good housing part? Nope! Food is in short supply, and it is only made worse because they pumped up the taxes on all food, which led to people going crazy and buying every food item they can before it took effect. Now the shelves are bare."

"They even bought vegan food," says Varil.

"Wow. That is desperation," says Don. "I had no idea it was this bad."

"How'd you have no idea it was this bad? You were literally undercover in Chester's group for months," says Gyrij with a harsh glare and flexed crest.

"I thought it was... I don't know, just a piece of society, not the whole society," says Don.

"Yeah, the *Great* Society," sneers Gyrij.

"Gyrij, please relax," says Rara.

"The houses are garbage, too, did you know that?" says Gyrij.

Don and Nesschter shake their heads.

"Of course not," scoffs Gyrij. "We can't even call them houses. They're more like clumps of shacks instead of houses, and the brick-and-mortar houses are more like apartments since the mortgages and rent eat a month's worth of wages without including utilities or anything else. So, for someone to own a house or apartment, you gotta stuff three, five-"

"Ten, twelve," interrupts Rara timidly.

"Maybe fifteen or twenty," adds Varil.

"Yeah, lots of people stuffed in apartments and houses," says Gyrij. He scowls and stabs at his plate. "Backyards are campgrounds, front yards are campgrounds, and you can't grow food because that's illegal, and the cops will burn the food and poison the dirt, so you don't do it again. That's why we're here in this abandoned place! There's no life in Shio!"

Don and Nesschter are stiff, and Rara gets behind Gyrij and gently rubs his shoulder, while he wipes his face. He sighs heavily a moment later and looks at Nesschter.

"Yeah, we get our government checks, our food stamps, our health cards, all that crap, and a lot of dumb fucks out there love the easy money, and I was one of them, too, but guess what? Those are also taxed.

"And with taxes up and inflation jacking up the prices, those checks will mean nothing. The Core will feel it, too. It may be clean, but supplies and taxes spread to everybody, and there is a lot of anger and resentment against the Core that you people don't know about because you're in your own little world. And that world will get wrecked. All it will take is one bad day."

Nesschter narrows his eyes. "Is that a threat?"

"A prediction," says Gyrij.

Nesschter sniffs. "If that's the case, I really need to get Ara out before that happens."

Don looks at Nesschter. "And just how are we going to do that?"

"I don't know. But we need to hurry. I don't know when Xajil will relocate her."

* * *

A pair of black pills land on Director Xajil Ojin's tidy desk. Next to them is a syringe filled with brown fluid, and it is next to an open container with more tubes of the brown fluid.

Xajil closes his anxiety medication container and opens a fresh bottle of water. As soon as he swallows the pills, a sharp tingle runs through his spine, and he shudders and coughs as the mix of water and pills travel down his throat.

As he coughs, he closes his water bottle. Then he removes his gray blazer, revealing his straps of knives, and he unbuttons his shirt. Various healed puncture wounds are on his shoulder, and healed scratches are on his arm and chest. The feathers and fluff have yet to return, so pink lines and cracks desecrate his athletic build.

Xajil takes the syringe, taps it a few times before giving it a squirt, and after a deep breath, he injects himself with it. He grunts as the foreign fluid surges through his veins, and his muscles tense and relax in cycles with the pulsing, as he removes the syringe needle and slips it into a "used" slot in the case.

After that is done, he locks the case, puts the medication away, puts his clothing back to where they should be, and goes through the files for Holden Hosenheim (with "Nesschter Hebediah Norkit" being a footnote at the end), Ara Giovine-Parsen, Caro Naji, and Donald "Don" Stein.

Don had also turned up missing, and no cameras have been able to track him, so Xajil figures he has something to do with the recent chain of events. In fact, a part of him is hoping that is the case since everything about Don annoys him, so Don going rogue to help Nesschter and Caro will be all the justification he needs to relocate him.

While Xajil is searching through their files, he finds that they are mostly unhelpful. Ara's was just started, Nesschter never went anywhere, and Don's information is relevant to Iselae City, but not to Shio. And Caro has no property outside of the Core.

Then there is the knocking, which doesn't help Xajil's concentration, but he obliges.

"Come in," says Xajil.

Darius Jules cautiously approaches Xajil's desk. When he reaches it, he salutes, and Xajil returns it.

"Director Ojin, sir," says Darius.

"What is it?" says Xajil.

"It is Ara Giovine-Parsen. We were scheduling her for relocation but found that she was put under immunity."

"I did that. Her being Balik's comforter means she had access to information we don't have."

Darius hesitates. "Sir, with all due respect, she is an N-Light junkie. Her memories are shot. She can't tell us anything."

Xajil exhales and stands up with his talons digging into his desk. "N-Light will jump start her memories, and it will be clearer when she has context to use. When we ask her for certain details, we give her the N-Light and the information will be clear and accurate."

"Oh…" says Darius. "Should we…?"

"No. Leave her be. She will be safer in her de-escalation room until we need her. Right now, our focus is finding Holden Hosenheim and Don Stein."

"We probably shouldn't have been so rough on Caro Naji," says Darius.

Xajil glares at him, and Darius swallows nervously. Several seconds of staring later, and Xajil returns the files to his locked desk and walks around to stand next to Darius. He stares at him some more, and Darius swallows again, with tiny beads of sweat trickling down his face.

"Let's go to the War Room," says Xajil.

Darius nods and follows Xajil out of his office with a shaky exhale.

When they reach the War Room, Xajil finds that everyone is still working on their computers. After a brief conversation with the supervisor, he finds out nothing of importance has been found, so Xajil takes the same seat he was in last time, brings up the feed for Ara's de-escalation room, and watches her while the clicks and clacks of typing float in the air. Dozens of minutes of this type of noise pass, and then the supervisor goes over to Xajil.

"Sir, we may have gotten a lead on our targets," says the supervisor.

Xajil stands up and follows the supervisor to a human.

"Show the director what you got," says the supervisor.

"Yes sir," says the Agent. He clears his throat, then speaks as if he is giving a presentation to a teacher. "Sir, Caro Naji was switching vehicles, but what I did was back track his moment of arrest from his appearance at the airport. He took a taxi to the airport, so I back tracked the taxi until it picked him up and kept going back in the footage. He took multiple taxis, and when he was walking, he was keeping his head down a lot, so I couldn't get any good readings. I had to cross reference walking patterns and clothes and height and whatnot, which wasn't easy, because of all the protests going on now, but I tracked him all the way to his car, which he left abandoned with his keys and windows down next to a bunch of druggies."

"Where?" says Xajil.

"The Outer Ring. Section One-One-Four, which is set to be remodeled with funds from the Improving the Impoverished Foundation. But the vehicle came from a blind spot. The blind spot leads to an area of abandoned businesses, apartments, and an abandoned museum."

"How many structures?"

"Records show eighty-five."

Xajil pats his shoulder. "Very good."

Xajil then makes his way to Darius.

"Send a drone to Section One-One-Four. We may have found who we're looking for," says Xajil.

***

Balik stares into the darkness of the Vagsten Tunnels. Light from floodlights shine past him, casting his shadow along the floor, stretching far and nearly touching the darkness. Glow sticks of various colors are hung on the walls, and faint screams echo in the tunnel. They are like wind, swirling and rising and falling in pitch.

Screaming, thrashing, ticking, tocking, locking, stocking, clicking, aiming, ready, aim, fire.

A gunshot echoes in the dark tunnel, and some Revivalist soldiers laugh about the popping engine sounding like a gun.

Balik's ears twitch and he stiffly sips his thermos. The chicken soup was cooked on the propane grill inside the shack. It tastes good, but it cannot distract him from the screams.

His fingers twitch. The agonizing screaming continues.

His eyes narrow in the dark as shadowy figures with glowing eyes move towards him.

The screams continue, getting louder as the figures get closer, and the watch ticks in his ear. The shadow figures reach the light, and it turns out to be a small vehicle with headlights and soldiers clutching its rails. The engine is smoking and one of the soldiers is calling for a mechanic.

Balik steps aside, and the vehicle grinds to a stop next to him. The passenger has a map, and in the back are empty boxes. The smoke from the vehicle's engine smells like burning bodies, and the black smoke looks like fingers wiggling past the grates desperate for a trapped body to escape.

"What's the news?" asks Balik, turning sharply from the vehicle.

"Well, aside from nobody changing the oil on this thing for years," starts the soldier.

"Important things only."

"We got the weapons delivered to the next team, but we need more glow sticks."

"We got plenty. Restock and go at it again."

"Sir, we've also had to make alternate routes because some of the areas are caved in. We marked the routes on the map, and we've set up safe zones as you instructed," says another Revivalist soldier.

"Kiss ass," mutters the first soldier.

"Good," says Balik. "Now restock and go at it again." He points at the first soldier. "As for you. You mouth off again and I'm welding a ball gag to your mouth."

The first soldier's ears drop, and Balik waves him away.

"Fuck off," orders Balik.

The two Revivalist soldiers hop on the vehicle, and it struggles on its way to the exit while Balik resumes staring in the dark.

A moment later, three trucks with long beds drive past him. The backs are filled with Revivalist soldiers, clutching their weapons, and are stocked with more weapons and other supplies. The vehicle headlights shine on the damaged walls, and the taillights look like shrinking red eyes.

Two more trucks roll by, and Balik goes into the shack's underground chamber. There is a new tunnel that has been dug out by their machine, and it is braced with beams. It is large enough for trucks to go through, and at the far end of the chamber are the Division 4 carriers that Talos Yeshniv confiscated when his territory was raided.

Teams of mechanics are working on their fronts, attaching large cattle guards and horizontal metal beams. Technicians are working on wires, while explosive experts are making bombs filled with nails, metal marbles, or barbed metal splinters. The ones completed are loaded into the carriers, which have had their sides thinned out, while their roofs have been reinforced. Then there are painters who are writing *"Mevmo Vagsten!"* or painting burning trees and cities on the sides. The last group by the vehicles are drawing straws.

The stash of weapons that Colonel Barzee has given Balik has been reduced to a fraction of its original size due to them being shipped down the Vagsten Tunnels. With careful planning and cartography comparisons, Balik, Jarvis, and a few others were able to determine where the tunnels would go beneath Shio and made the appropriate messages to the right people to meet them at said locations.

Next, they dug their way out and handed off weapons and supplies to their associates in the safety of abandoned buildings, or businesses under their control. They already had plenty of weapons and munitions in the slums between the Norkits and Caro's networks, but those were leftovers from the Aarde War or "lost" police weapons. The ones being trafficked through the tunnels are entirely Federation.

And speaking of Jarvis, the mute is approaching Balik with Khal. When they are next to him, Jarvis tilts his head to Balik while looking at Khal.

"What is it?" says Balik

"Mason is saying that the Outer Ring is getting stirred up, and our scouts agree," says Khal.

"Explain," says Balik.

"The taxes have skyrocketed on food and other supplies, and people are not happy about it. The protests are growing fast."

Balik's ears perk. "Really? How big are they now?"

"I'm thinking it's going to take the whole Outer Ring in a few hours."

Balik rubs his chin. "Interesting... And what about Nesschter? Is he still with the birds?"

"He is, and they had to chain him to a pole because he tried escaping."

Balik looks at Jarvis. "We should have done that."

Jarvis nods, and Balik looks at Khal again.

"Send a group to help Gyrij defend his little fort. If things get bad, take Nesschter and move him to the Tunnels. I'll send Gyrij a message about that. I don't need any misunderstandings."

Khal pulls out his phone and walks off while pressing it against his ear, and Balik points at Jarvis.

"You send out the signal. We're moving now. I want our soldiers in position when the protests fill the streets. Have our boys serve as agitators if need be," says Balik.

Jarvis pulls out his phone and starts texting, and Balik goes to the group working on the carriers.

"Hurry up, boys!" says Balik. "It is almost time to make Shio bleed!"

The teams hurry, and Balik goes to Khal. He has just hung up and is turning to Balik.

"I'm sending Fargo and his team to Gyrij and Nesschter," says Khal.

"Good. I have another task for you. Your task is to stay behind," says Balik.

Khal does a double take. "Forgive me for asking, but why?"

"Because..." Balik puts his hand on Khal's shoulder. "When I don't make it back, you'll be in charge of the Gacerae Pack."

"Balik, you can't talk like that. You will make it back. I can send Mason to help so you can make it back without worry."

Balik's hand tightens on Khal's shoulder, his voice dropping and cracking. "I don't want to make it back, Khal. I'm tired of all of it. All the screaming, the memories, bridges I can't cross... I hate all of it. I want it to end, but I can't just..." Balik points a finger gun at his head. "I got too many failures to make up for."

"Balik, listen to me. You're being irrational," says Khal softly, gently grabbing the finger gun hand and lowering it. "If you want to step down as Alpha while your mind heals, that is fine, I will gladly take your place while you are away. But to lose you after our family has lost so much... That is... Awful. You are too valuable to be wasted."

"But we're here because of my failures, and Jarvis is right. When Nesschter is returned, nobody will trust him, and the Gacerae Pack needs someone they can trust," says Balik. He puts his other hand on the back of Khal's head, locking eyes with him, his speckled amber eyes glazed. "No one else in the Norkit Branch is old enough to rule, which means that leaves you by law. So, assemble the oldest Lupinaks of each caste you can find. We'll get all this legalized before we move out."

Khal hesitates, then nods. "If that is what you wish."

"It is."

There is a moment of hesitation before Khal nods and leaves. After Khal is out of sight, Balik sighs, opens his thermos, and takes a sip. Much to his dismay, the thermos is empty, but he sips the emptiness one more time before closing it and staring into the darkness of the Vagsten Tunnels.

Chapter 7

Ti-Tick. Ti-Tock.

Ti-Tick. Ti-Tock.

Ti-Tick. Ti-Tock.

It is late in the afternoon. The pocket watch's uneven rhythm pokes at Nesschter's ears, bringing them to twitch every so often. His thumb rubs circles over the faded dove on his watch's cover. He sits on a chair in one of the higher levels of the museum, watching the world outside.

There are numerous structures in decay. Many are crumbling, some have plants overtaking them, and some are still standing, but losing their strength. All of them are covered in graffiti of some kind.

Towering above the structures is a massive billboard with lights on its border and equally placed holes through it. It has a picture of a near cloudless, sunny sky, with clean, crystal-like towering structures, and multi-level roads weaving through the structures. Light is reflecting off the spires, and a convoy of moving trucks are making their way to the city. Beneath it all is:

The future is coming.

Improving the Impoverished Foundation.

This message is in the three languages of Aarde, but despite the picture displaying a clean, bright future, Nesschter doesn't see that happening. He can't see much beyond the abandoned zone, but he can hear the chants and horns honking that has been steadily getting worse over the hours.

"So, what's the deal with you and that watch?" asks Don.

Nesschter looks at Don. The human is playing checkers with an Avus guard while two more watch them. All of them are armed with tranquilizers.

"Ness? Can I call you Ness?" says Don.

"Sure," says Nesschter.

"Cool. What's the deal with the watch, Ness?"

Nesschter shrugs. "I don't know. I just like it."

"Well, you might want to get it fixed, since it doesn't even work. That ticking is loud and janky."

"It works just fine."

Nesschter pops it open and looks at the time. The hour and minutes hand have stopped moving, but the seconds hand is swinging like a pendulum. Nesschter closes it and looks out the window again.

"How long have you had that watch, anyway?" asks Don.

"As long as I can remember," replies Nesschter.

"How long have you been brainwashed by Xajil Ojin?"

"No idea."

"And the knife?"

Nesschter looks at the knife on his hip. His throat tightens as he remembers watching the video of himself murdering the prisoner under Xajil's instructions. It was the same knife he has now, but he hasn't had the heart to get rid of it. Now that he thinks about it, the watch is probably a gift from Xajil, too.

"I've had this knife for a while," says Nesschter.

"Does the knife work or is it dull?" asks Don.

"Why do you want to know?"

"Just curious."

"Do you want to use it?"

"Of course I do! It's a nice knife! ... Checkmate, by the way."

"We're playing chess? I thought this was checkers!" says the Avus.

"Hey, relax, it was a joke," says Don, grinning widely.

The Avus hisses, flips the board, and storms out, and Don throws up his hands.

"Hey, not my fault you suck at this game!" says Don.

"So, was it chess or checkers?" asks a guard.

"Parcheesi," replies Don.

The Avus guard flips him off, and Don chuckles. Then Gyrij and Varil enter the room.

"Good news, Nesschter. You'll be going home soon," says Gyrij.

Nesschter silently stands up, and Don goes to his side. The guards in the room, including the one that left in rage, go to Gyrij.

"Balik is sending some people over for extra protection, and when he is done with whatever it is he's doing, you'll be free to go," says Gyrij.

"Caro said he was going after Xajil," says Nesschter. "Xajil has Ara, so I need to-"

Varil shoots Nesschter in the neck with a tranquilizer, and a guard shoots Don in shoulder with a dart. They both stumble, and Nesschter growls as a cotton feeling takes over his mouth. and his breathing become heavy. His legs wobble, and he struggles to stay standing while he glares at Varil.

"Why me...?" asks Don, his voice sounding distant and muffled.

Don crumbles to the floor, and Nesschter steps forward, leading Varil shooting him again, thus dropping him to his knees. He still glares at Varil, though.

"*Azool...*" growls Nesschter.

Then he falls face-first on the dirty floor and starts snoring.

* * *

Director Xajil Ojin's talon taps the desk. Slow and steady. In tune of the watch in his pocket.

Tick. Tock. **Tip. Tap.**

Tick. Tock. **Tip. Tap.**

Tick. Tock. **Tip. Tap.**

Tiny trembles shake his digit, and he fumbles to pour the black anxiety pills in his palm and chug from his bottled water. His heart races and his breathing is forced to stay low, puffing through his nostrils like a sick engine sputtering out exhaust.

While chaos unfolds on the big screen, Xajil's golden eyes flick between two screens on his desk. One is the recording of when the Observers violated Ara in her apartment. The other is a live feed for Ara's de-escalation room. She is huddled in the corner, and an untouched tray of food lays near the door.

Xajil briefly watches at what the other computers are doing. Many of them are monitoring Section 114, but a sizable number are watching the other sections through the camera network.

While they don't see it with his stoic expression, fear is wrapping around Xajil like a serpent. The streets of the Outer Ring have been filling up at a rapid pace with angry civilians, and the cameras have picked up agent provocateurs wearing masks, going through the crowds and getting them riled up.

All of them have been Lupinaks, and they have been running around with megaphones and throwing out fliers of Gorvin Yeshniv, his boys, and the teenage Lupinaks killed during the botched raid-extraction in Parudasi Fusas.

Others have been handing out bricks and other junk to throw, or cans of spray paint or buckets of paint and oil from the backs of trucks. Glitter bombs are also used, and the masked agents and the civilians they have riled have been liberally using the paint, oil, glitter, fireworks, and weaponized trash against police officers and government buildings. They have even managed to damage the cameras or outright rip out the poles using tools or the power of vehicle towing.

While watching the feed, Xajil's phone rings, and he sees that it is Kevin Asven.

"This is Director Ojin," says Xajil.

"Hey, Xajil!" says Kevin brightly. *"You seeing what's going on in the Outer Ring?"*

"I am," says Xajil.

"That's nuts, isn't it? But what are your plans to take care of this?"

Xajil frowns. "We have to confront the reasons in order for there to be de-escalation."

"De-escalation? That's boring. Beat them into submission and lock them up! Let them know that things suck because of them, and because they're little brats, things have gotten worse."

Xajil rubs his brow. "Kevin, these aren't kids."

"They're behaving like kids."

"Kevin, this is going to get ugly very fast. We must deescalate. We do not have the manpower to carry out your wishes at such a large scale "

"Deescalate? How? Lower the taxes? Give out cookies and apology cards?" says Kevin.

Xajil inhales heavily, then steadily exhales. "Kevin, I am watching the feed-"

"So am I."

"Then you see them getting incredibly more aggressive by the hour. It **will** get worse by nightfall. We **must** deescalate this. If we can't we will be forced to fall back to the Core."

"Good grief. Have the cops and agents fortify the important structures and let the peasants destroy their area. The whole thing needs to be bulldozed, anyway, and if they get violent... shoot them."

Xajil's hand tightens on his phone. "Kevin, you need to listen to me."

"No, you listen to me!" snaps Kevin. *"We must show them whose boss! We cannot be weak or else they'll abuse us again."*

Xajil raises a brow.

"You have all the camera feeds, all the phone and ID tracking, so we can retaliate with fire and brimstone if they really get ugly with us."

"Kevin..." says Xajil.

"Nope. Not going to hear it. Jasnee is going shopping for girly crap, so I trust you will keep the Core safe, even if the peasants cause trouble outside. And I am going to go to the movies to see that one movie made by that one guy who made that one movie. I heard it was awesome!"

"Kevin..."

"Fix this mess. I got fun stuff to do. Bye!"

Click.

Xajil pulls the phone away from his ear and stares at its screen. Kevin Asven's name and smiling face is still on display, but now a "Do Not Disturb" message is beneath it. Xajil sighs heavily, sets his phone down, and looks around before he wipes his face and pops a couple more anxiety pills in his mouth.

Then he grabs his phone, selects dozens of people in his contacts and goes for direct voice mail. After all of them are connected, he waits a few seconds before speaking slowly and heavily.

"This is Director Xajil Ojin. I am authorizing lethal force on violent protesters who inflict bodily harm on any GSAU employee or representative of the GSAU, regardless of status. Use nonlethal means in other cases. Disperse protesters before nightfall. That is a nonnegotiable order."

Xajil ends the message, and drops his phone on the desk and stares at nothing. He even numbly closes the videos of Ara and resumes staring off into space, watching the ceiling fans spin like helicopter blades and watching the shadows shift on the walls. There's even a water stain in the upper corner near the large monitor dominating the wall. So, Xajil takes out his notebook and makes a note to get that fixed.

After several minutes pass, Darius appears next to Xajil.

"Sir, we have interesting activity in regard to the museum," says Darius.

Xajil quietly gets up, grabs his phone, and follows Darius to the human that figured out where Caro came from. This prompts Xajil to write in his notebook to give the human a promotion, and when the human sees him, he briefly becomes energetic, but his professionalism returns before he becomes too giddy.

"Director Ojin, sir. Our drone has picked up something," says the human.

"What is it?" says Xajil.

"A convoy of vehicles have pulled into the museum. All of them are Lupinaks, and look..." The Agent switches the feed to show bodies moving around inside the museum. The bodies look like stick figures, so there is no detail to them. "We've been watching them all day, and from what we can see, two have been kept under close supervision, while what I am guessing are customers go through for a hit of drugs in the lobby and leave later."

Xajil studies the drone's feed, and his talons grip the human's chair as he leans forward.

"It's them. They are going to move Holden Hosenheim and Donald Stein," says Xajil. He goes to his desk, pulls out his phone again, and quickly selects multiple people for a conference call, skirting the mass voice mail feature entirely. It rings a few times before people start answering, and when everyone is accounted for, Xajil speaks. "This is Director Xajil Ojin. Send in the Observers to Section One-One-Four at the abandoned museum. Code red. Shoot to kill everyone."

* * *

At an apartment, Kwari is watching a soap opera with his wife, his beak bandaged, and four little Avus are in the corner playing with blocks. His phone buzzes, and he checks the message. It has an address with a red dot and a picture of Don and Nesschter. He sighs, stands up, and rubs his wife's crest.

"I got called into work. I'll be back in a little bit," he says.

"But you got back," says the wife.

"I know, but this is another high profile. They're calling everyone available in the sector."

"Hmm... Well, please be careful. The protests have been getting bigger by the hour, and I'm afraid they will do something stupid if they don't clear out soon," says the wife

Kwari smiles and rubs his wife's head again, and then he goes to the children and gives them quick hugs before he grabs his locked suitcase and leaves the apartment. He goes down the apartment elevator and enters a parking garage, ducks into a bathroom, and after checking the stalls, he puts on an armored vest and quickly assembled a shotgun and pistol. Then he dials a number. It barely rings before someone answers.

"Before you ask, I'm on my way with a van with five others. There are closer Observers who are watching the main roads to One-One-Four as well as the museum. It's going to get bloody. I can feel it."

"I know." Kwari pulls out a combat knife from his suitcase. "But I'm prepared."

"Right... I'll see you in five minutes."

The line disconnects, and Kwari checks his gear one more time before leaving the bathroom.

59

Chapter 8

Balik walks around the captured Division 4 vehicles, holding a folder, his thermos and knife clipped to his belt. He is marveling at how the mechanics have been modifying the vehicles for their coming tasks. He also loves the paint jobs the other team did. However, the workers are still looking at Balik nervously. Jarvis standing behind them isn't helping, either.

"Is everything up to your standard, sir?" asks one of the mechanics.

Balik looks inside one of the carriers and sees barrels with bags of nails and explosives strapped to it. He whistles and bangs on the side, loving the sound of weak metal.

"This is very good. I'm proud of you," says Balik,

The mechanics nearly deflate with their sighs, and Khal approaches Balik. Seeing him come brings Balik's ears to perk, and he weaves past the mechanics to go to Khal.

"Did you gather them?" asks Balik.

"I've gathered two dozen of the oldest Alphas, Betas, Deltas, and Omegas in our vicinity. They are in the conference room," says Khal.

"Very good," says Balik.

"I still don't know why I deserve this."

"Simple. You are the oldest in the cousin branch, so when I die, you'll take over. And I want to make sure we're clear about this."

"Right..."

"Right, indeed!"

Balik speed walks to the conference room. The room is concrete and crammed with a long table and folding chairs. It has a large fan hanging overhead and weak lights hanging off the walls.

Jarvis and Khal trail Balik inside, and waiting for the group are two dozen Lupinaks, whose natural colors are fading to white or graying with age, much like Khal. The elderly Lupinaks watch Balik go to the end of the table, and Jarvis takes a position behind Balik, his hands clamped in front of him.

Khal stands off to the side, and Balik looks at all the eyes on him. He smiles, but his heart is racing, and his hands tighten on his thermos.

"Good evening, representatives of the castes of the Gacerae Pack!" says Balik. "I know these conditions are not regal, but unfortunately the nice house was firebombed by the GSAU. To make things quick, I am naming Khal Mason Jarim my successor due to a lack of eligible Norkits."

The group looks at Khal, and he keeps a stoic expression. The group looks back at Balik.

"We heard Nesschter Hebediah Norkit is alive and in Shio... Working for Division 4," says one of the elders.

There are murmurs and nods, and Balik bows his head, sets the folder and thermos on the table, and presses down on his thermos.

"Yes..." says Balik, his voice tense and heavy. He takes a deep breath and looks up. "Yes, it is true. And I have associates that will bring him back to Revivalist territory."

"For trial, hopefully," says another elder.

"No. They did something to him. Brainwashed him. When he is returned, he will be rehabilitated."

There are groans and mutters of disbelief.

"I know he is not fit to rule," says Balik over the griping, "but when he is brought back, he **will** be rehabilitated. He is my brother. He is a Norkit. Most importantly, he is one of us and he was harmed beyond what most of us can comprehend. And when he is returned, no further harm will come to him, even when I pass away. Is that clear?"

Balik looks at Khal sharply, and Khal nods in agreement. Seeing that, Balik returns his focus to the group of Lupinaks. They also reluctantly nod.

"Very soon, I will lead an operation against Shio, against Xajil Ojin, and possibly Kevin Asven, depending on if he is still there. But Xajil Ojin is my primary target, and I have been planning this assault for a very long time; the stars just happen to align, and therefore my mission's time frame has been sped up. That said, it is still very dangerous, practically a suicide run, so in the light of me **very likely** not returning, I am naming Khal Mason Jarim as my successor."

The table is silent for a few moments, and then one of the elders leans forward.

"Balik, you don't have to go on this mission," he says.

"Yes, I do," says Balik.

"You don't have children."

"Says you."

"You haven't been Alpha long, though. It's disgraceful to quit now!" says another elder.

"I was never fit to rule. All of you know this," says Balik.

Another elder leans forward.

"Balik, if this is you trying to redeem yourself, there is no need for this. There was nothing you could do about Vagsten or Hebediah. You did what you could. What happened was out of your control," he says.

Balik's eyes narrow. "I'm going to make this easy for all of you. I'm the Alpha of the Gacerae Pack, and I will go to Shio and make things right. They will pay for what they did to Vagsten, to my father, to my brother, to Gacerae, to all of us. I will do this without regret, and when I die, Khal Mason Jarim will carry the torch. Any objections?"

Another hand is raised, and Balik slams his thermos on the table, growling and fangs bared.

"You weren't supposed to do that!" says Balik.

The hand drops, and Balik smiles.

"Good." Balik straightens himself out and picks up a folder and opens it up to two pages. One has a wall of texts, and the header has "GACERAE PACK ALPHA SUCCESSOR & WITNESSES." At the bottom are empty signature lines with circles next to them. The next page is blank. Balik adjusts the folder's position and clears his throat, and Jarvis pulls out a pair of pens from his pocket. He gives one to Balik and the other to the closest elder.

"Khal Mason Jarim of the Jarim Branch of the Norkit Tree of the Gacerae Pack, due to lack of eligible successors of the Norkit Tree you have been selected by me, Balik Hebediah Norkit, Alpha of the Norkit Tree and the Gacerae Pack, to serve as successor and Alpha of the Gacerae Pack. Upon the death of me, Balik Hebediah Norkit, you are to immediately assume command of the Gacerae Pack and all its functions to the best of your abilities. The Jarim Branch will become the new Tree and serve as the Alpha Family and will keep command until death or removal by more worthy parties. Our witnesses today are Vojehan and twenty-four of the patriarchs of all castes. Do you accept the position of Alpha?"

Balik looks at Khal. Jarvis looks at Khal. And all the aged eyes look at Khal. And Khal Mason Jarim looks at all of them separately before bowing to Balik.

"I accept," says Khal.

"Very good." Balik quickly signs and dates his signature line, and after that, he scrapes his thumb on his fang and presses his bloody digit on the paper. Then he turns it to Khal and gives him the pen. "Your turn."

Khal mimics what Balik did, and once that is done, he passes it down the table. Each of the old Lupinaks sign, date, and fingerprint the blank page, and after the last Lupinak signs it, Jarvis takes it and the pens, and gives the folder to Balik.

Balik blows on the pages to dry the blood, and then he closes it and gives it Khal. The elderly clap halfheartedly, and Balik smiles and shakes Khal's hand.

"I would advise you make enough copies for each of the witnesses," says Balik.

"Yes sir," says Khal.

Balik shakes Khal's hand a little bit longer, offering him a toothless smile, his eyes wet. After he releases Khal, he turns to Jarvis and exhales heavily.

"Alright, let's roll."

Chapter 9

Today would have been a good day if Nesschter wasn't shaved bald.

Because of his black mane's obliteration, be is wearing a green beanie hat that has slots for his ears to poke through. Normally he wouldn't wear it, because it is a bright day with sparse clouds, but desperate times call for desperate measures.

Now he is bald, has a beanie, and is walking down a path carved through the thick, fully bloomed trees of the Syrikel Forest, with Ara in between him and Balik.

The two males are wearing traditional tunics, Balik is carrying a pack of fishing poles, and Nesschter has a cooler. Ara has her dress and a backpack of snacks. She has her arms linked around both of their free arms, and all three have matching steps.

Their path is shaded by the towering trees and their thick branches. Up ahead, running river water gurgles and splashes.

"You're going to love it. I promise," says Balik.

"And what if we don't?" asks Ara.

"Well, you won't be my friend, and I'll have father disown Nesschter," says Balik.

Nesschter rolls his eyes and Ara's jaw drops with her smile.

"Wow. Rude," says Ara.

"What's rude is not appreciating my hard work," says Balik snobbishly, adding with a smile, "But you will love it. It has a great view, lots of space, and furniture… Maybe we can cut your bangs while we're up there…?"

He grins, makes finger scissors, and snips at Ara's large bangs.

"Nooo!" whines Ara playfully.

She bats Balik's hand away and turns Nesschter into her shield. Her hands grip his shoulders tight, and she peeks past him, while he stiffens.

"Keep your shoddy barber skills away from my bangs!" says Ara.

"C'mon, I'm not that bad," says Balik.

"I'm bald," says Nesschter flatly.

"It'll grow back," says Balik.

Nesschter frowns, and Balik moves ahead. His steps are light enough to where he is nearly hopping, and he makes his way down a small hill that ends at the river. The river is clear enough to see the rocks at the bottom, and the water beats against the rocks that have poked out. Trees arch over, and their roots weave around other stones and dig into the ground.

The sounds of the traveling water are music to Nesschter's ears, but his eyes are fixated on a tree house that is nestled between two trees. Its support poles have been inserted directly into the trees, it has a cone roof with a balcony, and its windows have shutters. The way up is a ladder, and Nesschter and Ara stare at the tree house with wide eyes while Balik smiles proudly.

"It's beautiful, isn't it?" says Balik.

"It is..." says Ara.

"You did this?" asks Nesschter.

"I designed it after a picture mom made, but Khal helped me build it and get the furniture up there... and he built the furniture for me."

Nesschter and Ara look at him questionably.

"You built a tree house but couldn't build a chair?" says Nesschter.

"The furniture instructions were weird!" says Balik defensively.

"I'm not judging, but–"

"I'd like to see you build a tree house," interrupts Balik.

"*Bayos!*" calls Ara. They stop bickering, and Ara takes a moment to collect herself, then smiles at Balik and holds his arm, much to the annoyance of Nesschter. "Tell us about your tree house."

Balik's smile returns, and he points at the support beams in the trees. "The beams are inserted directly into the trees, so when the tree heals, it'll seal the poles in place. It's on two trees for extra support, a balcony for fishing or star gazing, and the cone roof looks cool."

"Star gazing sounds like fun," says Ara.

"You're more than welcome to stay the night," says Balik.

"I think I will." Ara smiles at Nesschter. "How about you, Nesschter? Will you stay?"

Then a sharp pain strikes across Nesschter's cheek, and his eyes snap open. Rara is gripping his shoulders and screaming at him.

"Hey! Wake up! Snap out of it!" says Rara.

Nesschter's vision is hazy, and his heavy eyelids they flutter, with a mix of ringing, ticking, shooting, and screaming clashing in his ears. His tongue feels like cotton and his fingers sluggishly stretch and curl on his thighs.

"Whuz gohna ohn?" slurs Nesschter.

"We're being attacked!" says Rara. She goes to his side and removes the u-lock trapping him against the pole, as gunfire rattles inside the building. "We have to get out of here!"

Rara goes to Don and slaps him awake and quickly removes his u-lock as he blinks. Meanwhile, Nesschter's eyes close, darkness bleeds in, and his cheek hits the dirty floor.

"Don't you dare fall asleep!" says Rara, her voice floating in the void.

"*Will you stay?*" asks Ara.

"*Stay after class,*" says Mr. Verimoor.

Nesschter extends his hand in the dark. Small pockets of fire sprout up, creating flickering orange glows that reveal patches of burning buildings and trees. Gunshots crack the air, the world shakes, and Nesschter loses balance.

He falls into mud, and the dark sky is lit up as a beam breaks the clouds and strikes something in the distance. The shock wave pushes against him, and his muscles lock as he watches a ball of fire, smoke, and debris rolling into the clouds.

"What are you doing! Get up!" says Rara.

Nesschter's eyes open just enough to see Gyrij and Varil run into the room. He closes his eyes again, but he is quickly slapped awake. This time he sees Chester and a few humans and Lupinaks in the room, and Don is patting Nesschter's cheek while Rara is digging in her backpack. The gunshots are getting closer, and Don is having a hard time keeping his eyes open.

"What kind of darts did you use?" asks Don.

"Better yet, who did you call?" says Chester.

"How the hell am I going to call someone when I don't have a phone?" says Don.

"I should put a bullet in your head just to be safe, you damn rat!"

"Water under the bridge!"

Nesschter's eyes droop, Don slaps his face again, and Rara pops open a ton can, revealing the slightly glowing red gel pills of N-Light. She takes a pill and returns to Nesschter.

"I can't believe this, but... Open wide!" says Rara.

Nesschter opens his mouth and Rara chucks an N-Light pill in. He coughs and gags, and Don holds his muzzle shut until he swallows it. When he does, Don quickly releases him and scrambles back.

Nesschter coughs and hacks, and he props himself on his hands and knees, wheezing with a burning sensation surging through his veins and brain. Eyes wide and pupils trembling, his claws dig into the dirty floor.

Ti-Tick. Ti-Tock.

"You need more lessons," says Mr. Verimoor.

Muzzle flashes light up the dark. Shadows move through the trees with tracers streaking through the air. There are shouts in the distance, and Balik runs past Nesschter, barking orders and pulling a hunkered-down, scrawny Lupinak out of their huddled position behind a tree.

"Keep pushing! Keep pushing! We got them on the run!" yells Balik.

Ti-Tick. Ti-Tock.

Ara is holding Nesschter's hands and is guiding him across the frozen lake on their ice skates. Her eyes have never left his face, and her smile is bright.

"Isn't this great?" asks Ara.

"Yeah... I guess..." says Nesschter, holding Ara's wrists tight. He looks at the ice beneath them with a heavy heart and a rock in his twisted gut.

Ara giggles and pulls Nesschter close. Their bodies squish, and she wraps her arms around him with her tail wagging.

"You'll be fine. I won't let you fall," says Ara, adding with a playful smile, "on purpose, anyway."

Ti-Tick. Ti-Tock.

Nesschter is being dragged by his legs across a dirty floor with weak lights above him. His legs and wrists are bound, and his muzzle is trapped shut. In front of him is Xajil and the human in the black, faceless mask.

"I'll only say this once. You will determine how long this will last," says the human. "All the pain that will happen will be because of you. Cooperation makes it easy for all of us. Defiance will make it a nightmare for you. Choose wisely."

Ti-Tick. Ti-Tock.

"You caught a fish!" says Balik proudly.

"I caught a fish!" cheers Ara.

Ara, Balik, and Nesschter are sitting on chairs on the tree house patio with their fishing poles, and Ara is giggling uncontrollably and bracing herself for more leverage. The large, colorful fish on her hook is thrashing in the air as it ascends to its doom, and then there is Nesschter. He caught seaweed. Lots and lots of seaweed.

Ti-Tick. Ti-Tock.

"*Pay attention,*" says Mr. Verimoor.

"You destroyed my tree house!" screams Balik. "Do you know how long I spent on that tree house! The memories I've had with it!"

The people Balik are screaming at are captured human Federation soldiers, with more dead Federation soldiers stripped of their gear being tossed into a pile, while other Gaceraen soldiers are taking inventory of the confiscated supplies. The captured soldiers are sweaty and covered in grime and blood. They are digging a large grave, and dead Gaceraen soldiers are being lined up with their arms crossed, sprinkled with oil by a Gaceraen soldier muttering a prayer.

"I ought to put bullets in your heads!" says Balik.

"Balik, wait!" says Nesschter, his hand extended.

Ti-Tick. Ti-Tock.

"Are you crazy?" says Nesschter, his eyes wide with disbelief.

He is in his uniform and at the Giovine lakeside cabin, and Ara is in front of him, holding a basket of fruit and pastries.

"What?" says Ara. "It's a goodwill gift basket between my family and the AAHU. What's the worst that can happen?"

Ti-Tick. Ti-Tock.

A bright light blinds Nesschter when his head is pulled out of a bucket of iced water. As he coughs and sputters globs of frosty water, he is thrown against a metal table and a heavy arm pins his neck, while his feet and wrists are chained.

Nesschter thrashes and attempts to push back, but a club to the head knocks everything out of focus and leaves his ears ringing. Through the ringing he hears a ticking, and in the direction of the ticking are cold, gold eyes staring at him from the dark.

The eyes move forward, and Xajil Join comes out of the dark with a blank pocket watch in his hand and knives on his straps.

"Nesschter Hebediah Norkit, we will be here as long as we have to be. So, tell me, how do we breach the Vagsten Tunnels?" says Xajil.

Nesschter struggles some more, and a pair of clubs hits his ribs and the back of his legs. His legs buckle, but he is pulled upright, and Nesschter growls and glares at everyone while his limbs throb and burn.

"I'm not talking," says Nesschter.

"You will."

Xajil grabs Nesschter, slams his head on the table, and, after making a series of hisses, clicks and chirps, one of Nesschter's wrists is uncuffed. His arm is pulled across the table and held down by an Avus.

Then, Xajil draws a knife and traces Nesschter's arm, barely touching the skin beneath his gray fur. Nesschter's heart races, his claws extend, and he tries freeing his arm, but the Avus holds tight, digging their talons into his flesh. Xajil tilts his head to investigate Nesschter's eyes.

"Let's see how durable you are," says Xajil.

Then he stabs Nesschter's arm and-

Nesschter jolts upright and screams. He backpedals on the floor and hits Don, knocking him over.

Nesschter looks around, hyperventilating and sweating. Everyone from before is still in the room, weapons drawn, and a few of them are looking at Nesschter.

"Shit. What kind of memories does he have?" wonders a Lupinak.

Nesschter is still breathing heavily, and his mouth is clamped shut by Don.

"Quiet," says Don. "There's birdies lurking."

Nesschter's ears flick. Gunshots echo in the building, and he hears the squawks and screeches of the Avus. His watch is ticking loudly, and he pries Don's hand off his muzzle and goes to Gyrij.

"What's going on?" asks Nesschter, his voice raspy and heart still racing.

"Observers are attacking the museum," says Gyrij. "They went in guns blazing. Killed our customers and a few of our guys. We're going to have to fight our way out of here."

"Great," huffs Nesschter.

"The good news is that Observers are not usually heavily armed," says Don. "The bad news is that they are brutal sons of bitches."

"Quiet," hisses a Lupinak. "I hear them."

Everyone goes quiet and listens. Footsteps travel down the hallway, and the group jumps when wood shatters. There is a moment of silence. Then more steps and wood breaking. Nesschter looks around.

Wood breaks again.

He quietly approaches the wall and taps the brick in multiple places. Then he goes to Varil and motions for his short barrel rifle and his knife to be returned.

More wood breaks.

Varil reluctantly gives up the weapons and Nesschter waves everyone off to the sides and has them crouch.

Shattered wood echoes not too far from the room.

They do what Nesschter says, and he moves off to the side, matching the steps of the walking Avus. He has an angled line of sight to the doorway.

The steps stop outside the door, and Nesschter motions the ones on his side to aim at the wall. The others raise their rifles and pistols, and the door is broken off its hinges by a ram.

Broken wood and a doorknob fly. Nesschter fires three shots; two to the chest and one in the head for the Avus holding the ram, and the ones aiming at the wall open fire. The gunshots leave Nesschter's ears ringing and the pained squawks and screams of death mix with the wood and brick breaking from the unrelenting barrage.

Holes in the wall grow as bits and pieces of it crumble. Nesschter slides to the other side and peeks down both ends of the hallway.

On the side where the Avus came from, shadows break the late afternoon sunlight shining on the walls. When the first Avus appears, he shoots them in the chest with a controlled burst.

They stumble back, and Nesschter moves forward, keeping low so his body is hidden by the concrete barrier. He hears the other Avus shouting and screeching, and he moves forward, carefully stepping over the corpses. His heart is still racing, his hands are sweaty, and his ear is twitching from the ticking and overlapping voices in his mind.

"Stay low and move fast," orders Nesschter.

The group files out and Nesschter creeps forward a few steps before bullets strike the concrete barrier. Bits and pieces fly, and Nesschter lowers himself further.

While the bullets fly, an Avus at the end of the walkway fires blindly around the corner. Parts of the wall crumble and pieces of the floor pop up. Nesschter backpedals and falls against a corpse while shooting back.

After the shooting stops, he rolls back into the crouching position and keeps moving forward. His hands are still trembling, and he pushes himself against the concrete barrier.

The people behind him fire down into the lobby. The Avus fires blindly again, but this time the angle is much safer for Nesschter.

When Nesschter reaches the corner, he slides up, shoulders the rifle, and draws his knife, putting it in an ice pick grip. The Avus fires blindly again, but this time Nesshcter yanks him around the corner, slams him in the wall, and stabs him in the neck.

He removes a flashbang from the Avus's belt and chucks it around the corner. The loud bang and bright flash of light momentarily discombobulates Nesschter, but he quickly shakes it off and unslings his rifle before sliding around the corner.

The Avus are stumbling around, cursing and hissing, and Nesschter guns down all of them, splattering the wall with blood. The bullet shells clank and roll across the floor, and Nesschter ejects the spent magazine.

He keeps his eye on the doorway as he fishes for more magazines. When an Avus Observer runs up the stairs, Nesschter shoots them in the chest and head. Then a flash bang is tossed up, and there is a deafening bang and a flash of light with colored smoke rolling across the floor.

Nesschter snaps around, blinking away colorful blobs that infect his vision. His ears flick from the ringing and the sporadic gunshots.

Observers run up the stairs and Nesschter turns his rifle into a club, whacking the first in the head, shattering their beak. The Observer bounces off the wall and rolls down the stairs, and Nesschter rams the next one into his companion, leading to them falling down the stairs as a bundle of bodies bouncing and rolling off each other.

After they reach the bottom in a heap, Nesschter draws his knife and stabs the closest Avus in the chest. They squawk, and Nesschter elbows the next one in the face, scrambles up to slam the third into the wall, and stabs them through the ear.

They go limp, and Nesschter snaps around and throws his knife at the fourth Observer. The knife impales them at the base of their throat, and they stumble back, coughing and gurgling thick globs of blood.

The last Observer stands up and draws their pistol, just for Nesschter to put him in an arm lock, disarm him, and knock him out with a pistol whip. With that Observer limp, Nesschter throws him to the ground and looks around, panting heavily.

Blood has soaked the floor and furniture, and there are around twenty corpses of drugged-up Avus and their guards, plus a few Lupinaks and humans, all riddled with bullet holes. The floor has burn markings of a flash bang, and the makeshift garage door is still closed.

"Ness! Over here!" calls Don.

Nesschter looks across the lobby and sees Don across the room in a doorway, waving at him. He grabs his rifle and runs across the lobby and skids to a stop by Don. He looks past his friend and sees Chester, Gyrij, Rara, Varil, and a few other Lupinaks, humans, and Avus huddled down.

The hallway they are in stretches far, with dirty, broken windows going along its length. Light shines through them, illuminating dust, broken tile, and plants stretching along the wall or bullying their way through the cracks.

"Is there an escape route out of here?" asks Nesschter.

"There's the loading dock down the hallway and to the left. It was used by the museum for artifacts," says Varil. "If we can get there, we can fight our way to the vehicles and escape."

"Everyone, stay on your guard," says Gyrij. "Varil, you lead the way."

Varil nods, adjusts his grip, peeks down the hallway, and then looks outside. He hesitates, then goes forward with his weapon raised. A few seconds later, the rest of the group follows.

Around halfway down, there is a trio of pops, glass shatters, and Varil is blasted against the wall with a large hole in his chest. He crumbles, and the group yells and curses, and bounces off each other, as more bullets shatter the glass and cut down more of the group, including Chester.

"Get down!" yells Nesschter, tugging Don to the floor with him.

Gyrij pulls Rara down, right as bullets streak by them, shattering brick on the wall. Chester lays on the ground, twitching and coughing blood. More shots whiz overhead, striking those trying to run to safety, while the rest of the group ducks to the floor.

Chester's blood seeps towards them, his eyes are wide open, and he has become still. Rara is shrieking and trying to reach for Chester, but Gyrij has her locked in a hug.

"We have to keep moving!" says Don.

"Where? There's a sniper!" says Gyrij.

"We'll have to go through the abandoned area on foot. They're watching the vehicles and will hear them, but we can split up and move through the ruins without them. It's our best shot," says a Lupinak with amber eyes, a comb over brown mane, and gray fur.

"He's right. It's dangerous, but it's our best chance. Move forward and stay low," says Nesschter.

The group moves down the hallway, staying crouched as they do so. An Avus pokes their head up, and their head is immediately destroyed by a burst of gunfire.

"Jeeze!" says Don.

"Keep going! Stay low!" says Nesschter.

The group keeps moving, and when they reach the end of the hallway, Nesschter stays low as he pushes the door open. Sparks fly and holes appear as bullets strike the metal door, and Nesschter keeps it open, staying low and waving the others through.

"Go! Go! Go!" orders Nesschter.

The survivors rush forward, keeping to the crouching position. After the last of them go through the doorway, Nesschter ducks into the next area and slams the door shut. Light shines through the bullet holes, and Nesschter finds the new area to be a large room with old metal cabinets, broken glass displays, and spray-painted walls and pillars.

The room is crumbling from decay, and the scent of rot and mold clings to his nose and tongue. At the far end of the room is a large metal door that is rusted on the edges. The door is chained and padlocked shut, and Gyrij uses a key to remove the chains.

Once those are removed, Gyrij pulls open the door and is grabbed and stabbed in the chest with a large knife. He squawks and is pushed back while Kwari moves forward, using his body as a shield and shooting his pistol at the group.

The group scatters with a couple dropping dead, and seven more Avus Observers rush in with shotguns and start unloading on the group. Blast after blast shakes Nesschter's ears and leaves them ringing. The group fires back as they retreat, taking some of the Observers with them, but they are quickly gunned down, except for the gray Lupinak, Rara, Don, and Nesschter.

Kwari shoots Gyrij through the bottom of his jaw at an angle, tossing his lifeless body aside as he strolls into the room.

Meanwhile, Nesschter doesn't see where Rara or the gray Lupinak went. He dives behind a metal counter and covers his head as slugs destroy it and its contents in a show of sparks and shattering wood and glass. As the chaos consumes the room, Don slides next to Nesschter and checks his pistol while Nesschter peeks around the corner.

Rara screams and runs to the Observers, firing a pistol madly. She kills one of them, but before the body drops, Kwari rams her against the wall. His talon slash through her midsection, creating a thick flow of crimson. She screams in agony, and Kwari jams his pistol into her wound and fires three shots at an upward angle.

The shots rips through Rara, and she slides to the floor, staying on her knees, head slumped against the wall, soaked in a puddle of blood.

Kwari reloads and shouts an order in the chirping language of Avir. The four remaining Avus move forward. Three shotguns are raised and sweeping the area, and Kwari stays behind, moving slightly slower.

Don peeks out, retreats, takes a deep breath, and then peeks out again and fires off a few rounds from his pistol. An Observer drops dead, and a barrage of shotgun slugs and bullets shred the counter, forcing Don to scramble away.

With them distracted, Nesschter and the gray Lupinak move from cover and gun down the other two shotgunners, leaving just Kwari. He raises his pistol but stops when Nesschter growls at him.

"Drop it!" barks Nesschter.

Kwari stares at him, and Nesschter, Don, and the gray Lupinak slowly approach him with their weapons raised. Kwari crouches and sets his pistol on the ground.

"And the knife and shotgun," says Don.

Kwari sets his knife and shotgun on the floor next to the pistol.

"Hands on your head," says the gray Lupinak.

Kwari stays on his knees and puts his hands on his head, and the gray Lupinak kicks the weapons away.

"Who sent you?" asks Don.

"My boss," says Kwari.

"Director Xajil Ojin?" says Nesschter.

Kwari is silent, and Nesschter searches the Avus, pulls out his phone, and gives it to Kwari.

"Tell your supervisor that your targets are relocated, and have the snipers called off," says Nesschter.

Kwari glares at him, and Don and the gray Lupinak aim their pistols at his head. A few seconds of silence and ticking from Nesschter's watch passes, and Kwari grabs the phone.

"Put it on speaker," says Nesschter.

Kwari dials a number and puts it on speaker. It rings a few times, and then there is an answer of chirps, clicks, and whistles.

"It is," says Kwari in Aarden, glaring at Nesschter. "Pull the snipers away, too. We're done."

The other voice is quiet for a couple of seconds, and then, *"Very good. I'll see you in a few minutes."*

The other end hangs up, and Kwari's crest flexes, and Nesschter stares at him skeptically.

"Now what?" says Kwari.

"Now we tie you up and put you somewhere where you won't bother us," says Nesschter.

Don snorts a laugh, and Nesschter glares at him.

"What?" says Nesschter.

"You and your bondage stuff," says Don.

"Bondage stuff?" says the gray Lupinak.

"Ignore him. He's being stupid at a very inappropriate time," says Nesschter.

"I'm trying to lighten the mood!" says Don defensively.

Then Kwari springs forward. The three swear, and in a span of three seconds, Nesschter's rifle is disarmed and he is kicked into Don, and the gray Lupinak's face is slashed with Kwari's talons.

The Lupinak yelps and drops to the floor, holding his face. Don brings his pistol to bear, but Kwari quickly disarms him and flips him to the floor with swift, fluid motions.

Nesschter tackles Kwari into a pillar and punches him in the cracked beak. The beak nearly shatters, and Kwari screeches, kicks Nesschter back, and dives for his pistol. Don awkwardly kicks the weapon away from his position on the floor, and he rolls on his side, aiming his pistol at Kwari.

Kwari grabs Don's hand and slams it to the floor, causing the pistol to go off, the round barely missing Nesschter's foot.

Meanwhile, the gray Lupinak is on the floor, cursing and kicking. His hands and face are soaked in blood, and Kwari climbs on top of Don with his pistol hand still trapped against the floor.

The Avus raises his talons for his free hand. Right as he brings them down, Nesschter tackles Kwari. His claws tear into Kwari's shoulders, and he sinks his teeth into the Avus's forearm.

Kwari screeches and stabs Nesschter's arm with his talons, and the two roll around on the floor. Nesschter keeps a tight hold on Kwari's arm, and the Avus keeps slashing and pecking at him, tearing his flesh and clothes.

After a few rolls, Kwari kicks Nesschter off, picks up his knife, and lunges at him. Nesschter rolls away, swipes out Kwari's footing, and draws his knife, while the Avus falls on his back.

Kwari quickly gets back up and Nesschter isn't far behind. The Avus charges him with erratic swipes with his one arm bleeding profusely. Nesschter keeps a good distance, and Kwari screeches again and goes for another lunge.

Nesschter pivots around Kwari and slices the back of his leg. Kwari buckles and swipes at Nesschter, but his arm is swiftly trapped by Nesschter's knife hand, and his blade slices the Avus's tendon.

Kwari screeches and drop his knife, his fingers limp. Nesschter kicks the knife away, and Kwari awkwardly slashes at Nesschter with his injured hand.

Nesschter grabs and twists the arm behind Kwari's back, kicks the back of his injured leg, dropping him to his knees, and then he slashes his throat. Kwari drops dead soon after, gurgling and twitching.

Nesschter wipes his bloody knife on his sleeve, panting heavily and looking around. He sees the gray Lupinak sitting on his knees. He has his shirt serving as a bandage, and Don is tying the back of it tight. The Lupinak's gray fur is wet with blood, and he is shaking and looking around erratically.

"What's your name?" asks Nesschter.

"Fargo Khal Jarim," he says slowly, his voice trembling and slurred with bloody spit dripping past his mouth and down his chin. "I'm in a coushin brauhch of tshe Norkhet Fham-ly."

Nesschter nods and squeezes his shoulder. "Fargo, we're going to get you somewhere safe."

Fargo wipes his bloody chin with a shaky hand. "I hash to tahk you to a shafe haush."

"I'm not going anywhere until I get Ara. Xajil has her at Division 4 and she won't last much longer there," says Nesschter.

"Oh, thash where Bah-lk ish gog," says Fargo.

"What?"

"Oh... I should not hash shaid that... Can you draugh me osh shomewhere?"

"Yeah... Don, get a vehicle," says Nesschter.

"Why me?" says Don.

"Just do it!"

"There's a damn sniper!"

"And running out in the open will just get us killed because I guarantee you those snipers haven't moved. Plus, Fargo is missing an eye, so he really can't move well."

"And mah sheek ish shredded," adds Fargo.

"You're the super soldier. You do it!" yells Don.

"No!" snaps Nesscher.

"Why?" says Don.

"Because I don't know how to drive!" says Nesschter.

Fargo and Don look at him, wide-eyed.

"Seriously?" says Don.

"Dad'sh ghon love thish," says Fargo.

Nesschter rubs his brow, growling through his fangs.

"How do you not know how to drive?" says Don.

"My dad gish driving leshons on the shide to pups. He can teach shou," says Fargo.

"Just stop talking..." says Nesschter, and to Don, "You get a car!"

"Yeah, sure. Sure," says Don, walking backwards. "But when this is over, we're going to teach you how to drive."

"Go!"

Don runs away, and Nesschter sighs and rubs his mane, and Fargo looks at him, offering a weak smile

"My dad cahn do drishing leshons for free if money'sh pro-lem," says Fargo.

Nesschter's ears droop.

Chapter 10

Nesschter digs through Rara's backpack, retrieving the tin of N-Light while Don plucks a shotgun, its ammunition, and the ammo belt off an Observer's corpse. The stench of blood and gunpowder lingers in the air, and Fargo's pained seethes and quiet mutters hang in the air. Beyond the walls, the commotion of the protest grows.

"What'cha got there?" asks Don.

"N-Light. I know Xajil siphoned my money, so maybe we can bribe a doctor with some pills to fix Fargo," says Nesschter.

"Right..." Don peeks outside and sees shot-up vehicles and more dead Lupinaks and humans laying in pools of blood on the ground or inside the vehicles. Past them are crumbling or burnt-down structures that are being reclaimed by winding plants and gnarled trees, or grass and weeds through the broken pavement. Beyond the ruins, colorful smoke rises with the chants, honking horns and airships flying overhead. However, what he does not see are signs of a sniper. He doesn't like that.

"Hey, Ness," calls Don.

"Yeah?" replies Nesschter.

Don goes to Kwari and removes his vest, grimacing as his fingers are smeared by the blood.

"Gather every armored vest you can, and when I bring in whatever vehicle, I'm going to need you to put them against the windows," says Don.

Nesschter does a double take.

"You want to block the windows?" asks Nesschter.

"From sniper fire? Yeah," says Don.

"How will you see?"

"I'll leave a slot for me to peek through. Be ready to move fast like lightning, because I know for a fact that the birdie's buddies know we're still kicking."

"You got that feeling, too, eh?"

Don nods, and Nesschter moves towards the nearest dead Observer and takes a couple of flashbangs and starts removing the vest.

"Get the car. I'll handle the vest," says Nesschter.

"Whaht abaught me?" asks Fargo, still slumped against a pillar.

Nesschter gives Fargo a pistol and turns him to the hallway entrance.

"Keep your eye on that door and shoot anybody that isn't us," orders Nesschter.

"Sheer thang," says Fargo.

Nesschter resumes gathering, and Don returns to the loading entrance. He hesitates, checks his weapon again, and looks outside. The nearest car is a three-second sprint away, near a large, broken statue of birds. Its windows are cracked and splattered with blood, and a dead Lupinak lays on the ground next to it.

Don takes a deep breath... and runs.

The first second is fine.

The next second, a burst grazes past his head.

The third second, he slides to the ground and pushes himself against the car, hyperventilating and clutching his shotgun tight. His hands tremble, his heart aches, and blood from the graze trickles down his cheek.

Don wipes his face and raises his head enough to see the interior. The driver, a Lupinak, has his head and chest torn apart by bullets and broken glass, and his blood has soaked the seat, steering wheel, and dashboard. The car keys are in the driver's hand.

Don cautiously opens the passenger door and flinches when bullets strike the windshield and break the dashboard. He retreats, breathing heavily and wiping blood off his cheek again. Then he crawls inside, cringing and tensing as bullets hit the car again. He grabs the car keys and stretches his arm to open the door and push the corpse out.

More bullets strike the door. Staying low, Don starts the ignition and puts the gear in reverse, using his shotgun to hit the gas. The engine revs and the car zooms back, until the door is broken off by the statue.

The statue provides enough cover for Don to adjust his position. Now that he is sitting, he zooms forward, makes a sharp turn, and speeds inside the receiving area. It takes only a few seconds for him to go from outside to slamming on the breaks and narrowly missing Nesschter.

Nesschter rushes to help Fargo get to the car. After Fargo is seated, Nesschter helps Don fortify the windows with the vests. They use bricks to hold them in place, and clothing hooks to hold up the vests on the passenger windows. Up front, Nesschter is jamming the vest on his side and on the windshield. Don jumps inside and sets his shotgun in between himself and Nesschter.

"There is still a sniper somewhere, so I'm going to drive fast," says Don.

Fargo buckles up, Nesschter adjusts his grip on his rifle, and Don slams on the gas and speeds out in reverse. He has his head out just enough to see a sliver of his environment, and once they are outside, bullets strike the trunk and back window.

Fargo shrinks down and the vests on the back buckle. Don makes a sharp turn, putting the vehicle in a spin. Loud pings and cracking glass mess with the squealing tires, and Don zooms forward.

He drives blind for a few seconds before he and Nesschter can remove the vests. When that happens, they see a blue car speeding towards them.

"Jeez!" yells Don.

He spins the wheel, and the two cars bang into each other on Don's side. Nesschter aims his rifle at the opposing car, and Don slams on the gas. They surge forward, and the car gives chase.

"Fargo, we got company!" says Nesschter.

Fargo shakily checks his pistol, and Nesschter tightens his grip on the rifle and looks at the mirror, his ears perking at an unpleasant sight.

"What do you see?" asks Don.

"We have three cars chasing us," says Nesschter.

"What!?"

Suddenly, their car jerks forward, and everyone screams and swears as the vehicle spins. The vest in the back window falls. In the rear-view mirror, Don sees three blue cars behind them, and the trunk of their vehicle smashed. Observers on the two front vehicles lean out with their short barrel rifles aimed at them.

"Get down!" yells Don.

All three duck, and a barrage of bullets tear into the trunk and break through the remainder of the back window, shatter the windshield, and destroy the rear-view mirror. Don screams out a stream of swears and gives the vehicle another sharp turn into a section of crumbling apartments and burnt-out stores.

Fargo fires blindly out the back hole, while Nesschter peeks out and fires a controlled burst with his rifle. The vehicle bounces and swerves from the aged rubble and broken road, giving the wheels and their shocks hell.

"Get me closer!" says Nesschter.

Don slams on the breaks. The car directly behind them slams into their back, while the other two speed by them. The occupants of the car behind them become disoriented, and Nesschter fires rapidly at the car passing his side.

Bullets move side and up and down like a wave, ripping into the vehicle's side, shattering its driver's window, splattering the interior in blood, and tearing apart its wheel and rim. Torn rubber flies, the vehicle spins out of control and smashes into an old fire hydrant, crunching its front and popping it into the air. The vehicle lands, sparking and ejecting bursts of electrical fire, and Don speeds forward, dragging the back bumper on crumbled pavement. Nesschter slips a fresh magazine into his rifle, and Fargo shoots blindly again. Then they hear a pop, and their car swerves erratically, despite Don's best efforts. Sparks fly from the back, and Fargo's bloody hands tremble while he reloads.

"I shmell shmok," slurs Fargo.

Don and Nesschter look behind them and see smoke rising from the trunk, and the car that hit their back goes next to them with the Observer aiming their short barrel rifle at them. The second blue car turns towards them.

Don switches gears and puts their vehicle in a spin, knocking their closest target off balance. The Observer still shoots, but the bullets strike the already damaged engine, and jets of fiery smoke accompanied with loose sparks burst out.

Don makes another sharp turn and crashes through a rotted display window, obliterating a naked Lupinak mannequin covered in graffiti. The closest car follows them inside, but the next one veers off.

Headlights and sparks light up the dark, dusty department store, knocking over crumbling displays and crushing garbage under their tires. Nesschter and the Observer exchange gunfire, both striking the vehicles or the scenery.

A jet of flame bursts from the trunk. Nesschter pulls in and Don makes another sharp turn. He fishtails on the dirty tile, and right before their pursuer finishes passing them, he rams them and keeps pushing.

Tires squeal, and Nesschter unloads the entire magazine into their window, destroying the glass and splattering the blue car's interior with blood. Don keeps pushing forward, smashing the Observer's car into a pillar.

Chunks of the concrete pillar break off, the blue car's frame bends, and its remaining windows shatter. Don goes in reverse, briefly taking their target with them before their front bumper snaps off. Their engine whines and sputters, and each sputter shoots out sparks and black smoke, and the popped tires tear into the decayed tile.

The group is silent the entire time Don reverses out. When they reach the street, the engine sputters and whines, and the car jerks forward, going slow, then fast, then stuttering, and then back to slow and jerking to fast again.

"I shthink we should evacht the cahr," says Fargo.

"You sure?" asks Don.

A puff of black smoke erupts from the trunk, and Nesschter nods.

"Might be a good idea... What was in the trunk anyway?" says Nesschter.

"I dunno. Flahmble shtuff fer grilling?" says Fargo.

Suddenly, tires squeal from a short distance away, and all threesee the last blue car speed out from an alley. Don groans, Fargo bangs his bloodsoaked head on the seat, and Nesschter taps his skull against his rifle, growing in aggravation.

"Oh, for Pete's sake," says Don. "Fargo, give me a flashbang."

Fargo gives Don a flash bang as the last blue car speeds towards them. All three nonchalantly duck when more bullets rip apart their vehicle.

As they putt-putt along, the last blue car reaches Don's side, and the Observer aims their short barrel rifle at them. Donchucks the flashbang in their vehicle.

The Observers scream and veer off, and then there is a bright flash of light that shatters their windows and sends the vehicle swerving and crashing into the corner of a building. Soon after, the group's vehicle groans, sputters, and stops in the middle of the road. The smoking and sparking are thick and intense.

Don sighs and wipes his hair. "Well... That was–"

The engine bursts into an inferno of electric flames and oily black smoke, and fire erupts from the trunk.

"Oh shit!" yells Don.

"Out! Out! Out!" yells Nesschter as all three scramble out of the vehicle.

They run and stumble away as multiple pops, screeches, booms, and sparks echo over the desolate cityscape, and fire and black smoke roll into the sky. Then the engine and trunk explode, jerking the car in a circle and leaving it to be consumed by the fires.

Nesschter and Fargo stiffly watch the scene unfold with wide eyes, and Don hobbles next to them, panting and wiping sweat and blood off his face. There is a moment of silence between the three due to them being mesmerized by the flames dancing in front of them.

A moment later, Don looks at Nesschter and says, "You're not allowed to ride with me, anymore."

Chapter 11

Gears crank and chains rattle. The darkness of the tunnel fades and its ruins are gradually replaced with an empty warehouse, its air thick with dust and smelling of oil and sweat. Balik sits in the front passenger seat of his modified Division 4 carrier, which has metal bars attached to the front, an extra layer of metal plating on the sides and roll bars on the windshield and door windows.

The small crane guides the carrier to a secure area, and then gently lowers it to the concrete floor. After the vehicle touches down, humans and Lupinaks quickly work to remove the chains.

Balik, his troops and Jarvis, who was sitting in the back with the soldiers, exit the carrier and the crane returns to the hole to grab the next vehicle.

The warehouse is large and serves as a lot for other modified, and numerous humans and Lupinaks are arming themselves with Federation weapons.

Balik isn't using any Federation weapons, but he, Jarvis, and their soldiers are wearing a spinal shield generator. Excellent against ballistics, garbage against more personal attacks.

Balik and Jarvis do a quick visual inspection of the dozens of Revivalist soldiers camping out in the warehouse. Balik likes how quickly everyone has set up their vehicles and equipment. No one has slacked off. Everyone is ready to go. However, he is not seeing a particular person of interest. Surely, they would be here by now, and there is no way this person slipped by them in the tunnels.

Balik keeps one eye open for Nesschter or Fargo as he silently continues inspecting the Revivalist soldiers, their equipment, and vehicles. Then a Lupinak with a shotgun slung on his shoulder approaches him, and with him is a small group of humans and other Lupinaks.

"Sir, we have our people in place doing what they can to cause trouble. We're just waiting on your word for the next phase," says the Lupinak.

"Excellent," says Balik. He rubs his hands and looks around the warehouse. "But before we go, where's Nesschter?"

The group goes quiet. Balik stares at them, and Jarvis scans the area. The group looks at each, and one of the Lupinaks nudges a human next to him, bringing Balik to look at them.

"Where's Nesschter?" asks Balik, his voice darker.

"That's the problem, sir... He isn't here," says a human. "We haven't had any contact with him or the extraction team for some time."

Balik's eyes darken. "What?"

The human swallows. "He's not here, sir. None of them are. We haven't been able to get a hold of anyone from the group, either. Not even Chester or Fargo."

Balik stares at the human. His lips are tight and his eyes are narrowed. The human shifts uncomfortably, sweating profusely and heart beating loud enough for Balik to hear. The Lupinaks step back.

Balik takes a deep breath and presses his palms together in front of his snout. "Is that so?"

"Should we send someone to investigate?" asks the human.

"Yes, you should. Right now." Balik pops open his watch and observes the seconds hand swinging back and forth like a pendulum, the hour hand drags itself along way too fast for an hour, and the minute hand going back two minutes before lurching forward three. He closes his watch and puts his hand on his shoulder. "I'll give you eleven seconds to assemble a team to investigate the museum or I am smashing your head flat into the nearest concrete pillar... Eleven..."

The human bolts away, shouting random names, and pointing at the people he called and ordering them in the nearest vehicle. Once all of them are in, the car speeds out of the warehouse, and Balik sighs, removes his green beanie, and runs his fingers through his stubby mohawk mane.

"We'll find him, sir," says the Lupinak.

"For your sake, you better, or it's your face being flattened instead of the human's," says Balik heavily. He returns the beanie to his head and marches to his vehicle. "Get everybody loaded up! We're moving out now!"

The Revivalist soldiers vocalize their affirmation and hurry to their vehicles. Soon engines rumble to life and headlights flash on like beasts waking up from slumbers, their engine rumbles swallowing the faint noises outside.

Once the convoy starts leaving the warehouse, Balik watches the vehicles go, one by one. When it is his turn to leave, the driver eases forward, and Balik pulls out his phone.

The setting sun's orange glow shines on Shio, and its orange hue is tainted with thick colored smoke rising over the rooflines. Even with the distance, he can hear the chants and the banging, and as the vehicles make their way through the warehouses, more vehicles join them from other buildings that have "closed" or "under renovation" signs.

They aren't the repurposed Division 4 vehicles, but they are a mix of vans, cars, SUVs, and trucks, all fitted with armor plates, and the trucks have turrets mounted on them. Balik sees a camera drone over the roof watching them, and he smiles and waves at it. Then he sends only one thing on the encrypted group chat: "11"

Chapter 12

Xajil is in the War Room, watching the theater-sized screen as the swarm of protesters is captured on multiple cameras. The ones that are causing the most trouble with violent acts, or carry signs or flares, have their bodies highlighted in red or yellow boxes, and their profiles are brought up on the computers monitored by individual agents.

Most are wearing masks, but their IDs and state-issued phones provide direct tracking. The profiles on the screens of the smaller computers display their names, addresses, occupations, bank information, and phone and social media information.

"Orders sir?" asks Darius.

"Yellow blocks, dock them twenty points and confiscate fifty-five percent of their financial accounts. Red blocks, dock fifty five points and confiscate ninety percent of their finances and freeze their wages and government checks. Then search their internet history, phone calls, and texts, and dock them double points for every violation. If they reach zero points, relocate them," says Xajil.

"Excellent call, sir."

"Leave the chanters and walkers alone. They are just sheep following a shepherd. They will scatter when they see us act against the agitators."

"Of course."

Darius relays the message, and Xajil rubs his talons together, silently watching the footage. The crowd is halfway made of Avus, but there are a sizable portion of Lupinaks and humans joining the rush.

Random alien immigrants have joined the fray, too. The signs are mostly about the high taxes and food prices, but some have signs dedicated to inflation, wages, and cost of living. The ones with the flares have different colors, and Xajil noticed that the ones with red flares are nearest where police blockades are.

Green appears to be at grocery stores and convenience stores, which are being looted, despite the best efforts of the police and the drones. The police are launching tear gas or pepper bombs into the crowd, and a couple have manned hoses to spray at the protesters, while camera drones fly around, zapping their targets and taking pictures.

Before one of the camera poles is torn down, it captures a drone being tugged down, beaten with wrenches and hammers, and then dragged down the road by a chain attached to a car that is full of Avus launching fireworks.

Yellow flares are around camera posts, and after the post is torn down, by whatever crude method the crowd sees fit, the flare is put out. The user runs off to another camera post and lights another yellow flare.

Xajil also notices that all the flare users are Lupinaks who so far do not appear in the systems, and yet the drones are still picking up cell phone signals from them. Which means they are using modified phones, and either left their ID at home, or are from outside of Shio. Xajil is leaning towards outsiders.

"This is too coordinated for it to be spontaneous," says Xajil to Darius. "Immediately confiscate all finances and property and relocate anyone using yellow flares and tearing down the camera poles."

"Yes sir," says Darius.

"Director! Sir! We have a problem!" says an operator.

"What is it?" says Xajil.

"Camera drone one-zero-zero-five-five-two-B in Section four-twelve picked up a lot of movement that came out of the warehouses."

"Put it on the big screen."

The feeds are all replaced with a single live recording of a large convoy leaving the warehouse district of the Outer Ring. He sees that half of them are the missing Division 4 vehicles from the botched raid in Talos Yeshniv's territory.

They have been modified with various attachments and have slogans and pictures painted on them, but they are the property of the state, desecrated by violent vagabonds. The rest of the convoy is comprised of an assortment of vehicles, all armored, and all filled with Revivalists.

Xajil's crest goes limp, and his eyes widen, and Darius' jaw drops. The rest of the room has similar reactions, and Xajil's eyes narrow when he sees Balik smiling and waving at the camera as his modified Division 4 vehicle passes by.

"What the hell?" says Darius, his eyes flicking in every direction possible to take in the details of the feed. "Where did they come from? That's a small army! And why is Balik on the front? Does he have a death wish?"

"This protest is a cover. The agitators are working for Balik Norkit and the Revivalists…" says Xajil. He grabs Darius and pulls him out of the room with him, speaking as he goes. "Get Division 4 tactical teams out there, right now. Get every Observer out there, arm all the police officers and I will call in the military."

Darius nods and Xajil pulls out his phone and types in a command. Immediately after, an alarm sounds and red lights swirl.

"Where are the Asvens?" says Xaji, his voice cracking into a frantic shake.

"Mrs. Asven is out shopping at the Gailo Mall, and Mr. Asven is at the theater," says Darius.

"Get them back here and put them in the safe room. And make sure the civilians are locked in their homes."

"Yes sir!"

Darius breaks off and Xajil runs to his office and speedily types on his computer an urgent message to the nearest GSAU military base. The message header: ***Insurgency in Shio.***

Next, he types in a command that has the TVs in the working areas switch from propaganda to messages ordering civilians to return home immediately and lock their doors.

The following slide orders all available firearm certified agents to defend their respective work locations. Outside his office, the crowd of desk jockeys rush out with other agents to the armory.

As Xajil watches the mess of bodies he chucks a few anxiety pills in his mouth, and drowns them with his water. Then he checks his knives on his straps, and after that, he checks the time. The faceless clock tells him plenty, so he slams it shut and exits his office.

Outside, he sees a group of Avus guards returning from the armory, fully armed and wearing armored vests. He orders them to follow him to De-Escalation Chamber C.

The alarm is ringing inside, and the prisoners are shouting and banging or shaking their bars. The guards pace around nervously. They salute when Xajil enters with his security detail, and he makes a quick salute in return, without slowing down. He grabs one of the guards for the De-Escalation Chamber and drags him straight to Ara's cell.

The obnoxious prisoners are demanding to be released or wanting to know what is happening, but they are ignored. When they reach Ara's de-escalation room, Xajil clamps his hands in front of him as he stares at her, his eyes tracing the fading scratches on her body.

Ara pushed herself in the corner, trying to escape through the concrete. When the guards unlock her door, she whimpers and shakes her head. Then the guards file in with cuffs, a gag, and muzzle.

"No!" cries Ara.

Ara grips the bed frame, and the guards swear in Avir with loud hisses and sharp squawks as they tug on her and pry at her hands. Xajil can't see much due to the bodies crowded around her, and he impatiently checks his watch.

"Get off of me!" sobs Ara.

The guards manage to pry Ara off the bed frame and drag her across the floor as she kicks and screams, hitting some of the guards. They retaliate, hitting her with their clubs.

"Hey what are you guys doing to her!" yells a prisoner.

"Leave her alone!" shouts another prisoner.

Xajil ignores them, too busy watching Ara is still thrashing and crying.

"Stop! Stop, please!" sobs Ara over the shouts. "STOP IT!"

Ara bites an Avus. It squawks and beats her head while she sinks in and shakes her head, tearing his flesh and throwing him down. The other Avus stomp on her, making her yelp and release her victim.

Then one pins her down by pressing on her spine and forces her head back and mouth open. Ara's claws scratch the concrete, and the gag is shoved in her mouth. The muzzle is strapped, while her hands and ankles are bound.

After that, she is hoisted up with blood on her face and her knees weak. She and Xajil lock eyes, and her breathing becomes erratic. She tries pushing back, but she is shoved out into the hallway. She stumbles, and Xajil catches her with the help of another guard that grabbed her arm.

Xajil holds her muzzle, and his gold eyes stare into her bloodshot, green eyes. Tears soak her cheeks, and more roll down, mixing with the blood that has stained her white fur. Xajil inhales, and slowly exhales, as he brushes some tears away with his talon and straightens her hair. This only makes her stiffen and whimper, and she tries backing up again, but the guards hold her tight.

"I know you are scared, but there is nothing to be afraid of. I will fix you and protect you from what's coming," says Xajil.

Ara's reply is sharp breaths and trembling.

"Take her to the safe room," orders Xajil.

Ara's scream is muffled, and she shakes her head with a new wave of tears and digs her feet in, but it is useless. The guards easily overpower her and elect to drag her down the hallway. Xajil follows close behind, talons twitching, and the grip on his watch tight.

He can feel it in his bones. The end is coming for someone.

It is only a matter of time.

Chapter 13

Wailing alarms and angry chants is the ambience of the Outer Ring of Shio. Large groups of protesters move through the streets, waving flares, signs, flags, and banners. They are shouting, they are chanting, and some are breaking windows or attacking parked vehicles.

Police vehicles are weaving their way through the crowds, honking, revving their engines, and jerking forward against the swarm in a threatening manner. The sky is getting darker, so the various colors of the flares stick out, and the lampposts shine on the swarm. Lights from airships and camera drones sweep the area high above the reach of the people.

Nesschter, Don, and Fargo use the chaos for cover as they make their way through the streets. But the downside is that it is difficult to stay together. The crowd moves like a river of sludge with multiple currents, so the group must force their way through it and keep a hold on their clothes to stay together.

While this happens, Fargo has gotten worse, to the point where Don is nearly carrying the Lupinak with him.

It takes them a while of nudging and shoving their way through the crowd, but after they reach an opening at a filthy alley, the group hurries forward. Nesschter slides to a stop by the wall, and Don follows his lead.

Nesschter pulls out his pocket watch and pops open its lid. His hand trembles, and the ticking is clear in his ears, despite the deafening chants of the crowd moving through the streets. Flags are waved with fervor, flares are directing the crowd, banners are held up high, and an airship flies overhead with large speakers.

Its orb-shaped engines twist and turn to guide the airship over the crowd, and Nesschter's group ducks down as a convoy of armored police vehicles speed by with their lights flashing and sirens blaring. The crowd throws garbage and bricks at them, but they keep going without slowing, forcing the protesters to move out of the way, lest they want to be crushed by tons of steel and rubber.

"You are not authorized to gather! Disperse immediately!" instructs the airship.

The message is repeated over the speakers on the lampposts, and Nesschter closes his watch, stuffs it back in his pouch, and adjusts his grip on his rifle. Don sets Fargo against the wall and goes to Nesschter's side.

"So, we're still going to Division 4 HQ, right?" says Don.

"Yes. That's where Ara is, and that's where Xajil is going to be," says Nesschter.

Then movement above catches Nesschter's eyes. On the upper floor of a rundown apartment, there is a Lupinak watching the scene, but he is a little too attentive to be a civilian watching. His eyes are closely following the police vehicles, and he is speaking on his phone.

"And so is Balik, and you do know that Balik wants to kill me, right?" says Don. "Also, we need to get Fargo to a hospital."

"No... No hoshpitahl," says Fargo. "Theresh a chlinic on fahv-fahv-oh-three Harshon Ave."

Nesschter looks further down and sees a pair of masked Lupinaks climbing a ladder, disappearing from sight when they reach the roof.

"Harshon?" says Don.

"H–A–R–V–O–N," says Fargo.

"Harvon. Gotcha... Where's Harvon Avenue?"

Nesschter stuffs his rifle underneath his coat and leans further out. The police have set up a barricade, and police officers have hopped out with a shield phalanx.

"You are not authorized to gather! Disperse immediately!" repeats the airship.

Nesschter looks at the alley across from them and sees a van and a car gliding along. He can't see much with the van, but the car is full of Lupinaks, and they are readying weapons. Nesschter curses under his breath and goes to Fargo and Don.

"We need to get you to that clinic, right now," says Nesschter.

Fargo nods and holds Don's arm tight. "You go. I tahlk direcshons." He points with a shaky finger. "Down there."

Nesschter grips his weapon tight and goes down the alley. He wants to run, but with Don having to practically carry Fargo, that is out of the question. His fingers are also itching, and his hand feels like a rope is tugging him towards the N-Light in his pouch.

The craving, the ticking, the chanting, the sirens, the scent of the smoke and urban rot is playing hell with his senses. His heart races and his mind spins, trying to figure out what will happen next with the Lupinaks he saw.

"Hey! Hey! Ness, slow down!" calls Don.

Nesschter looks over his shoulder and skids to a halt. Despite his best efforts to stay slow, he still managed to outpace Don and Fargo. So, he waits for them. Finger tapping his rifle's trigger guard and flinching when he sees a camera drone flying by.

"What's going on?" says Don when he reaches Nesschter.

Nesschter turns and takes slow, heavy steps down the dirty alley, loathing the smell of sewage and rotten food seeping into his nose.

"I saw a group of Lupinaks getting in positions civilians don't take," says Nesschter.

"Shit... You think they're Balik's?" says Don.

"Probably."

"They are," says Fargo.

Nesschter and Don look at him, and he swallows bloody spit and leans against Don, shaking and having difficulty focusing.

"Itsh hish redeshon," says Fargo.

"What the hell is that supposed to mean?" says Don.

"We tahk right... down three blohcksh... Left two... Fren-ly Clinic."

Nesschter nods. "Alright. Let's go."

The three move forward again, and Don looks between Nesschter and Fargo.

"But the cryptic part," says Don.

"There's nothing cryptic about it," says Nesschter. "Balik was a ranking officer of the Gaceraen military. They lost the Aarde War, and he thinks whatever this is will restore some of his honor."

"Or maybe he's just crazy," says Don.

"That too."

Nesschter stops by the edge of the alley and peeks down. A crowd is passing him, with a few masked Lupinaks holding red flares, and another holding a yellow flare. The one with the yellow flare is surrounded by a group of Avus and humans tearing down a pole with a ring of cameras. The ones with the red flares are leading the crowd to the police barricade.

The riot shields phalanx holds fast, and the armored vehicles have lined up to create another layer of the blockade. The airship returns and shines a light on the protesters, and camera drones fly above the crowd, snapping pictures.

"Shit. The clinic is past the barricade," says Nesschter.

"Can we go through the crowd?" asks Don.

Nesschter looks at the crowd. It is very thick, and some are throwing junk at the camera drones and flipping off the airship or shining laser pointers at it and the camera drone.

"You are not authorized to gather! Disperse immediately!" instructs the airship.

"Extreme punishment is authorized," says a nearby camera drone.

The protesters shout back and wave their flags and signs and push against the barricade. The police officers hit back with their batons and shoot tear gas in the crowd. Some scatter, but most keep pushing forward, or drive ahead with large fans on their vehicles to blow the gas back.

"Stop starving us!"

"Remember Vagsten!"

"Fuck you, GSAU!"

Nesschter looks at Don and Fargo.

"We can try to get through, but it'll be rough," says Nesschter.

"We'll just have to take the long way," says Don.

"I know lohg way," says Fargo.

"Good." Nesschter looks at the crowd again. "We'll have to..."

Nesschter's voice trails off and his eyes gravitate to the masked Lupinaks with the red flares. They drop the flares and sink into the crowd. Then, Nesschter's eyes go to the roof of a building behind the police barricade, and another nearby. There are multiple flames flickering on the roofs, and he sees movement in the windows of those same buildings and people aiming rifles.

Nesschter snaps to Fargo and Don. "Get down!"

Flaming bottles are thrown from the rooftop. When the bottles shatter behind the barricade, balls of fire erupt, engulfing the officers. The officers scream and flail, and muzzle flashes appear from the upper floors of the building across from them and near them, dropping more of the police officers.

The police phalanx shatters, shields toppling and batons flying as officers are cut down in waves of fire and gunshots. The crowd is a whirlwind of triumphant roars and terrified shrieks.

Bodies clash as the protesters either retreat or bull rush their way through to attack the officers. The surviving officers scramble to hold up their shields while their comrades burn and wail around them, struggling to protect themselves from the storm surge of bodies.

* * *

Xajil returns to the Division 4 War Room just in time to see the fires erupt on the large screen, much to the horror of the agents, and himself. The burning officers flailing reminds him too much of the bodies being eaten by the fires in the Vagsten Tunnels.

The screams and cracking skin and splitting bones surge into his ears. His legs go weak as he steps back, bumping into Darius, who is also horrified by what he is seeing.

Every pixel becomes a slab of violence and chaos. The Outer Ring has rapidly turned into an urban sprawl flooded with blood and fire. The carnage plays out in real time, dozens of camera angles shoved together into a sick panorama. The helmet cams broadcast the officers' screams and up close, vicious faces, some masked and others not, as the officers are beaten or dragged.

Street cams and drone footage catches civilians fleeing in terror and rabid rioters scurrying through the streets, and red flares arc overhead and burning bottles exploding like cheap fireworks. Every corner of the grid is filled with writhing, surging bodies.

Xajil smells the reek of fur, sweat, and greasy food on them. He smells their blood, hear their screams, and his wife eyes flick erratically at the various feeds, seeing specters move through the crowd, gunning, stabbing, tearing, burning, breaking.

They are breaking everything he fought for, bled for, killed his soul for.

They are breaking everything.

They are breaking it all.

'*Fix it,*' says the voices.

Xajil's talons tremble as he digs into his pocket. The flashes of red on the screen pop in and out, like signal flares.

'*Fix it.*'

The specters move through the crowd. The screams, the fires, the gunshots, he hears it all. The rapid click sand clacks of the keyboards sound like bullets being loaded, the frantic speech of his techies sounds too much like the mentally broken squabbles of his brothers in arms facing the gunfire and explosions.

'*Fix it!*'

The fires and smoke snapping out like hands from Hell wanting to drag people down. Drag him down.

Xajil pulls out his anxiety pills and shakes the container in his hand. Nothing comes out. Xajil's heart stops.

'*Fix it!*'

Xajil shakes it again. Still nothing. He shakes it again. Still nothing. Shakes it again. Still nothing.

Shaking. Shaking. Shaking. The screen is burning. The specters are around him. The gunshots, the screams, the fire, all of it is there. Shaking. Shaking. Shaking.

There is nothing!

'*Fix it!*'

Xajil's beak grinds together as he fights not to scream. His thumping heart aches, watching the vermins break apart his work."

'*FIX IT!*'

Xajil shakes his empty pill container one last time before he throws it across the room.

"KILL THEM ALL!" screams Xajil.

The silence is immediate. All eyes turn to him, now focused on him instead of the filthy rats breaking his work.

"Sir?" says Darius.

Xajil grabs Darius by his throat, seething and glaring into his eyes, his talons becoming wet with Darius' blood. "KILL THEM ALL! KILL ALL THE RATS IN THE DE-ESCALATION CHAMBERS AND KILL ALL THE RATS OUT THERE!"

Xajil throws Darius aside and grabs his observation desk, eyes pulsing, a long, ragged hiss leaving his beak, and his crest twitching sporadically.

"They want to break everything we've built. They cannot be spared. It's for Aardesl's sake," says Xajil, his voice heavy and trembling.

There is a moment of tense silence, then the War Room erupts into frantic movement. Operators jam buttons, alarms go off, and the city map blooms with new signals as kill teams are activated. The list of targets is unlimited. Xajil watches as every square marking civilians, no matter the color, switches to red, and information scrolls across monitors as their scores and bank account are zeroed out.

Darius steps away, but Xajil snaps his talons to him before he can get far, freezing him in place.

"Stay," hisses Xajil. His heavy, golden eyes, rimmed in red, lift to the large screen, shoulders bobbing from his heavy breaths. "Watch me fix this."

* * *

"*Live ammunition has been authorized!*" says the airship flying above the crowd.

Nesschter's ears drop, and he backpedals with Don and Fargo.

"Oh no…" says Nesschter.

Large guns roll out of the airship, and the rioters scramble away as more police jump out of armored vehicles, brandishing rifles.

"RUN!" yells Nesschter.

Bullets scream and rattle from the weapons, flashing the air with pockets of light and spraying the walls and asphalt with blood. The crowd screams and scatters, and Nesschter and Don duck and weave, holding Fargo tightly as bodies drop around.

"Keep moving! Don't stop for any reason!" orders Nesschter.

The Shio police officers shoot at the buildings and into the crowd. Broken glass and brick fall, and dozens more protesters drop. Red and yellow flares cloud the air, and the flags, banners, and signs lay scattered on the road.

The officers move up and continue shooting at the protesters in the smoke, and Division 4 jeeps and other police vehicles speed ahead. Agonizing screams and cries linger, more gunshots ring out, and large armored personnel carriers roll forward, the gun mounted on its roof unleashing a salvo of bullets that shred people trying to climb fences.

"Shit!" says Nesschter. "Into the alley!"

His group takes a sharp turn into the nearby alley, and Nesschter aims down his rifle as he walks backwards. The colorful smoke covers the alley entrance in a thick fog, but Nesschter can still see the silhouettes of the officers and their vehicles passing by, with the squeaks and clanks of their treads crushing the items and bodies left behind.

More loud bangs and rattles of gunshots echo, and there is another flash of fire that quickens the group's pace and brings another wave of retaliation from the officers. Two more airships fly overhead, spraying the area with heavy gunfire. Don stops by a door and tries opening it, but when it doesn't budge, he kicks it open and pulls Fargo in with him. People scream and Nesschter follows the two inside.

The room they enter is stacked with boxes of ingredients, and people in colorful Klumsy K's restaurant uniforms are hunkered down, all shouting over each other and holding their hands up or cowering further into their spots.

"Stay quiet!" orders Nesschter. "You two, follow me."

Nesschter runs past Don and Fargo. Don closes and blocks the door by pulling a rack down before following Nesschter and Fargo to the front of the eatery. The lobby has white tables and simple chandeliers, and the two crouch behind a counter.

There are customers crouching or laying on the floor. Most are whimpering or shivering, and Don and Nesschter barely see the armored personnel carrier rolling by with the police officers and Division 4 agents marching forward, firing down the streets.

Nesschter checks his rifle. "Don, are you ready?"

"No, but I'll pretend to be," says Don.

"Good enough. How about you, Fargo?"

Fargo gives a shaky thumbs up, and Nesschter hops over the counter and runs to the entrance. Don stops next to him, and he peeks outside, dropping down when a truck with a turret speeds around the corner, firing erratically at an armored Division 4 jeep chasing it.

The Division 4 jeep rams the truck, causing it to crash into parked vehicles. The turret operator is flung off, and the Division 4 agents rush out and shoot at the occupants until they are dead, and then shoot them some more.

The turret operator is executed with a shot through the head, and the Agents quickly return to the jeep and speed off. Their lights are distorted in the colorful smoke, but that doesn't stop them from speeding off with no care of the bodies they run over.

When they are out of sight, Nesschter looks at the civilians.

"Stay low and nobody leave. You'll be safe if they don't see you," says Nesschter. Then to Don and Fargo. "Let's go."

Nesschter leads the way across the street, and Don and Fargo hobble after him. They pass mutilated bodies and try to avoid the puddles and streams of blood.

They run down the block and take cover in an entryway when Division 4 jeeps speed by and an armored personnel carrier follows them with an Avus manning a turret. Above them is an airship and a few camera drones.

"All civilians are to return home immediately! Violators will be incarcerated!"

announces the airship as it guns down another group of people trying to flee.

Nesschter watches them until they are out of sight, and then he pats Don's arm and motions him to follow him. The three continue their path, and civilians run in the opposite direction. One is carrying a bleeding Avus and another yells at the group.

"Crazy Lupes! Go the other way! They're killing everybody!" yells the Avus.

They reach the second block, and they witness a trail of smoke launch from the third story of a rundown building. An armored police vehicle explodes, and an airship banks towards the structure.

Nesschter grabs Fargo and pulls him into a looted convenience store with its door torn off. All the shelves are empty, the coolers are shattered, and a TV hanging above the register displays an emergency message. An old Avus shouts at them, but quickly ducks down when a barrage of gunfire and explosions shake the area.

"Stay down!" orders Nesschter.

Fargo slumps to the floor and Nesschter and Don look out the window, flinching when the airship flies away and camera drones fly past the store. Armored police vehicles and Division 4 jeeps speed by a moment later. The Division 4 armored personnel carrier trails them. The turret operator is chewing on a red lit cigar and is shooting madly at another building.

"We're going out the back," says Nesschter.

Nesschter stays low when he backs away, and Don and Fargo follow his lead. They go through the back door and enter an alley that is crowded with civilians huddled against the walls. Various languages and pitches of crying mix in the group, and fiery smoke rises into the dark sky.

Nesschter's group passes the building that had the missile, now engulfed in flames and crumbling. Flames snap out, like tendrils trying to grab the group, and they run faster, reaching the third block.

Avus civilians dressed in colorful clothes and their feathers painted in tribal symbols run out of an apartment covered in graffiti, armed with various weapons, and go in the direction the convoy went. They turn a corner, and more gunshots follow.

The burning building collapses and fire rolls into the alley and in the street. Nesschter's group takes a left on Fargo's direction. His voice is weak and Don is having trouble keeping him up.

When they reach the new block, a human civilian grabs Nesschter and points down where he came from.

"Don't go down there! They're killing us!" says the human. He runs to Don. "Observers are going through the apartments! They're killing the protesters! They have our faces!"

He runs away after that, and right on cue, gunshots and screams echo from a building, and broken glass falls to the street. Nesschter's group takes cover behind some parked vehicles and waits.

A minute of tension and heavy heartbeats later, and a group of Avus Observers exit the apartment building. Nesschter's group carefully slides along the parked vehicles, keeping out of sight.

Nesschter watches the leader checking their phone and pointing to another structure. They go across the street, and Nesschter's group shifts their positions to the sidewalk side of their vehicles. The Observers enter the building, and Nesschter's group runs.

The road is littered with destroyed vehicles, shattered glass, and dead bodies. Flares sputter in the streets. The stench of death and gunpowder makes Nesschter gag, and his ears twitch from the constant gunfire, screams, and ticking.

But there is a silver lining. There is a sign hanging over the sidewalk, flickering and swinging. It says, "Friendly Clinic."

Nesschter smiles for a moment and quickens his steps.

"I see it!" says Nesschter.

Don and Fargo struggle to keep up, and when Nesschter reaches the door, there is a red band over the top. "CLOSED" is displayed on the door with a digital sign. Nesschter knocks on it, anyway.

"Open up!" yells Nesschter. He knocks again and kicks at the door, growling. "Open the damn door! We need help!"

Don and Fargo reach Nesschter, and he shakes his head and turns Don toward the alley.

"To the side!" says Nesschter.

Nesschter leads Don and Fargo to the alley, and the door they need is marked by the clinic's logo and is being watched by a camera.

"Let me handle this one," says Don.

Nesschter crouches and aims his rifle down the alley. Don sets Fargo against the wall and politely knocks on the door.

"Hey! Anybody there? We got a badly injured guy here! We can really use some help!" says Don.

The camera swivels and adjusts its lens, and Don bangs on the door again. Fargo's breathing is shallow, and his eye is distant, and Nesschter hears the creaking of treads and rumbling engines. A car speeds by, and shortly after it leaves his sight, a missile streaks from the sky and hits its target.

There is a flash of fire with the explosion, and metal scrapes along the pavement before some glass shatters. The creaking treads get closer and Nesschter backs up, watch thumping in tune with his heart, his grip on his weapon tight, and his breathing heavy.

"Opening now would be really nice!" yells Don.

Then the door opens, and an old Lupinak waves them in, speaking Gaceraen in a hushed voice.

"*Ishe, ishe. Nafa! Nafa!*" he says.

Don pulls Fargo in, and Nesschter ducks in with them, right as the armored personnel carrier passes by. The old Lupinak closes and locks the door, and a pair of younger Lupinaks grab Fargo and take him to the back. They set Fargo on the cot, and a third one immediately works on getting the supplies.

"What happened?" asks one of them.

"An Avus tore his face open," says Don.

"Strap him down and get him cleaned," says the second one.

They work on strapping Fargo to the cot. Nesschter hurries up front, passing empty rooms, and he sees that their windows and doors have the added protection of steel bars. Nesschter looks through the cracked window and sees a drone flying overhead and airships shining lights on the buildings and streets. Nesschter shakes his head and goes back to Don.

Don is in the room with Fargo, watching with a pale face as the doctors clean the deep gashes and torn cheek that is just flaps of flesh. His scratched eye is a bloody pocket. The talon scratches have made their way down to his neck to his shoulder, coating the gray fur on his shoulder and chest in blood.

"We have to go," says Nesschter.

Don does a double take and points toward the front of the clinic.

"Out there? You serious?" says Don.

"Fine. I'll go. You can stay here," says Nesschter.

Nesschter is about to leave, but Don chases him.

"Hold on!" says Don. He gets in front of Nesschter and puts his hand out. "You're not going out there alone."

"You don't want to go out there, though."

"Of course I don't! It's a warzone! And Fargo is messed up. We can't leave him alone."

"I can't leave Ara to Xajil, either. He *will* kill her because she had N-Light. So, you can stay, and I will go and take care of the problem."

"Alone."

"Yeah. Alone."

"It is best you go with him. Fargo will be fine with us. We're friends with the Revivalists, so he is in no danger," says one of the doctors.

Nesschter and Don looks at them, then at Fargo. Fargo can barely lift his hand when he gives a thumbs up and weak nod.

"Don't keep him too long. The GSAU is watching," says Nesschter the nearest doctor.

"We figured out a way to fool them. That's how we've been able to operate as we have. We'll keep Fargo here until it's safe, or someone picks him up," says the doctor.

"Oh... Well..." Nesschter digs into his pouch, pulls out his stash of N-Light, and gives one to each doctor. "Thank you for helping him. If anybody asks, we're going to Division 4 HQ."

All the doctors' ears perk.

"Unless it is some GSAU guys asking," says Don.

"Right. If it is the GSAU, we weren't here and Fargo is a bum," says Nesschter.

"That got in a cock fight."

Nesschter looks at Don. "A what?"

"A cock fight... You've ever seen roosters fight? They're vicious. I mean, normally it is two roosters fighting, but people do get attacked by those bastards. And when they attack, good God is it horrifying."

"Why are you going to Division 4?" asks one of the doctors suddenly.

"To get some things sorted out," says Nesschter, and then to Don, "Let's go."

Don follows Nesschter, and the old Lupinak takes them to the side door. After checking the camera on his pad, he opens the door. The two thank him and exit, and the door is slammed shut and locked behind them.

They take a moment to collect themselves, and then go to the alley's edge and peek at the hellscape. The flare's smog has eased a bit, but thick smoke from burning buildings and vehicles is still clouding the sky.and stinking the air.

The lights are flickering, and bodies lay next to shot-up or burning vehicles. The scent of gunpowder and blood is thick, and the rattles and pops of gunfire mix with the crackling flames and structures collapsing.

A group of Avus led by Seni Nesi runs past them, equipped with backpacks and holding cameras on selfie sticks or attached to their shoulders or heads, and some are laughing and chirping excitedly in their language while they record the carnage.

"Man, this is going to be great material for a movie! And I know just the guy who can star in it! He was in that one movie directed by that one guy!" says Seni Nesi, his voice fading from distance like his body disappears in the smoke.

"Oh, I love that movie!" says another Avus, his voice faint and his body shrouded by the carnage.

Nesschter and Don watch Seni Nesi's group until they are out of sight, and then Don looks at Nesschter while he checks his watch.

"I guess the last one there is a rotten egg," says Don.

Nesschter snaps his watch shut. "You're weird."

Chapter 14

"It's a lovely day... lovely day... lovely day..." hums Balik to himself.

Outside, people are running, buildings are burning, stores are looted, cars and government vehicles are being mauled by bats and crowbars, and gunshots echo in the distance.

As Balik's convoy speeds through the chaos, multiple vehicles split off for suicide runs. Their objective is to keep Division 4 and the Shio police bogged down while the main vehicles complete their objective before the GSAU military arrives.

Bullets ping off their vehicles, and police and Division 4 work together to fight the swarm of rioters that are hurling bricks, launching fireworks or going after them with crude weapons or stolen guns. As they go through the city streets, the augmented Division 4 vehicles bash aside abandoned vehicles and rushed barricades.

Then Balik's phone rings and he sees that its Fargo's number. He quickly answers.

"Fargo where are you?" says Balik.

"*This is Doc. Fargo is with us and in bad shape. He asked us to call you,*" says an old Lupinak in Gaceraen.

Balik wipes his face. "What happened?"

"*Talon gash on his face, neck and shoulder. We're having to use blood transfusion to get him back to health and he needs a lot of stitches.*"

"Was he with anyone else?"

"*Yes. A gray Lupinak and human with an ugly nose. They said they were going to Division 4. Fargo said we had to let you know immediately. Said their names were Nesschter and Don."*

Balik growls and punches his door window. "Damn it!"

"Sir?" says the doctor.

"You're fine. Thank you for calling me. Keep Fargo safe. I'll send some people over there to protect you."

"That won't be–"

Balik hangs up and dials another number. This time the human he sent out answers.

"Hey, Balik, boss, sir, I was just about to call you. Everyone's dead, man. Total massacre. We're still looking through the bodies," says the human.

"Fargo is with Doc. Get your team there and protect him with your lives," orders Balik.

Before the human can reply, Balik hangs up and grabs his radio.

"First gift basket, you need to speed it up. Everyone else, keep your distance," says Balik.

In the convoy, one of the vehicles with *"Mevmo Vagsten!"* painted on it zooms forward, despite the bullets from the guards and the electric shocks from the camera drones hitting it. Its augments clear the way, and it rams the Core wall's gate. The gate breaks, and the vehicle detonates.

The blast tears apart the wall, and the shock wave shakes Balik's vehicle, leaving his ears ringing and his eyes momentarily blinded by the flash. Fire and debris soar into the sky and knocks an airship and many camera drones out of balance. The airship crashes into a building, spirals out of control, and spins into the street, crumpling and exploding on impact.

Balik fumbles with his radio, ears throbbing and colorful blobs interfering with his vision.

"Back up! Back up! Back up!" yells Balik into the radio.

The tires squeal and the vehicle goes in reverse, swerving to avoid the broken concrete, shrapnel, and twisted metal raining down around them.

The shrapnel decimates everything around it, and falling debris crashes into buildings, lands on abandoned vehicles, and breaks the streets. Rioters and police officers alike that weren't killed by the blast run for cover, and the driver reverses Balik's vehicle around a corner.

When the last of the debris falls, all that remains are broken sirens wailing, and a multitude of moans, cries and shouts while smoke and dust rolling through the streets. Flickering lights from the lampposts provide inefficient lighting, and the shuffling people move in and out of view like apparitions.

"Go slowly," orders Balik.

The driver inches forward, and Balik's eyes widen at the gaping hole in the Core's wall, allowing him to see the pristine buildings on the other side.

They keep going forward, and the rest of the convoy follows Balik's vehicle. When they reach the opening, the driver lowers the plow attachment and presses forward.

"Honk your horns and draw them in," orders Balik through the radio.

The convoy honks their horns, and some of the Revivalists shout *"Mevmo Vagsten!"*, which is repeated by a few others. Some of the protesters gather scattered weapons or debris to use as blunt weapons, and they follow the convoy into the Core.

The plow pushes through the rubble with some difficulty, but it does the job of clearing the way. As this happens, police officers and Division 4 on the other side hastily set up a barricade to replace the one that was destroyed, using their vehicles as well as the destroyed ones.

The bullets bounce off Balik's vehicle. Each shot makes the driver flinch, and Balik pats his shoulder.

"Steady... Steady... Keep pushing. You're doing good," says Balik.

The rubble is soon condensed to a large pile and is pushed against the barricade. The swarm of dazed, yet angry rioters flow through, seeping past the convoy, and Balik smiles.

* * *

Xajil Ojin is in his office with Ara bound and gagged, and watched by the guards and Darius Jules. Chairman Kevin Asven has also just arrived in the building, his steps light and posture completely relaxed.

But what Xajil is far from relaxed after seeing the large plume of smoke and gaping hole in the Core's wall.

He switches to another camera feed, watching Balik's convoy moving in, honking and firing off their guns or fireworks, and rioters pouring into the Core. The police and camera drones are doing what they can to hold back the crowd with a mix of non-lethal and lethal rounds, but they are quickly overrun. And the residents of the Core scramble for shelter, their trance shattered at the last line desperate of defense breaking

Seeing that mess, Xajil quickly types on his computer and the bookcase behind him slides to the side, revealing a large metal door with a camera above it. Another command is entered, and the door opens to a large room with warm lights, wood panel walls, a collection of beverages ranging from alcohol to sodas, and bottled water. There are also snacks, another bookshelf with reading material, and various couches and chairs, plus a workstation.

"Destroy every file in this building. I don't care if you take axes to the computers. Destroy everything. Burn everything," orders Xajil to Darius.

"Yes sir," says Darius.

He quickly leaves the room and orders a group of Agents to follow him. On Xajil's computer, every file is being scrubbed. And while that happens, Xajil points to the safe room.

"Chairman, if you will," says Xajil.

"Where's Jasnee?" asks Kevin.

"She'll be here soon. Now please, for your safety, get in the room."

Kevin growls, but he goes in the room with his protection detail. When Xajil sees that his files have been completely deleted, he pulls out his pistol and shoots his computer multiple times. After that, Xajil drags Ara into the safe room with him, and a few more Agents follow him in. Once everyone is inside, Xajil closes the door and keeps a tight hold on Ara until the door seals shut. Then he drags her to the couch. She makes muffled protests and wrestles against him the whole time, and yelps when he throws her on the couch. Ara struggles to get off the couch, but Xajil holds her down by her neck and makes a cuff chain to lock her onto the couch leg.

"Stay," orders Xajil, pointing at Ara's nose.

Ara growls, and Kevin paces in circles while his security detail is watching the door intently. A pair of Division 4 Agents work on the computers, scanning the camera feeds. Everything becomes quiet for a while, but the silence is broken when Kevin turns to Xajil.

"Where is Jasnee?" says Kevin.

"She should have been here by now," says Xajil.

"Well, she's not here. Where is she?"

"We'll find her, and we can open the door when she arrives, but it will remain closed until then. It is for your safety, which is more important than hers, if we're to be frank."

"That's my wife!" Kevin jabs his finger into Xajil's chest. "And you snagged a... a... comforter before my wife was secured!? What the hell, Xajil!?"

"Dora has valuable information on Balik that will be proven to be useful in the long run, so she will be detained as long as necessary," says Xajil.

"That's Ara. Who the fuck is Dora?"

"I said Ara. She will be useful to me after I fix her."

Kevin steps closer, towering over Xajil with his hands on his hips and lips twitching. And Ara yells garbled words again and shakes her head as she tries wiggling off of the couch

"Jasnee is far more valuable than any other toy or investigation you have. Send people to get her, right now."

"Your wife has security detail," says Xajil.

"Yeah, where the hell is her security detail? Where's Aki, Sakura, Mi, and that bird!? Whatever his name is!" says Kevin.

The Agents on the computers frantically search through the systems, and one looks at Kevin, face pale and posture stiff.

"Chairman Asven, sir..." says the Agent.

"What is it? Spit it out!" snarls Kevin.

"Put it on the screen," orders Xajil.

The Agent transfers the feed to a screen on the wall, and Kevin's ears droop. The Gailo Mall is in shambles. Fire is pouring through one of the stores. Broken glass shines on the tile, and the area is littered with spilled and trampled bags of goods, bloodied bodies of protection detail and civilian bystanders, as well as dead humans wearing black armor with no markings.

The camera feed switches to the parking garage, and Kevin falls to the couch.

The vehicles are destroyed, and more of their guards and the mysterious humans lay dead. But Jasnee and Aki's group is nowhere to be seen.

"Where are the Agents and law enforcement?" asks Xajil. Then louder, and with a growl, "Where is the assistance? Where is the team to get Mrs. Asven!?"

"You sent them out there to beat back those hooligans," says Kevin heavily. "This day is nuts. Everything about today is nuts! But they don't have her. They don't have Jasnee. If they did, Aki would be one of the dead. So, they'll be here soon."

Kevin chuckles, grabs a cup and a bottle of alcohol, and pours himself a drink.

"It'll be fine." Kevin gulps it down in one go. "It'll all... be fine."

Xajil says nothing at first. Then he goes to the intercom and turns it on.

"Attention all Agents. Defend this building with your lives," says Xajil. Then he looks at the other Agents. "Prep the escape. We can't stay here."

* * *

Balik watches with great interest as the rioters swarm through the Core like locusts, destroying everything in their path.

They move as a single, unstoppable mass, the sound swelling to a thick, suffocating roar. Storefront windows and glass doors are shattered. Rioters claw through the gourmet markets and luxury boutiques, stripping down every display, knocking down racks and shelves. The air is a toxic cloud of ozone, smoke, luxury perfume, and spilled blood.

The Core residents seek shelter wherever they can, but the Outer Ring insurgency isn't slowed by locks or cameras. They force their ways past the barriers, easily overpowering security and civilians trying to fight back by sheer numbers.

Food is raised down to the last crumb, from pristine to expired. Specialty breads, blocks of cheese and meat, bottles of expensive wine, and everything else edible is claimed by hungry hands and stuffed in bags or pockets. What is t stuffed away is eaten on the spot, leaving faces smeared and sticky. Taste isn't registered, just calories and the feeling of a full stomach. Hands reach and grab, taking more than they can carry just to deny it to the Core.

But what really electrifies the mob are the shrieks and the begging. The moment Core residents try to run, they are swarmed. They are dragged out, stripped of whatever is valuable or shiny, and sometimes just stripped for the hell of it, and reduced to bloody pulps by a barrage of kicks, punches, and broken bottles. Bodies dent cars and bounce off robot security drones as the crowd piles on, eager to be part of the carnage. Someone screams and tries to crawl away, only to have his face stomped down so hard his teeth spray across the pavement, blood marking every boot and paw that tramples over him.

And it isn't just the wealthy citizens being targeted. Even Core workers who work the mundane jobs at grocery or fast food or retail are assaulted by the bloodlust fueled Outer Ringer insurgents. Even taxi workers and chaperones are dragged out and their vehicles stolen or burned.

The mad swarm go after the women next, dragging shrieking shopgirls by the hair, wrestling Core mothers and luxury wives from behind glass counters or the safety of trembling security bots. Workers wearing simple uniforms are tugged from over the counters and dragged out of the stores, kicking and screaming. Every scream draws the mob tighter, hungrier, hands clutching bodies and ripping clothes.

Core girls in tailored skirts and school uniforms, still clutching their bags, are yanked into the chaos, unable to escape. Nobody tries to help. The mob hoots and howls at every beautiful woman captured, every well-groomed Core wife or assistant or nanny, even down to fry cooks and register worker. Screams and animal shrieks blend with the pounding feet and glass-shattering, the hoarse voices shouting and laughing as stores and vehicles are set ablaze, and females and food carried off like prizes of a prehistoric raid.

Inside the safety of his vehicle, where the Hellish noise is partially damp-ened by metal and glass, Balik notices the driver's trembles and the wetness on his eyes as he watches the carnage unfold. Balik smiles and squeezes the driver's shoulder.

"Hey, relax. This is what they did to Vagsten. This is divine judgement, and you and I are it's instruments," says Balik.

"It just seems a little... Much," says the driver.

His wet eyes flick at the sight of a female Avus police officer screaming and flailing as she is carried into an alley and thrown down to be swarmed by male Avus. Nearby, a limo is set on fire while another Avus in a suit is tied to a pole.

Balik forces a laugh. "Are you seriously disturbed this? Kid, when I was your age, I saw Vagsten burn. The shit they did to us... Let's just say this is only a fraction of what they deserve and a tiny taste of what they did to the Vagsten residents. But now we're doing it, and now they hear it, too."

The soldier swallows. "Hear what, sir?"

"The screams."

The driver's ears drop, and Balik motions him to look ahead while he pulls the Radiohead off the dash board.

"Convoy, the GSAU military will be arriving shortly, so it is donor die. Speed it up and let's get this job done," says Balik

The engines rev, and the converted Division 4 carriers zoom ahead, while the remainder of the convoy splits off and engages government vehicles and their drones. The rattling gunfire and screams are enough for Balik's hands to clench and his eyes to glaze over with a twitching smile.

Balik's convoy speeds through the streets, bashing aside civilian and government vehicles. Drones, Division 4, and police shoot at them and give chase, but the bullets bounce off the augmented vehicles.

The same can't be said for the rest of Balik's convoy that intercepts and engages. The vehicles ram, swipe, shoot. They do very tactic they can think of to distract or destroy the defense. In the door's mirror, Balik sees a few of their vehicles already burning with electric fire and others getting gunned down and crashing.

Balik's convoy swerves. An airship comes around the corner and unloads on them, destroying one of his armored trucks and a few more of the Revivalist vehicles in an onslaught of bullets. But it is shot down by a missile launched from a van.

Its burning wreckage crashes into the street, and Balik's convoy swerves past it while the van is targeted and swarmed by drones and Division 4. It too explodes when its munitions detonate, flinging fire and rubble into the air. Seeing this through the mirror, Balik makes a quivering laugh and turns his head to look at the carnage behind them before looking at the driver.

"This brings me back to the war!" says Balik, his body jerking and bouncing as the driver bashes his way through the streets of Shio.

The driver says nothing. His glazed eyes are focused on the road and his hands are tight on the wheel, masking the trembles, and sweat is trickling down his face.

"You know, of I wasn't destined to die today, I'd pick you as my driver," says Balik. "You're a little squish, but nothing experience can't fix."

"Thank you, sir," says the driver.

"Oh wait." Balik slaps his thigh, forcing a laugh. "You can be Kahl's driver! And I'm going to say you're a Delta. Am I right?"

"You are, sir."

"Ha! I knew it! I love Deltas. Real team players. Talk to Kahl when you walk out of here and consider your family promoted to Betas, my orders. Do you got any kids?"

"No sir."

"Get yourself a nice Beta and make one. You won't regret it."

The driver sneers, and steers the vehicle around another corner, coming face to face with the Division 4 Headquarters. It towers over the Core, its pristine glass reflects the lights of the city, and the GSAU flags hanging from it are like banners, challenging anyone to defy them. A challenge which Balik is more than happy to oblige. In front of the building are concrete barriers, and there are some very nice steps leading to the entrance, which is a mix of glass and concrete, and a line of fancy doors.

"There it is…" says Balik, and then into his radio, "You know what to do! Go! Go! Go!"

The last carrier with *"Mevmo Vagsten!"* zooms forward, and the carrier's augments shatter the concrete barriers. It drives up the steps and breaches the entrance with ease. Shattered glass and debris spill into the lobby, and a barrage of bullets strike it as the Agents inside unload everything they have on the carrier.

It keeps going. Despite the added protection, the windshield very quickly becomes completely covered in spiderweb-patterned cracks, and within seconds it shatters, and the driver jerks and twitches as the bullets rip through him and the seat, but he keeps going.

He slumps on the wheel, and the carrier hits the wall on the other side of the lobby. Then comes a massive explosion, launching fire, nails, metal beads, and barbed metal. The Agents in the lobby and working area are thrown back and shredded into bloody pulps, and the upper floor caves in. Burning smoke and dust spills into the streets from the gaping hole in the Division 4 Headquarters, and Balik bangs on the dashboard.

"GO! GO! GO!" barks Balik.

The driver speeds forward. The vehicle rocks from the rubble in the road, and everybody rattles when the carrier goes up the mangled steps. The plow front pushes aside the debris, and it goes through the gaping hole in the lobby.

The tires shred on the mangled metal, glass, and shattered concrete, but they keep going and speed into the burning working area. Broken brick and loose metal falls on their vehicle, and Balik laughs while the carrier runs through the desks and half-walls, and strikes a few disoriented Agents.

The other carrier is close behind, and Balik's carrier swerves to a stop, tearing up the floor as it does this. He slips on sunglasses and hops out, grinning from ear to ear with his rifle ready. He marches into the smoke, passing broken desks, mangled bodies, and pools of blood, and he snaps his rifle up at the first Agent he sees.

"GUESS WHO, BASTARDS!" yells Balik.

He guns down that Agent, and then unloads on the other Agents that are still struggling to regain their composure. Their vests hold for the most part, but it still knocks them down, and the bullets striking Balik are broken by the shield covering his body.

The spinal shield generator brightens and his shield crackles with bright light, but he doesn't mind it. He is loving the dampened punches. They hurt a lot less than a bullet going through him.

"BALIK'S BACK!" yells Balik as he marches forward, shooting wildly at the

Agents, while his team spreads out and takes more controlled shots. "YOU THOUGHT YOU COULD BURN ME!? FUCK YOU!"

Jarvis jumps out of the other carrier with his team, and they spread out, shooting at anyone that moves. Their shields flicker and crackle, and Jarvis's aim is pinpoint, taking head shots and heart shots with ease.

The Revivalists rush through the rubble, gunning down and executing anyone that gets in their way with ferocious speed. Their masks protect them from the smoke, and their earmuffs protect their ears from the thundering gunfire.

However, Balik is loving the pain in his ears and the burning sensation in his lungs and nose. It is bitter, and yet satisfying, knowing that going through this hell again means that Xajil's time is running out.

Balik shoots some more Agents and trails others to gun them down. His team is keeping with their methodical executions, and Jarvis is showing no signs of slowing as he guns down Agent after Agent. One, two, three. Down they go.

One. Two. Three. Four.

Tick. Tick. Tick. Tick.

Balik's watch is loud in his ears, and his grin is wide. The bullets hitting him are merely punches rather than deadly objects. He loves it. And he loves gunning down Division 4. None of this would have been possible without the stars aligning.

Maybe Vojehan is wanting to see the GSAU fall for what they did to his creations? Or maybe the universe hates Xajil Ojin? Whatever it is, Balik has no complaints. The Mandate of Heaven has spoken, and he is its instrument.

Balik keeps shooting until he is out of ammunition, and he switches to his pistol and shoots a wounded Agent dead. Then he sees some Agents running for cover, and they shoot at his soldiers.

He can see a few of his troops have already fallen, so he charges the Agents. He leaps over broken desks, tackles an Agent, and sinks his teeth into their neck. The Agent squawks and thrashes, and Balik rips out a chunk of their neck. He pounces on the next one, slashing their throat and drawing his knife to rapidly and viciously stab the next closest Agent.

They try fighting back at close range, but he is rabid. The pain influences him to go faster, go harder. He snaps their bones, tears their flesh, and he slashes their veins. The bullets do almost nothing against Balik because of the shield, but he feels the bruises growing on his body. I'm

One by one, they go.

One by one, they die.

It is all a blur for Balik as he attacks the Agents. Their blood covers his face, his clothes, his hands. Avus and human blood on his lips and tongue is tantalizing. He wants more. **Craves** more.

Every slash, every stab, every punch, every bone breaking under his brute strength, every scream of fear and pain as they fall to him brings him back to the battles of the Aarde War. Charging the enemy, taking what they hold most dear from them, just as they have done to him.

They burned his country, his forest, his home. They took his teammates; they took his friends and family. They burned, they killed, they erased, and now they have the nerve to show fear when retribution comes.

Tick. Tick.

They need to die.

Tick. Tick.

They can run. And they are running.

Running. Running. Shooting. Shooting.

Tick. Tick.

They run, they shoot, but judgment has come at last. They cannot escape it.

They can scream. They can shoot, stab, slash, peck, punch. It won't stop judgment.

Tick. Tick.

He will kill them all.

Tick. Tick.

Kill all of them.

Tick. Tick.

Vagsten and the Norkits will be avenged!

Suddenly, a hand grabs Balik's shoulder and he whirls around, snarling with his claws and knife raised. A strong hand grabs his knife and swiftly pins it down to a safe location and his claws are blocked with a machine-like stiffness.

It takes a moment for Balik's erratic, rabid breathing to settle to an easier breathing, and his amber-speckled, dark brown eyes lock on to Jarvis Vaan Luken's emotionless blue eyes.

The black bags under Balik's eyes are covered in speckles of blood, and sweat trickles down his face, cleaning off streaks of more blood, and his mane is a mess. His outfit is also stained in the blood of his enemies, as well as his own, and tears have exposed old and fresh wounds on his body.

Jarvis nods past Balik, and he looks over his shoulder and sees dozens of Agents lying dead in mangled messes. Bones have breached their skins, their heads are smashed, some have torn organs laying out or chunks of their bodies ripped off from Balik's fangs.

The carpet and walls are heavy with blood stains, and the alarm is now a weak hum. The red lights swirl and flicker, putting the bodies in a mix of red and shadow. At Balik's feet is a dead Avus Agent with a flat head and rib cage shattered and poking through his caved-in chest.

Balik looks back at Jarvis, and Jarvis steps away from Balik and motions to his thermos. Balik unclips it, and Jarvis tilts his hand to show him "drink." Balik licks his lips and drinks the chicken soup in the container. The mix of chicken, vegetables, and broth is an odd mix to have with the taste of blood, but Balik swallows it anyway.

Jarvis puts his hand on Balik's shoulder and takes him away from the massacre. Balik wipes his face, and Jarvis leads him to Xajil's office. The room has been ransacked, and behind a bookcase that has been moved aside is a large metal door with a camera above it. There is also a row of hostages, which include Darius Jules, Sower, and Hajir among the eight.

The Revivalists in the room look at Balik. Some have wide eyes and drooped ears, and others avert their gaze while he walks toward the camera. When he reaches the camera, he waves at it, and then looks out into the working area.

Corpses of Agents and Lupinaks alike litter it, and he can hear some shooting somewhere inside the building, too. But one door catches his attention, so he goes to one of his soldiers, takes him to the working area, and points at a door marked as "DE-ESCALATION CHAMBERS."

"Get a small team and free everyone down there. Then take them to the Tunnels as recruits," says Balik.

"Yes sir," says the soldier.

He grabs a few of the Lupinaks and hurries off with them, and Balik sighs and rubs his snout as he returns to the office. There, he sees Jarvis standing off to the side, watching the line of hostages with his pistol in hand.

Balik paces in front of the hostages, listening to their heavy breathing and whimpers. Some are muttering. Some are cursing. Some are silent. Balik looks at the camera again, his whiskers twitch from his quick smile.

"Good afternoon, everyone. I am Colonel Balik Hebediah Norkit, former ranking officer of the now disbanded Gaceraen Defense Force, and now a ranking officer of the Revivalist Militia. I am a veteran of the Aarde War. Or War of Unification. Or the Aarde Conflict. Whichever one you think is the proper name, it does not matter to me, the events are the same... Now, do you know where you are?" says Balik.

The hostages remain silent, and Balik looks at each of them for a few seconds at a time. Then he points at Sower.

"You. Where are you?" says Balik.

"Here," sneers Sower.

Balik sighs, draws his pistol, and shoots Sower through the head. The hostages yell and curse, and Balik holds up his hands and motions them to quiet down.

"Let me be clear. I don't have time for sarcasm. I want an answer to my question! WHERE ARE YOU!?" screams Balik. He goes to Hajir and aims his pistol at his forehead. "Answer the question, birdie."

"Division 4 HQ. Shio Branch," says Hajir, his voice heavy and his crest flexing.

Balik clicks his tongue and looks around. "Well, you're not wrong, but at the same time you are. Those are always funny." He looks at Jarvis. "Isn't that right?"

Jarvis nods, and Balik paces in front of the hostages, tilting his pistol towards their heads as he passes them.

"Yes, this place, this Connected City as you call it, is named Shio, but originally it was called Vagsten," says Balik. "Vagsten, fun fact, was the crown jewel of the Gacerae Pack. Said to have rivaled Iselae City in its beauty, and it was a fortress city, too. It withstood centuries of attacks from, and during the Aarde War it was a city that the Federation of Sol Systems and Aarden Avus Humans United could not take. Attacks, air raids, orbital bombardments, you name it, we withstood it! Then one day it fell. Burned from the bottom up and destroyed by an orbital bombardment that was like the wrath of Hell burning the Saints away!"

Balik grabs Darius and drags him to the front of the hostages. He presses his pistol at the crook of Darius's neck and peers into his eyes, growling, and fangs and eyes gleaming with hatred. Darius is silent. His eyes are wide and despite his best attempts, he still shakes and sweat trickles down his head.

"They bombed us. Bombed us! Over and over again. And again! AND AGAIN!" screams Balik. He grabs Darius's chin and forces his head up when he tries looking away. "What happened next, Darius Jules?"

"Y-You surrendered?" says Darius.

"You're right." Balik grins and rubs Darius's sweaty head. "You're very right. We did surrender. But before that, your boss, Xajil Ojin, the AAHU before they became the GSAU, took the survivors of Vagsten, executed the soldiers, and took turns torturing and raping the women, the men, and the children, before selling them off as slaves or putting them in mass graves! And believe me, I am all too familiar with how Xajil tortures people."

"I-I didn't know that!" says Darius.

"BULLSHIT!"

"I didn't know!" cries Darius.

Balik pistol whips Darius to the floor and pulls him back up. His face is bleeding, and bloody teeth are on the floor.

"Lie to me again," growls Balik. "Lie to me. Tell me you didn't know one more time!"

"*Let him go,*" says Xajil over the speaker.

Balik's ears perk, and he turns to the camera, still pressing his pistol at the crook of Darius's neck.

"Xajil Ojin. I finally get to hear your voice again." Balik smiles, his sharp teeth gleaming and drool dripping from his fangs. "How have you been?"

"Let all of them go, Balik Norkit," says Xajil.

"No time for chit chat?"

"Let them go."

"Don't worry, I will... Once you open the door."

Xajil is silent, and Balik presses the pistol into Darius, making him wince, and Balik narrows his eyes.

"Am I going to have to kill people?" says Balik.

"I will not open the door for you or anybody else. But I can promise you this. The longer you stay, the slimmer your chances are of surviving, and harming the hostages will greatly reduce those chances further," says Xajil.

"Oh, Xajil..." coos Balik. "What makes you think I want to walk out of here alive?"

He pulls the trigger, and the bullet rips through Darius's neck and bursts through his liver. Darius's legs give out, and he pukes blood as more gushes from his wounds. Balik kicks him to the floor and grabs Hajir.

The hostages are screaming and swearing, and the Revivalist soldiers shout back at them and beat some of them down with their weapons. Harij stares ahead, crest twitching and breathing heavy, and Balik paces behind him.

"OPEN THE DOOR, XAJIL!" screams Balik. He takes a deep breath, takes off his beanie, and runs his fingers through his mohawk. He glares at the camera, speaking in a low, even tone. "I just want to talk."

Suddenly, there are rushing, heavy steps, and muffled screaming being overtaken by sharp shouts. Balik turns around with his pistol raised, and his group races to the office door and aims their weapons towards the noise.

"Don't shoot! We're friendly!" shouts someone. A fair-skinned human with white hair and dirt brown eyes, wearing black armored pads and a gray scarf, comes from behind one of the breaching carriers with his hand and rifle raised. "We got her."

Balik tilts his head and goes out of the office.

"Got who? And who are you?" asks Balik.

"Mercs on Khal Mason Jarim's payroll. He sent us here to help you," says the human. "And my name is Mason Garintine. I lead the mercs."

Balik lowers his pistol and rubs his brow, but the Revivalists keep their weapons aimed at the group.

"Damn it, Khal," says Balik. He drops his hand and looks at Mason Garintine. "So, you're Mason, eh? That's very interesting."

Mason nods. "Us sharing a name was the start of the friendship. We've been doing security detail in the Core for his section of N-Light trafficking. And let me tell you, that ain't easy."

"I bet... How many of you are there?"

"Twelve of us are left, myself included."

Mason turns to the side, whistles, and waves people forward. Eleven humans come out from behind the two breaching vehicles, wearing the same armor as Mason. But all of them are battle-worn, and they are dragging a barefoot female Lupinak with them.

She has her hands and muzzle bound, a chain is wrapped around her, and she is thrown to the ground. Her knees scrape against the rubble, the humans chuckle. Balik slowly steps forward, unsure if his eyes deceive him, or if he is the victim of a weird prank.

The female Lupinak, middle-aged, gets on her knees, and her brown eyes are red and puffy, with tears trickling down her dirty cheeks. Dirt, grime, and soot cover her light gray fur, black snout, and the thin black bands that trail her cheeks. Her thick, white and gray banded mane is ruffled and burnt and stained with the same junk on her body. And her modest dress is torn and bloody in some spots.

Jasnee Asven's eyes widen at Balik. Her breathing becomes heavier as Balik kneels in front of her.

"Interesting. There's a face I haven't seen in a very long time," says Balik.

He removes the appendage trapping Jasnee's muzzle and holds her head up, so they are eye to eye.

"B-Balik? Is that you?" says Jasnee.

Balik blinks, thinking of vague memories of her visiting the Norkits for an international meeting of some kind. It was years before the Aarde War. A time of simplicity and joy. A time that should have never been burned away.

Burned away by the Asvens and the Gailos for their GSAU ambitions.

"Balik, please... Let me go..." whimpers Jasnee.

Balik shakes his head slowly as he strokes her chin, using the hand scarred with "11."

"I can't. This is the end for all of us," says Balik.

Chapter 15

Nesschter and Don slip through the gaping hole in the Core's wall, scrambling over broken concrete and bent rebar. A path of rubble and destroyed barricades lead to the city. Police officers and Division 4 Agents lay on the ground, bloodied, dead, stripped of weapons and gear. Gunshots, explosions, and screams echo in the smoky fog taking over the streets.

Flickering fire and spinning red lights illuminate pockets of the smoke, and dark silhouettes sway to and from view like ghosts from street to street, building to building, always moving. A bus stop is smashed, the digital clock above it displaying numbers breaking and flickering to various times.

The stench of blood, burnt wires, gunpowder, sweat, perfume, and a dozen other things are carried in the wind, clinging to the smoke and burning Nesschter's nose and throat.

His run devolves to a stumbling, hasty walk, his breathing ragged and eyes wide. He sees the Obelisk burning in the distance, like giant torch. A female shrieks somewhere, and a van speeds away from a nearby alley.

They reach the edge of the block but quickly retreat when a line of Core police officers masked by the smoke shoot at them, chipping brick and concrete, creating a line of flashing lights and thundering pops.

"This way!" orders Nesschter, hurrying to the alley where the van came from.

As they enter the alley, a group of rioters scurry past them, carrying looted alcohol, food, and expensive gadgets and clothes. Soon after, a group of Revivalists drive towards the police, shouting madly. They round the corner and chaotic gunshots of booms, pops, and rattles echo through the broken city.

Nesschter and Don keep moving, only slowing when they pass a shredded police uniform, a broken vest, discarded shoes, and torn undergarments. Claw marks scratch the concrete surface and wall, feathers stick to the grime, and tire marks lead from the clothes to where the pair came from.

Nesschter stares at the clothes, and he slumps against the wall, hand trembling as he pulls out his watch. The ti-tick ti-tock continues, but the hands are not moving. Nesschter shakes it, which makes the hands spin loosely, but they don't move with the ticks and tocks. His eyes glaze and his heart rattles from the gunshots and screams.

"Ness?" calls Don. "Ness, buddy, are you okay?"

Nesschter shoves his watch back in his pocket and hurries down the alley. Don follows hi, briefly looking over his shoulder as the police from earlier pass by the alley, their vehicle riddled with bullet holes and the cops, wearing red and gold warpaint.

"I need to save Ara and stop Balik," says Nesschter.

"Well, slow your pace a little. I still have to cover your six," says Don.

Nesschter and Don stop by the edge of the alley, both panting and holding their weapons tight. Rioters rush past them, brandishing crude weapons or stolen police firearms. They engage the police officers wearing the war paint, the fight going very badly for the rioters as the officers ruthlessly use their own weapons and talons to slaughter them.

As the massacre happens, Nesschter and Don swiftly cross the street, cutting through another alley. They stop at the other end of the alley, and Don wipes sweat off his face while Nesschter peeks around a corner, quickly retreating when an airship flies past him, unleashing a stream of hot lead on a speeding vehicle launching fireworks. The vehicle is torn apart, and it crashes and burns into a line of parked vehicles. The airship veers off and speeds away, and Nesschter waves at Don.

"Let's go," says Nesschter.

The two resume sprinting, legs burning, lungs tight, and throats scratchy. Shouts and gunshots echo from down the block, and the pair reach a fence. They quickly climb over it, jump down to the other side, and seek shelter by a dumpster. A few seconds later, multiple vehicles speed past them.

Nesschter pokes his head out just in time to see the last Division 4 vehicle pass by with police cars and drones following it, all brandishing the gold star GSAU flag. Seconds later, there are multiple thuds and flashes of light, followed by a burning tire and a group of Avus racing down the street, cackling maniacally, armed with a rocket launcher and other weapons. All of them are gunned down the airship returning.

After the airship is gone, Nesschter and Don use the smoky fog for cover, passing roving gangs made of primarily Outer Ring Avus. With them are a few Lupinaks and humans, and random aliens, terrorizing the streets by smashing windows, looting stores, or setting fires to vehicles.

"*Mevmo Vagsten!*" shouts a Lupinak, shooting in the air.

"*Mevmo Vagsten!*" repeats another Lupinak further down, also shooting in the air.

Then headlights swerve around the corner. The cops in the war paint return, their engines roaring as they ram their vehicles into the group, snapping bones or crushing them under their tires. The survivors are executed, and the cops speed off again, blaring a heavy metal instrumental.

Once the mad cops are out of sight, Nesschter and Don bolt across the street. They weave their way through the streets, avoiding the large crowds going through the streets of the Core. Rioters are keeping the police and Division 4 busy and trapped. Both sides exchange gunfire and explosives at every opportunity.

They keep going, not stopping, and when they near the Gailo Mall, Nesschter sees smoke pouring out of it and rioters swarming it, breaking and stealing what they can. The parking lot is filled with smashed vehicles, and people are launching fireworks into the sky, at surrounding buildings, or nearby vehicles.

"Shit..." says Don, panting heavily and using a lamppost for support as he watches the mall's destruction.

"We need to keep moving," says Nesschter.

"Yeah, yeah, I know, I'm right behind you."

"Holden!" shouts Aki suddenly.

Nesschter stiffens, Don perks up in confusion, and the pair see Aki, Mi, Sakura, and Gajo running towards them, armed with short barrel rifles and ammunition belts on them. All of them have seen their fair share of battle. Their personalized outfits are torn, revealing damaged armored vests, and the fabrics are speckled in blood and covered in grime. Aki's golden tail bands are gone, and the group's colorful fur and plumage is a ruffled mess and stained with the same gunk covering their clothes.

"Holden!" calls Aki again.

Her speed picks up, and Nesschter approaches her.

"Aki?" says Nesschter.

When Aki's group reaches Nesschter and Don, Aki keels over, wheezing and panting, and Nesschter put his hand on her shoulder.

"What happened?" asks Nesschter.

"Human mercenaries kidnapped Mrs. Jasnee Asven," says Aki. She grabs Nesschter's arm, and he helps her stand up as she continues. "We had to fight our way out of Gailo Mall. It is overrun with Revivalists and rioters."

"They're all insurgents at this point," says Mi.

"We're going to get Mrs. Jasnee back. Do you want to help or are you off duty?" asks Sakura.

"Off duty?" asks Nesschter.

"You're dressed weird, so I thought you were off duty," says Sakura.

Nesschter looks at his traditional Lupinak tunic, which is torn in spots, and has its fair share of blood and dirt staining it.

"I was fired. Didn't you hear?" says Nesschter.

"What for?" asks Mi.

"None of your business."

"Fired or not. Will you help us, Holden? I'm sure you will get a handsome reward and lots of points if you help us get Mrs. Jasnee Asven back," says Aki.

"My name's not Holden. It's Nesschter"

Aki's group gets a blank look, and a few seconds later, Aki sneers.

"Since when?" asks Aki.

"Since always. I just forgot for a while," says Nesschter.

"How do you forget your own name?"

"It's complicated."

Garlo checks his wristwatch, Aki's ears splay back, Sakura arches a brow, and Mi nods in understanding.

"Just like that book with the spy that has amnesia," says Mi.

Nesschter squints at Mi, and Aki waves dismissively.

"Whatever, we'll talk about this later. But Holden–"

"Nesschter," says Nesschter swiftly.

Aki huffs irritably. "Whatever. I need your help."

Garlo clears his throat.

"*We* need your help," says Aki. "And despite our falling out–"

"That you started," says Nesschter.

"That **you** started," says Sakura.

"You're not part of this conversation," snaps Nesschter.

"But you repeated the same pattern for all three of us," says Mi.

"You shut up, too," says Nesschter, pointing at her.

"Ness, we talked about this," says Don.

"And I'm ignoring it," says Nesschter.

"This is why I dumped you," says Aki.

"Why?" says Nesschter.

"Because you're a stubborn prick," growls Aki.

Nesschter rolls his eyes, and Mi puts a comforting hand on his shoulder.

"What she means is that you built a wall around yourself and never let us in because you're afraid of getting close to people," says Mi.

Nesschter rolls his eyes in the other direction.

"There you go doing it again!" says Aki.

"Doing what again?" says Nesschter.

"That thing that led to my fist going to your face," says Sakura.

"You punched Ness?" says Don.

"I did," says Sakura proudly.

"I punched her back harder," says Nesschter.

"Damn, dude," says Don.

"She started it!" says Nesschter defensively.

Garlo coughs loudly and taps his wristwatch while glaring at Aki.

"Right! Right! I know," says Aki. "Look, Holden-"

"Nesschter."

"Nesschter. We need your help. Can you stop being a pill and help us!?"

"No," says Nesschter. "I've been fired from Division 4, alright? So... tough luck."

"I know you were fired. But despite what happened between us, I know you're capable, so for old time's sake, will you help us?"

"No."

Aki frowns. "Why not?"

"**Because** I'm **not** Division 4. Plus, Division 4 tried to kill me, and even if I wanted to help you, I can't. I need to get to Xajil and save Ara. I already wasted enough time arguing with you."

Aki blinks, then her orange eyes widen and glow like a switch being flicked. After that, her eyes narrow, a wolfish grin spreads across her muzzle, and her thick tail swishes. This in turn causes Nesschter to furrow his brows, and Don's eyes flick between the two. Garlo, meanwhile, hisses irritably.

"I've got good news for you. I heard the mercenaries say they were taking Mrs. Jasnee Asven to the Division 4 building, which just happens to be where Xajil is," says Aki.

Nesschter frowns, and Aki leans forward and tilts her head up, so their noses are mere centimeters apart.

"That means we're heading to the same place. So, will you help me save the Chairman's wife? For old time's sake?" asks Aki in a more alluring tone.

Nesschter's nose twitches. Aki's pheromones are partially covered by the gun powder and grime, and the blood of her enemies, but her tone also provokes his tail to twitch. With an aggravated sigh, Nesschter turns around and walks ahead.

"Fine. Let's make this quick," says Nesschter.

Aki snickers and returns to her team. "Works like a charm with Holden."

"Nesschter," corrects Nesschter.

"Whatever."

Nesschter keeps walking, and Don goes next to him. He casts a glance at the female Lupinaks before looking at Nesschter.

"So…" starts Don slowly. "Any tips you got about that Aki chick? Like, is she single, or…?"

Nesschter stares at Don.

"Never mind," says Don.

Nesschter shakes his head and jogs down the road, and the rest follow suit. It takes them a few minutes of weaving through the battle-torn streets of the Core to reach the Division 4 Headquarters. When they do, they take cover behind a flipped Revivalist vehicle and stare at the gaping hole. Their jaws are slack, and their eyes follow the smoke spilling out of the numerous holes in the building. Gunshots echo out and muzzle flashes appear sporadically from the holes peppering the building, and Garlo hisses.

"They're clearing out the building," says Garlo.

"Holy shit, that guy talks," says Don.

Aki slaps him on the back of the head, making him wince, but he still grins at Nesschter and mouths, *I like her.*

Nesschter slaps him on the back of the head this time and puts his focus back on the building.

"Now's our chance to get in there. The Revivalists are distracted and Division 4 is fractured. We can get to Ara and Xajil easier, and if Balik is there, then the mercs would have taken Jasnee to him. We can end this without having to confront many Revivalists," explains Nesschter.

"Let's get this over with, then,," says Garlo.

Garlo hops over the flipped vehicle, and the group follows him. Their steps are light, nearly hopping as they move across the broken ground. They pass scattered debris, and glass shards and pebble-sized rubble crunches under their feet as they make their way through the burnt lobby.

Wires dangle and eject sparks, the alarm alternates between loud screeches, weak whines, and warbled tunes, and the red lights flicker and swirl. Dust is illuminated by the fire, and blood and mangled bodies carpet the floor. Nesschter clenches his jaw to keep the stench of death from making him hurl as he leads the group through the lobby.

They pass broken desks and half-walls, corpses of Division 4 Agents and Revivalists, and when they reach the two converted Division 4 vehicles, they take shelter behind them and listen. Nesschter hears the alarm, but he also hears people talking. He doesn't recognize their voices at first, until...

"Well, Mason, when you see Khal again, slap him on the back of the head for me. I told him I didn't want your help, and him going behind my back like this is rude," says Balik.

"Hey, I'm just a merc, alright? I get a job, I get paid, the end. But if you want, we can just take the missus with us and have Khal watch her. Have them pay a ransom for her," says Mason.

"Nah. Having hostages didn't work out last time for me. Besides, if she's here, that means Chairman Asven is here. Which means he's behind this door."

"It's not a guarantee, though."

"Who cares? She's high profile. My primary concern is Xajil, and if he doesn't open the door, then Jasnee dies, which means Kevin suffers a little bit. Which I'm fine with that. The guy's a douche bag."

Nesschter growls and storms out from cover.

"BALIK!" bellows Nesschter, his booming voice echoing in the desolation.

There is a moment of silence, and then Balik steps out of the office with a few of his guards plus Mason and his mercenaries. Don, Aki and the rest of the group follows behind Nesschter, and Balik grins theatrically at Nesschter.

"Well, **helllooo,** Nesschter! Someone said you were coming, and now here you are!" says Balik. He motions at his guards to lower their weapons. "Ease up, guys. This is a time to rejoice! I am finally reunited with my brother!"

Balik's guards barely lower their weapons, and Nesschter stops walking and glares Balik while the rest of his group flanks him.

"What's the meaning of this, Balik? Do you have any idea what you've done?" says Nesschter.

"Of course I have an idea, I'm standing right in the middle of it. I'm not blind," says Balik.

"You got a lot of innocent people killed!"

"Debatable."

"And now you want to hurt Jasnee."

"Well, yeah. She's an Asven. What else am I supposed to do with her?"

That is when Nesschter notices Balik's state. The older Lupinak's face is covered in bleeding cracks, his dark brown and amber-speckled eyes are wide, and his trembling hands are bloody.

Sitting in front of the door to the panic room is Jasnee Asven, Hajir, and six others. The desk and furniture have been moved aside, so the hostages are able to be seated in front of the camera in a row. All of them are bound, Jasnee is gagged, and armed guards comprised of humans and Lupinaks are in the room.

Then Jarvis steps into view. Nesschter looks to the side and sees Darius and Sower lying in a heap just outside the door, in pools of blood, with a trail leading to the office. His eyes narrow on Balik.

"What have you done, Balik?" growls Nesschter.

Balik looks at Jarvis, then at Mason, then at Nesschter, and raises a brow.

"Is this a trick question?" asks Balik.

"This isn't time for games Balik!" says Nesschter.

"You're the one asking stupid questions."

"Mrs. Asven, are you okay!" shouts Aki.

Jasnee's voice is muffled, and she whimpers and shudders when Balik grabs her and pulls her outside. He gently shushes her and rakes his bloody hand along her mane and cheek, and he smiles at Aki.

"She's fine for now," says Balik. Then to Nesschter, "Are you teaming up with Division 4 again?"

"We just crossed paths. But you need to let those hostages go. There's no point in having them. You'll just paint a bigger target on yourself," says Nesschter.

Balik shakes his head. "They aren't going anywhere. Not until Xajil opens the door."

Nesschter pauses for a moment, and looks at the door past Balik.

"Xajil's in there?" asks Nesschter.

"Where else would he be?" says Balik.

"Holden, don't you dare switch sides," growls Aki.

"I'm on nobody's side!" snaps Nesschter. "All I want is to get Ara and get out of here!"

"You still got a thing for her? I got over her a long time ago," says Balik.

"I don't need your commentary. I need that door open so I can deal with Xajil and get Ara!" says Nesschter.

Suddenly, the speakers in the working area crackle and pop.

"*Are you sure that is all of it?*" says Xajil over the speakers.

The group looks at the camera in Xajil's office or the speakers hanging from the walls.

"*Are you sure you don't want anything else? Balik Hebediah Norkit did kill your team, after all. Wouldn't it be nice to end him as well?*" says Xajil.

Balik chuckles and strokes Jasnee's cheek. She shudders and her knees buckle, leading to him tugging her upright.

"Trying to divide us, eh? It's not going to work, Xajil. We all have a bone to pick with you," says Balik.

"You tried to have me executed! And you warped my memories, you psycho!" yells Nesschter.

"*Only because you wanted me to,*" says Xajil.

"What? Memory warping is a thing?" says Mason

"*Make me forget. Your words. Not mine,*" continues Xajil.

Balik's smile fades. He looks at Nesschter and his grip tightens on Jasnee, making her whimper again.

"What is he talking about?" asks Balik.

"*Go on, Nesschter. Tell him what you did for me,*" says Xajil.

Nesschter is stiff and silent. His hands tighten on his rifle. Balik throws Jasnee into Jarvis and takes a step towards Nesschter, growling and fur bristling.

"**What is he talking about, Nesschter!?**" yells Balik.

Nesschter's breathing becomes heavy, sweat coats his face and hands, and his knees become weak. He takes a step back, all eyes are now on him. The only ones not looking at him are Don and Garlo.

Don is fixated on Balik, and Garlo and Jarvis stare at each other. Garlo's crest twitches, and Jarvis tilts his head slightly, confusion briefly flickering on his blank face.

"*Tell them what you did, or I will,*" says Xajil.

"You bastard. You made me do it," says Nesschter weakly.

"Do what, Nesschter?" asks Balik.

"Keep your mouth shut, Ness," says Don.

"A rat telling someone to keep their mouth shut. How cute. I'm going to love killing you," says Balik.

Nesschter snaps his rifle to Balik. "You touch him and you're dead!"

Everyone on both sides raise their weapons, and Balik laughs darkly.

"I have a spinal shield generator. The most you'll do is give me a headache," says Balik with demented glee, then adding darkly, "but I'm still curious about what you did for Xajil."

Nesschter's breathing is warbled and heavy. His body trembles, and he backs away when Balik steps closer, his head tilted slightly and his eyes reflecting the red light.

"Come on, *Ness*. Tell me what you did," says Balik.

"Don't do it," says Don.

There is a hard, wet lump in Nesschter's throat. His eyes are glazed and his ears and tail sag.

"He made me do it," says Nesschter.

"Stop talking," orders Don.

"What did he make you do?" says Balik, taking another step closer.

Aki steps next to Nesschter and aims her rifle at Balik's head.

"Don't come any closer!" orders Aki.

"I want to know what you and Xajil did," says Balik, his eyes locked on Nesschter. "Now tell me. **What did you do!?**"

Suddenly, the speakers crackle and pop again, and Nesschter's voice floods through the building. His voice is weak and shaky, but it is his.

"*They are very advanced. Basically, a city below a city,*" says Nesschter over the speakers.

Balik stares at the speaker above Xajil's office, eyes wide, ears perked, and lips tight.

"*They are also heavily fortified, but there are weak points,*" continues Nesschter.

Nesschter is also looking at the speaker, and when he looks at Balik, his older brother slowly turns to him, breathing heavily with his lips twitching and a growl rumbling in his throat. His fur bristles and his fangs become exposed, and his claws extend.

"I was stationed in the Blue Sector. I can show you where the weak points are, and then we can end this war and finally have peace," says Nesschter's recording.

Jarvis's eyes snap to Nesschter, and his grip hardens on his spearhead and Jasnee.

"You..." growls Balik.

Nesschter steps back and holds out his hand defensively.

"Balik, wait, I can explain," says Nesschter.

"What is there to explain, Nesschter?" says Xajil. *"You betrayed your family, you betrayed Balik. The Norkits and the Gacerae Pack lost because of your betrayal. Vagsten burned because of you. The Federation and AAHU solidified their victory in Gacerae because of you. Without you, there would be no Shio. No GSAU."*

"YOU TORTURED ME!" screams Nesschter with tears streaming down his face. **"YOU TORTURED ME, YOU SICK FUCK! AND YOU WANT TO DO IT AGAIN TO ARA!"**

Balik goes to a nearby desk. His muscles tense, his back arches as he looks down. His claws dig into the wood, while a loud growl rumbles from him. Sakura and Mi exchange looks, Don gets in front of Nesschter, and Aki puts her hand on his shoulder.

"Come on, Nesschter, let's go," says Aki.

Nesschter shrugs off Aki. "Balik, I just started remembering everything very recently. Ara gave me N-Light. I remember bits and pieces, and I remember being tortured by Xajil and a masked human. They tortured me. I didn't want anything to happen, but they forced me to do it."

Mason steps next to Balik and focuses on Nesschter.

"Well, I hate to say it, but whether we like it or not, you fucked up and gotta pay somehow," says Mason.

Balik takes a long, deep, and heavy breath, and glances at Jasnee, who is still being held by Jarvis. Only now she has the spearhead against her throat. She whimpers and shakes her head, and Balik looks at a nearby camera when

Xajil speaks.

"I remember you, Balik," says Xajil. *"You withstood what we put against you and stayed silent the entire time. You are very durable. The opposite of Nesschter. He betrayed everyone to escape the pain you easily withstood. He made you a failure. Without Nesschter's betrayal, none of us would be in the positions we are in today. You, the Revivalists, Mason's mercenaries, all of you are now in the presence of the greatest asset of the AAHU and the reason for the GSAU's power over Gacerae,"* says Xajil.

Nesschter steps forward, and the Revivalists and mercenaries step closer and keep their guns trained on him.

"Balik-" starts Nesschter.

"Nesschter," interrupts Balik.

Nesschter stops, and Balik's claws dig deeper into the desk as he looks at him out of the corner of his wet eye.

"I'll give you and your friends eleven seconds to run," says Balik. "Starting now... Eleven... Ten... Nine..."

Don pulls on Nesschter's arm and Aki and her team back up as the Revivalists and the mercenaries raise their rifles.

"Ness let's go!" says Don.

"Come on! We need to go!" yells Aki.

"Eight," growls Balik.

"Balik, wait a minute. Let's talk about this," says Nesschter.

Nesschter backs up and Don continues pulling.

"Seven." Balik stabs the desk with his knife. "RUN, NESSCHTER!"

Don tugs on Nesschter harder. That plus Balik stabbing the desk convinces Nesschter to flee with Don and the others.

"Six," echoes Balik. "Five... Four..."

Nesschter slams his shoulder against a stairwell door, and he and his group race up the stairs.

***

Balik's misty eyes stare ahead, his hands tremble, and his lips twitch as he whispers with an unsteady voice, "Three... Two... One..."

Balik bows his head and looks at Jarvis.

"Kill him," orders Balik.

Chapter 16

After Jarvis leaves with a group of Revivalists and mercenaries to kill Ness-chter, Balik takes Jasnee back in Xajil's office, his eyes distant and Jasnee's cries and the alarms muffled in his ears.

He doesn't feel the floor beneath his feet. His mind is completely silent. There are no screams, no memories, no concept of time. All there is, is now, and how he wishes he was not burdened with ordering his brother's death.

The words from the remaining Revivalists are garbled. Balik doesn't look at them as he gently sets Jasnee on her knees, giving her messy mane a gentle rub before he grabs a rolling chair.

Balik sits in front of Jasnee, his legs losing all strength, and he stares over her head. He sips from his empty thermos and checks the time on his watch. There is no ticking and none of hands move.

He counts eleven seconds before returning the watch to his pocket. Then he draws his pistol and exhales slowly as he watches his thumb rub its barrel.

"Balik?" calls Jasnee, her voice soft and yet defined in murky noise around him.

Balik's ears twitch. He looks at Jasnee, his eyes glazed and shoulders slouched. Jasnee's dirty face stares at him, tears cleaning streaks of grime off her striped fur. The noise of his carnage is still whispers in his ears. It is just him and Jasnee.

"Balik, listen to me. You can stop this. You're hurt. I can see it. Let me help you," says Jasnee.

"You don't know me," says Balik numbly.

"I knew your mother. She was my family's public appearance servant before she married your father. You have her eyes."

"Nesschter had her colors and patterns. I have a fraction of her."

"But you still have a piece of her. I know there's good in you. You can't let the pain win. Let me help you."

Balik's lips twitch, his wet eyes hardening. "Pain?"

Balik looks down at his pistol again, stroking its surface, every imperfection magnified under his finger.

"The past is pain. The future is pain," says Balik. "When I am not hearing the screams, I'm thinking about what the Asvens took from me.

Balik's eyes flick to Jasnee.

"I remember when the Asvens visited Vagsten. My father wasn't happy, but my mother was. You and Kevin weren't married yet since you were too young, but you two were inseparable. It was fascinating for me back then to see other full-blooded Iselaen Lupinaks besides my mom. It was... memorable... Do you remember that day?"

Jasnee nods, and Balik leans forward.

"What was the weather like?" asks Balik.

Jasnee hesitates. "S-Sunny. Warm. Your father gave us a tour of the Vagsten Museum and other areas of cultural significance. The Asvens and Hebediah pretended to get along for the public."

Balik smiles thinly. "Yeah... They did..." His smile fades. "After Iselae won the war, your husband and Milo Gailo had that museum emptied, the artifacts destroyed, and it was left abandoned.

"The family you married into, the family you love and pledged allegiance to, flattened Vagsten, and cleansed my people, to build Shio. And you keep going. Taking, taking, taking, killing, killing, killing. A ticking clock. That doesn't stop. Your family keeps going. Going. Going."

Tears stream down Jasnee's face in thick rivers, and she whimpers and shakes her head.

"Balik... I didn't know. I swear I didn't know that was the plan. It was war, an awful war, but I didn't know what Milo Gailo's goals were," whimpers Jasnee.

Balik's exhale is shaky, tears beading down his cheeks, making his speckled eyes and brown fur shine.

"I want to believe you, but I can't," says Balik.

Jasnee bows her head and sobs quietly. Balik slouches in his seat and checks the ammo of his pistol. The noise of the outside world is still damped in his ears. But the screams are coming back, gradually, but surely, they are coming.

"You know, sometimes I wonder if I am insane. Or if I got mixed up in a weird timeline jump, because I remember Vagsten. But nobody else does," says Balik. "'Remember Vagsten' is a slogan of defiance, but they don't remember *it* as a city. They don't remember the cobblestone streets, the gold-tipped cathedrals and their bells, the arches, the domes, the pillars with stories carved in them. The chatter of voices, carefree pups, chimes and chants of cathedrals and believers. The smell of bread and cooked meat. The white flowers, the winding trees... Every piece to make Heaven."

Balik looks down and taps his pistol against his head.

"It was beautiful... And it was destroyed. Hundreds of years of history gone. Hundreds of years of inspiration gone... All gone."

Balik stands up, exhaling heavily and walking towards a hostage. The screams get louder, and so do the broken alarms and distant gunfire Mason watches Balik closely, and Jasnee lifts her head, trembling and eyes wide in horror.

"Vagsten inspired me to be an architect. I designed and built a tree house based off a picture my mom made as a starting point. I wanted to go to the Vagsten Academy of Architecture. But it was razed after the war, and now here I am," says Balik.

Balik brushes his hand against Hajir's crest. The screams are now deafening in his ears. Screams, gunshots, explosions, the smell of blood and burning flesh, the sting of gunshot wounds and stabs. Its all there, tearing him, ripping him, killing him.

"I never wanted this life. I wanted to be an architect," continues Balik in an even tone, still going down the line of hostages, rubbing their heads and tapping the pistol against his leg, ignoring the uncomfortable looks the mercenaries and Lupinaks are giving each other. "I wanted to *build*. Not destroy. I wanted to be... Me."

Balik stops behind a hostage squeezing his shoulder and lowering his eyes, staring at nothing.

"But I put my life on hold to make my dad proud. Then I put it on hold again to make my CO proud. Then I had to make my country proud, and my team and my little brother proud. I wanted them to see me."

Balik returns to Hajir and plays with the feathers on his head, gently fluffing them and twisting the colorful plumage in his bloody hand.

"In the end, all I got was screaming. The constant. Screaming. This life I lived for others gave me torment, and now Aarde is finally hearing what I hear."

Balik releases, a wet, bubbling sigh and numbly aims his pistol at the back of Hajir's head. Hajir's breathing quickens and his crest flexes, but he keeps quiet and stares ahead.

"Aarde is finally hearing the screams," says Balik.

Then he pulls the trigger.

* * *

Nesschter's group runs up the stairs. The banging door and stampeding steps of their pursuers shakes their bones. Bullets ricochet off the railings and chip at the concrete. Each shot brings a thundering echo with it that leaves Nesschter's ears ringing. He snarls and shoots down at then, but the combatants keep approaching, rapidly catching up to the group.

* * *

"Xajil, for their sake, open the door," says Balik.

The door remains closed, and Balik shakes his head and executes the next hostage. Jasnee screams and pushes herself against the wall, and Balik stands behind the next hostage.

"Are you scared, Xajil?" says Balik.

* * *

Nesschter slings his rifle, draws his knife, and stabs the neck of his nearest target, a Revivalist Lupinak.

With the knife still in the neck, Nesschter draws his pistol and fires multiple shots into a Revivalist Lupinak's head at close range. His eyes burn from the bright light of their shield generator blocking the ballistics. However, due to the proximity of the gunshots, the Revivalists crumbles with his eyes and nose bleeding.

The target rolls down the stairs, causing others to stumble, and the rest of Nesschter's group engages. Stabbing, shooting, bashing, biting, clawing who they can. The stairwell is a hellish vortex of screams, gunshots, yelps and crackling energy that comes with flashes of light from the shields blocking the gunshots.

The gunshots slow down the Revivalist Lupinaks and all the noise brings a hot pain to Nesschter's ears that only fuels him to go harder and faster to end the pain.

* * *

"No door?" says Balik, staring at the camera above the blast door. "Fine."

He executes his next target and goes down the line, unaware of Mason inching towards the door. Balik grabs the hostage's shoulder and squeezes as he glares at the camera. The hostage is shaking and sweating, and goes limp when Balik puts a bullet through his head. The corpse is shoved down, and Balik goes to the next hostage.

"Your men are dying for you, and you can't even open a door for them. Pathetic," sneers Balik.

* * *

Nesschter slams a human mercenary's head into the concrete wall and throws him over the railing. A Revivalist tries shooting Nesschter, but he whacks the rifle aside, stabs them, and pushes forward, leading to them rollingdown the stairs, snarling, biting, and clawing.

They knock down other combatants, which gives Nesschter's group time to push back or gun them down. When Nesschter and his target stop rolling, Nesschter rips out a chunk of his target's throat with his teeth.

Then he is bashed on the head.

***

"Open the door, Xajil," says Balik.

The door remains closed. Another shot, another screaming sob from Jasnee. The remaining hostages curse, Mason is by the door now, and Balik moves to the next hostage.

"Do you hear those screams, Xajil? Those are for you. Now open the door," says Balik evenly.

***

Nesschter's head throbs from the head injury, and he retaliates by slashing the leg of his assailant. They scream and buckle, and Nesschter slams their head on the corner of the concrete step. Bone breaks, blood pours, and Nesschter throws his knife at another Revivalist.

They fall back, clutching their shoulder, and Nesschter wrestles with other Revivalists and a mercenary, using his claws and pistol to slash and club, finishing them off with bloody strikes.

***

"You can try to ignore the screams all you want, but they will never go away," says Balik.

He aims his pistol at the next hostage.

"Save your men. Open the door," orders Balik.

Mason slips out with the remaining mercenaries, the door does not move, and Balik pulls the trigger.

* * *

The Revivalist with the knife in the shoulder yanks out the weapon, snarls, and charges Nesschter. He swipes wildly, nicking Nesschter's arms and chest, but eventually Nesschter locks the knife wielding arm.

He snaps it at an awkward angle, making the Revivalist howl and drop the weapon. The Revivalist slashes at Nesschter with his injured arm. Nesschter tilts his head, but the Revivalist still gets his cheek and his ear slashed.

Blood pours down Nesschter's face, and he delivers swift, brutal punches to that Lupinak's face. Breaking teeth and cracking the eye socket, and then Nesschter finishes him by shattering his forehead against the railing, bending the metal upon impact.

* * *

Balik's disappointed sigh trembles as he paces behind the remaining two Division 4 hostages. The last of the human mercenaries and some of the Revivalist Lupinaks slip out, leaving just a pair of Lupinaks to guard Jasnee. After some seconds of pacing, Balik goes to the camera.

"Open the door, Xajil. Save your men. Save Jasnee. Open the door," says Balik.

Silence.

Balik's eyes harden, his lips hook into a quivering frown, and he puts a bullet through the head of one of the hostages, before looking around and seeing he has mostly been abandoned. His hardened eyes flicker to confusion and dart left to right before locking on the last two soldiers by his side.

"Where did everybody go?" asks Balik.

* * *

Nesschter picks up his bloody knife and unloads his remaining ammo on a Revivalist Lupinak. Both are blinded by the shield generator's flashing light, and the Revivalist fires blindly.

Nesschter ducks, the bullets tear into the concrete wall, and he slashes their tendon, bringing them to drop their weapon. Then he plunges the knife through their heart.

The Revivalist drops dead, and Nesschter looks around, panting and shaking with numerous wounds plaguing his body, ranging from bullet grazes, to claw cuts, knife slashes, and sharp concrete bits that nicked him, as well the multitude of throbbing bruises.

Nesschter's breathing is shaky and wheezing, and blood trickles all over his outfit. His vision is blurry, with a ringing, ticking, and heavy heartbeats battling in his ears. He sees Don waving at him, and between the two is a lot of corpses and a waterfall of blood on the stairs.

Nesschter takes a deep, scratchy breath, sheath's his knife, and runs up to Don, legs shaking and hands trembling.

* * *

In the office, the two remaining Revivalist Lupinaks look at Balik with worry.

"They left, sir," says one of the Revivalist Lupinaks.

"And you didn't try to stop them?" says Balik.

The Revivalist Lupinak shakes his head and Balik nods.

"I see," says Balik.

He goes to the last hostage. The Division 4 Agent looks at him with a wet, red-eyed glare. He is breathing heavily and covered in sweat, and Balik rubs his hand on his head and goes behind him. Once behind the hostage, he looks at the camera.

"I'm sorry your commander didn't love you," says Balik.

Balik fires twice into the hostage. Once through the head and another into their back. He ejects his empty magazine, pulls out his watch and checks the time. Then he holds it up to the camera, so they can see the jumbled numbers and hands hanging limp on its face.

"So that's it... The hostages are dead, except for one. This is your last chance. You have eleven minutes to open that door. If it is not opened within that time, Jasnee Asven dies," says Balik.

Chapter 17

Nesschter barges through the stairwell door, panting and stumbling forward. His trembling hands ache, his legs feel like they are going to burst, and his lungs are tormented by a prickling sensation that leaves a copper taste in his mouth.

Nesschter opens his watch, shifting his weight from one foot to the other. He can barely see with the sweat and blood trickling into his eyes, making the numbers blur together.

The others file in after him, and Nesschter puts his watch away and slumps against the wall, wheezing and coughing. Sweat and blood has glued his ruined tunic to his body, and he wipes his face while Garlo and Don check the stairwell. Aki goes to Nesschter, and Mi and Sakura slump slide to the floor, panting heavily.

"We made it," says Aki tiredly.

"No…" Nesschter coughs. "No, we didn't. We still have to deal with Balik and Jarvis."

"Where the hell is Jarvis, anyway?" says Don.

"It's better if we don't run into him," says Mi. "We should head back, get rid of Balik, and avoid Jarvis at all cost."

"Scared?" teases Sakura with a shaky, raspy voice.

Sakura adds a giggle in there, but Mi glares at her.

"If you read his file you'd be scared, too. That guy is a demon," says Mi.

"Nah, he's just a demented mute. He'll bleed and die the same as anyone else," says Don dismissively.

Then a door slams somewhere down the hall, and Nesschter's ears twitch as light footsteps make their way to them. Sakura and Mi stand up, and the rest aim their weapons down the dark hallway. Red lights flicker, and while the Lupinaks can hear the steps, Garlo's eyes narrow and he adjusts his grip on his weapon.

"He's here," says Garlo.

Seconds later, tiny, sharp blue eyes appear in the dark. They get closer, and with them comes the shadowed silhouettes of a figure. The closer they get, the louder their steps become.

Soon, Jarvis appears in the red light. His emotionless blue eyes stare at the group, but he doesn't have a ballistic weapon on him.

"Shit," says Don.

Mi's ears droop and she steps back. "D–Demon."

Jarvis Vaan Luken's sharp blue eyes shine in the dim red environment. His shadow spreads along the floor and walls as the red lights swirl. He draws his spearhead and walks forward, and Garlo approaches him, much to the horror and surprise of everyone in the group.

"What are you doing? Get back here!" says Aki.

Jarvis continues walking forward, and Garlo stops by a vending machine with his pistol drawn.

"You thirsty?" asks Garlo.

Jarvis wiggles his hand side to side, and Garlo shoots the lock off the vending machine. Then he pulls it open, removes a soda, and looks at Jarvis.

"Orange, right?" asks Garlo.

Nesschter's group looks at each other, Jarvis returns his spearhead and nods, and Garlo tosses it to him. Then he grabs a grape soda. The two open their cans with some fizz dribbling out, and gently tap them together before drinking. After taking their gulps, Garlo looks at the group.

"You guys should probably take a drink while he lets you," says Garlo.

"If that's the case…?" says Don.

Don goes to the vending machine and grabs a root beer.

"Bring me a Caffeine Rush if they have one," says Nesschter.

Don grabs a green can of Caffeine Rush and Aki slaps Nesschter's shoulder, bringing him to look at her.

"What?" asks Nesschter.

"Have you lost your mind?" says Aki.

"I'm thirsty.".

Aki slaps him again, and he quietly thanks Don when he gives him the Caffeine Rush. Meanwhile, Sakura goes to the vending machine and grabs a cherry soda.

"Do you two want anything?" asks Sakura.

"Sakura, you can't be serious?" says Aki.

"We're in the presence of the Jarvis Vaan Luken, and he's letting us have a drink, so I'm going to take advantage of this. It'll be fun to talk about after we kick his ass," says Sakura.

Jarvis's eyes focus on Sakura as he sips his drink again.

"Garlo, what is going on?" asks Mi uneasily.

"Me and Jarvis go way back," says Garlo.

"Friends?" asks Nesschter.

"Close. Enemies. Me and him engaged plenty on the battlefield, but we just could not kill each other. I thought I finally got him in the Vagsten Tunnels, in the Blue Sector, when I shot a rocket at him. But one day I took N-Light out of morbid curiosity and it showed me this day and this hallway. Now here we are."

"Did we live?" asks Mi.

"The vision didn't go that far, but I think we'll be fine if we gang up on him."

Jarvis smiles thinly and slightly raises his can. Nesschter's tail and ears twitch. He does not like that smile. It is like a face of flesh stretched on a mannequin.

Garlo sips his drink again. "Also, we need to remember he is wearing a shield generator, so bullets will just annoy him." Garlo drops his rifle and draws his knife. "Fortunately, I have this."

Jarvis finishes his drink, crushes his can, and drops it in the recycle bin. He holds out his hand to Garlo.

Garlo tosses him his empty can, which also goes in the recycle bin, and the Avus looks at the group.

"Finish up and give him your can when you're done," says Garlo.

"I hate everything about this," says Don.

"Me too," says Nesschter.

They give their cans to Jarvis when they are done with their drinks, but Mi drinks the slowest, using little sips at a time, as she stares at Jarvis with her ears, hands, and whiskers quivering. Jarvis stares at her, too, and when she finishes, she reluctantly crushes the can and gives it to Garlo. He gives it to Jarvis, and Jarvis puts it in the recycle bin.

"Alright..." Garlo takes a deep breath. "Let's do this."

Garlo lunges with his knife, and Jarvis slides to the side, deflects, and rams Garlo into the wall. He brings his spearhead down. Garlo grabs his wrist and twists Jarvis, but the mute uses the momentum to throw Garlo aside.

With Garlo on the ground, Mi shoots sporadically at Jarvis. Gunshots thunder in the hall, bright light blinds the group, and sparks from the shield crack the air.

When she is done, Nesschter's ears are ringing, and colorful blobs cloud his vision. Then he is shoved aside by Aki.

Aki and Sakura rush forward, while Mi reloads. They take swipes at Jarvis, but he easily deflects their swipes and quickly stabs Aki in the shoulder, before grabbing and twisting Sakura's knife out of her grip.

Then he twists Sakura's arm into a lock and rams her into Don. The two crash into a door, and when Jarvis pulls away, his spearhead slashes Sakura's arm, opening her cephalic vein along its length.

Sakura shrieks and clutches her bleeding arm as she drops to the floor. Her hand and arm quickly become slick with blood. Nesschter rushes Jarvis and tries stabbing him downward. Jarvis deflects and attempts a stab. Nesschter slides to the side and puts Jarvis in a chokehold while attempting to stab him in the ear.

Jarvis grabs Nesschter's wrist and forces the knife away. He gags when the pressure on his throat is increased.

Don removes his jacket Sakura's wound. The fabric quickly becomes overwhelmed with blood, and Sakura whimpers as the fiery light fades from her eyes.

Garlo and Aki rush Jarvis, blades ready for the kill. Before they can reach him, Jarvis pushes himself back, slamming Nesschter into the wall. Then he elbows Nesschter in the side and throws himself forward, flipping Nesschter into Aki and Garlo.

As the group stumbles to regain themselves, Jarvis adjusts his posture. Aki and Garlo go for more stabs, Jarvis elbows Aki back, punches Garlo, then kicks Aki into a door when she sprints towards him. After that, he tackles Garlo into the open vending machine, breaking the shelves and sending soda cans rolling and breaking. Many cans hiss and spray their contents over the floor and clothes, and Jarvis' shield flares when Mi shoots him again.

Jarvis grabs a full soda can and smashes it against Garlo's head. Garlo kicks Jarvis back, and while he staggers, Aki rushes him.

She leaps, he ducks and flips Aki over his shoulder, and throws another can at Mi. She dodges it, and the can explodes down the hall. Mi aims again and almost shoots Garlo due to Jarvis turning him into a meat shield.

The. Don kicks Jarvis in the side, knocking him into the broken vending machine again. Garlo snaps around with his knife and stabs Jarvis, pushing him further in with broken shelving and springs digging into his back.

Jarvis growls, extends his claws, slams them into Garlo's chest and pushes himself out. The two slip on the soda coating the floor, but Jarvis is able to roll to his feet, and he slashes Don with his claws, grabs his spearhead, and leaps toward Garlo.

Nesschter blocks Jarvis's stab, and Garlo slides to the side for an attack, which is quickly deflected by Jarvis. Nesschter and Garlo press forward with their attacks, and in quick, fluid motions, Jarvis uses his spearhead and hand to block and deflect their slashes.

During this, Don jumps on Jarvis' back and stabs him in the lung. Sparks fly, and Jarvis snarls and flips Don off. He grabs Nesschter's arm, twists it, disarming him with a loud crack that makes him yelp.

Then Jarvis punches him down and kicks him into Don. The two become tangled, and when Garo goes for another attack, Jarvis parries, locks his arm down, pulls out Don's knife, and stabs Garo in the neck.

Garo crumbles to the floor without a sound, soaked in blood, and Jarvis wheezes, sparks popping from the wound in his chest.

Aki wails and rushes Jarvis. She makes sporadic, mad swipes. Mi weaves side to side, trying to get a good shot, but the deadly dance between Aki and Jarvis makes it impossible for her to get a good shot.

"Aki, get out of the way!" yells Mi.

Jarvis deflects one of Aki's attacks, disarms her with slashes and punches, kicks out her footing, and then throws her through a door. Aki slides across the room, twitching and bleeding. While this happens, Nesschter and Don rush Jarvis again.

Jarvis quickly disarms the pair, and with a flurry of punches, he strikes down Don and Nesschter. Nesschter attempts to get up, but Jarvis kicks him to the wall, breaking its outer layer.

Nesschter collapses with broken wall and a coating of dust on him, and Jarvis wheezes as he picks up his spearhead and goes to Don. But he stops when a bullet strikes him in the head, making him stumble and causing his shield to emit a bright flash of light and crackling energy.

After regaining himself, Jarvis looks down the hallway and staggers back when another bullet strikes him in the head. The shield holds, and another bullet hits him. Again, the shield holds. Now Jarvis marches towards Mi with narrowed eyes and his lips twitching from his growling.

Mi whimpers and keeps keeps shooting while Jarvis approaches her, taking the bullets in stride. Her eyes widen and her ears droop when Jarvis' march turns to a run.

She ejects her magazine and slips in a new one. When she aims, Jarvis grabs and locks her arm so her pistol is aimed at underneath her jaw. Mi whimpers and begs, and she tries pushing back, but Jarvis holds fast.

His eyes focus on Mi as he slips his finger over the trigger. She shakes her head and keeps trying to push back, as tears soak her cheeks.

"Please.... Please... Don't," sobs Mi.

Jarvis pulls the trigger three times and Mi's brain matter and bloody skull bits splatter on the wall. Mi crumbles, and Aki stumbles out of the room just in time to see Mi's lifeless body fall.

"No!" cries Aki.

Aki charges Jarvis, but Jarvis effortlessly deflects her stab. He disarms Aki and slams her head against the wall, leaving an indent. He pulls her head back and slams it into the wall again, and again, and again.

After the last one, Aki falls to the floor with a bloody face covered in white dust. Jarvis kicks her knife away right as Nesschter charges him.

Jarvis dodges the jab, and when he attempts to stab Nesschter, his attack is deflected and he gets elbowed in the face. Then a belt is wrapped around his neck and is pulled back by Don.

Don is grunting and he adjusts his grip on the belt to tighten the impromptu noose. Jarvis retaliates with sharp elbow jabs to Don's side, followed by kicking Nesschter away.

The force from the kick pushes Jarvis back, and with him, Don. They trip over Mi's body, and Jarvis wiggles out of Don's grip and pins him just to be tackled by Aki. Jarvis uses her momentum to throw her off, and when he stands up, he sees Nesschter wrapping his arm and hand in Don's belt.

Nesschter's breathing is heavy and raspy, and his glare is focused on Jarvis. After the belt is secure, Nesschter adjusts the grip on his knife and marches forward with streaks of sweat and blood covering his dirty face.

"Don, get Aki out of here. I'll finish this," says Nesschter.

Don helps Aki up, and the two hobble away. Jarvis grabs his spearhead and rushes towards Nesschter.

They engage in a furious display of fast jabs and swipes, with most of them being being blocked or deflected. Every counter is coupled with a punch or kick that is also countered in some way.

The pair bounce off the walls and nick each other with slashes every so often. They move in circles, trying to no avail to get an effective flank.

The belt covering Nesschter's arm and hand is enough to protect him from Jarvis' blade, whereas Nesschter's knife slowly adds more cuts to Jarvis' arm, on top of the fresh bruises and breaches in skin from the previous strikes.

After several, possibly dozens, of moves and counter moves, the two bloodied and sweaty Lupinaks get into a close lock, and turn in circles, both growling and straining their muscles as they attempt to overpower each other. It is taking every bit of Nesschter's strength to keep Jarvis at bay. He feels his joints straining and his bones struggling to keep their form.

Jarvis wheezes and his lips twitch to expose his fangs, while Nesschter glares at him. Jarvis kicks out Nesschter's footing, snaps his hand down, and in a swift flick, the knife is popped out of Nesschter's hand.

It skids out of sight. Nesschter grabs Jarvis' spearhead, twists and guides it away from his side, and repeatedly uses his fist as a hammer against Jarvis's head as he forces him back.

They hit the wall, Jarvis kicks Nesschter away, leading to him stumbling and tripping over himself near his knife. Nesschter quickly grabs his knife and scrambles away when Jarvis lunges at him.

With Jarvis now open, Nesschter charges and attempts to pierce his ribs, but the mute turns too quickly and deflects. However, the momentum is too much, and Nesschter slams his entire weight against Jarvis.

They break through the door and bounce and roll down a flight of stairs, hitting the wall and railing. Each impact sends a flash of sharp, hot pain surging through them. When they land, Jarvis's spearhead slides away and tumbles over the edge, and Nesschter's knife stops not too far from them.

The two grunt and snarl as they shift on the floor, both covered in pockets of sharp, throbbing pain and blood. Then they see the knife.

Jarvis leaps to it first and elbows Nesschter in the jaw, making his head hit the railing. After Jarvis grabs the knife, he goes for Nesschter's gut.

Nesschter slides to the side, grabs Jarvis' elbow and hand, and presses his arm against his body. Jarvis growls and punches Nesschter in the head and ear as he is forced into the concrete wall of the stairwell.

Flashes of pain surge through Nesschter's skull, each punch rattling his brain and tearing flesh. Nesschter snarls as he twists Jarvis to the floor. Jarvis braces himself with his free hand, and Nesschter turns Jarvis's knife hand and forces the knife into his gut.

Jarvis pauses. His ears perk, his eyes widen, and he looks down at the dribbling blood. Then he looks at Nesschter, blinking. Confusion giving life to his soulless eyes.

Nesschter growls and pushes the knife again, forcing Jarvis into the wall. Then he rips the knife across Jarvis' gut and the two slump to the floor, with

Jarvis against the wall and Nesschter against the railing.

The two stare at each other with sweat and blood sliding down their faces and soaking their clothes. Jarvis' lips twitch to a flicker of a smile. He puts his hands on his bleeding gut, closes his eyes, and bows his head. Seconds later, his breathing stops, and his blood drips down the stairs.

Nesschter's heavy breathing, his pocket watch's ticking, and Jarvis' dripping blood is all there is in the stairwell. He stares at Jarvis' lifeless body. He keeps staring, unsure of how long he has been sitting there, but by the time he moves, Jarvis' blood has touched his clothes, and he wipes the bloody knife on his sleeve before standing.

Nesschter grips the stair's railing tight as he gingerly makes his way upstairs. When he reaches the hallway, he slumps against the wall and stares at the gore.

Blood and soda have seeped into the carpet. Sakura, Mi, and Garlo lay in pools of blood, and their shadows stretch and condense from the swirling red lights. Nesschter takes a deep breath and slowly walks down the hallway, taking a brief moment to search every room for Don and Aki. He finds them held up in an office at the end of the hall. Both of them are sitting against a wall and aiming their pistols at him. After they lower their weapons, Nesschter walks forward, and kneels next to Aki. He puts his hand on her shoulder.

"Are you okay?" asks Nesschter.

Aki shakes her head, ears drooped and lips quivering. "They're dead... They're all dead...."

Nesschter squeezes her shoulder. "Go somewhere safe. Me and Don will handle Balik."

"No. I have to save Mrs. Jasnee Asven," says Aki.

"Balik is dangerous."

"He is responsible for my team's death. He needs to pay. And I need to save Mrs. Jasnee Asven. Her safety is more than just a job for me."

"He will kill you."

"That's a risk I'm willing to take. And I'll either go with you or go alone."

The two stare at each other in silence for a few seconds before Nesschter sighs and stands up with his hand held out to Aki. She grabs his hand and is pulled up, and Nesschter helps Don up right after.

"Xajil will be in the safe room with Chairman Asven. And since he has an infatuation with Ara, that's where she'll be, too," says Nesschter. "We rescue Ara and then we escape with no harm done to the chairman... Unless he forces me to hurt him."

"I thought Xajil was going to relocate her because of N-Light," says Don.

"I did, too. But after thinking about it, he stares at her a lot, gave her a lot of attention, and set her up to be watched by him constantly. He wants her, and if he gets the chance, he'll do to her what he did to me. I will not let that happen."

"Okay, fair assessment, I guess. But now for the ugly part. How are we going escape?" asks Don.

"I can turn a blind eye," says Aki numbly. She and Nesschter look at each other, adding, "For old time's sake."

Nesschter nods. "Thank you." He looks at Don. "And you'll be driving us out of here."

Don scoffs. "Of course I am."

Nesschter gingerly walks towards the office doorway, wincing from the biting pain chewing at him. "Let's finish this."

Aki and Don nod and follow Nesschter out, and the three travel together to end Balik's madness for good.

Chapter 18

Nesschter leads Aki and Don through the Division 4 Headquarters, rubble crunching and soaked carpet squelching under their feet. Mutilated bodies carpet the floor, blood paints the walls, and the sparks and flickering lights guide them down the halls like pixies leading them to Hell.

Upon reaching the working area, they find Balik sitting in a rolling chair, with Jasnee on her knees next to him. He is sipping from his thermos and flanking him are two Revivalist Lupinaks. Everyone else is gone.

"Where's the rest of your group?" asks Balik, looking at Nesschter out of the corner of his eye.

Nesschter's eyes narrow and Aki's ears flatten as she growls. Balik, stares ahead, his fingers fluffing Jasnee's mane, making her whimper and quiver.

"I see... Where's Jarvis?" asks Balik.

"Dead," says Nesschter.

Balik breathes through his nose. "Of course he is. Was it you that did him in?"

"Yes."

"I'm not surprised. Fate gave you the soul of killer. Death walking." Balik gently sets his thermos and stands up, looking at Nesschter, his gaze heavy, like he is about to fall asleep standing. "Dad tried to make me like you. But I didn't have your... natural state. Even after he pulled strings to make me a ranking officer while he let you stay on the field, killing for us."

"Liar," growls Nesschter. "You were the psycho, killing with glee. I hated every moment of it."

"Of course you would say that," says Balik wearily. "You and I remember things differently. I remember me being a puppet on strings, killing. Killing. See me See me. The dread of watching structures burn fading every day to numbness. But you?"

Balik wags his finger.

"No... You, Nesschter... You were in your natural element. Calm... Death incarnate," says Balik.

Nesschter quietly glares at him, and Balik puts his hands on Jasnee's shoulders, squeezing them, his weighted eyes still on Nesschter.

"I forced myself to be a killer," says Balik. "Every life I took, I took for dad, for mom, for you, for Gacerae, for Vagsten. Yet they only saw my uniform. They saw you just fine. The youngest son behaving as a better Alpha than the eldest... When you disappeared, they said, 'Balik, you must become Nesschter.'"

Nesschter stares at Balik, silent and eyes stone cold, and Balik moves his hands to Jasnee's head, stroking her mane again, eyes downcast, focused on the white and gray strands sifting and seeping through his fingers. Jasnee whimpers, her brown eyes bloodshot and thick tears streaming down her cheeks. Eleven seconds of silence pass before Balik checks his watch.

"I'm late. Follow me," says Balik. He pulls Jasnee to her feet and guides her inside, and he puts his hands on the shoulders of Revivalists when they back up. "You two, I have one more order for you."

"Yes sir," says one of the Revivalists.

"Leave."

The two look at him, shocked and confused, and Nesschter's group mirrors their expressions.

"Sir...?" says the second Revivalist.

"Both of you leave. Tell Khal Mason Jarim that I accomplished my mission. It has been an honor to fight by your side, but this is the end of my road. Now, travel yours," says Balik.

There is a moment of strained silence. Then the Revivalists reluctantly leave. At first their steps are slow, but once they pass Nesschter's group, they run out of sight. After they are gone, Balik sighs heavily and turns around, so they see the glowing spinal shield generator on his back.

"Let's talk inside. That door should be open by now," says Balik.

The group cautiously walks inside Xajil's office, and Don gags and Aki gasps when they see the executed hostages piled in a corner.

"Balik, you're insane," says Nesschter.

"They wouldn't open the door. But now we're all here, and we can see the excitement together," says Balik.

"You literally just tried killing us," says Don.

"You killed my friends," says Aki.

"Yeah, I did. And I still want to kill you three and Xajil. But it has now been **twenty-one** minutes and the door still hasn't opened, so..."

Balik yanks Jasnee in front of him, turning her into a meat shield, and he presses his pistol against her head. Aki, Don, and Nesschter aim their weapons at Balik, and Nesschter and Aki step closer, both growling.

"Let her go, Balik!" says Nesschter.

"Let her go, now!" orders Aki.

"We've been over this. I have a shield. Your bullets won't work very well on me," says Balik.

"We'll just shoot you until the shield breaks, then," says Don.

"You're a clever one. What's your IQ? Three hundred? Wait, don't answer that. I got a better question. **WHY ISN'T THE DOOR OPEN!?**"

The door suddenly groans and hisses, and it slowly slides open. The three Lupinaks' ears perk and Don's eyes snap to the door. Balik turns to the side, and the group watches the large door slide open, revealing ... an empty room.

"What?" says Balik.

He drags Jasnee into the room, ignoring her yelping and whimpering. Balik looks around and paces in a circle, dragging Jasnee every step of the way.

"Where are they?" says Balik. He turns to the group and presses his pistol against Jasnee's skull. "Where is Xajil Ojin!? Why is this room empty!?"

"It's empty because we left a while ago," says Kevin over the speaker. *"I personally wanted to stay and see my lovely wife and perhaps talk some sense into you, Alpha to Alpha. But I had to leave. And seeing as how I saw you execute those hostages, and how you want to do the same to my wife, I'm wondering, have you even thought this through? What do you think is going to happen, Balik?*

Executing Division 4 hostages is one thing but killing Jasnee is just an all-around bad call."

Balik trembles and tightens his grip on Jasnee, teeth bared and a growl rumbling in his throat.

"I don't want to talk to you, I want to talk to Xajil," says Balik.

"Well, you can't. Xajil is gone with Ara, and you holding my wife hostage means you talk to me," says Kevin.

"Where is he?"

"I'm not telling you."

"I HAVE YOUR WIFE HOSTAGE!"

"Yeah, I can see that, genius. But here's the thing, hurting her will only benefit me and my PR team," says Kevin. *"It will be a dream come true for us! Go ahead! Kill her! Make my day, make my PR's day. This is spicy, juicy, wonderful content that we can make a masterful media tapestry with! Killing her will give me immense support from everyone and damn you and your movement to Hell!"*

Jasnee gasps with tears pattering to the floor, and Balik's eyes widen as he looks between the camera and Jasnee. Even Aki's face is frozen with shock, and Don's jaw is slack. Nesschter, however, keeps his eyes on Balik.

"Oh, what's that look, Balik? Horror? Wondering how I could be so cold?" mocks Kevin. *"Well, unlike you, I do not harbor guilt or regret for anything, even if it means leaving my wife out there to die. She understands, too, because all that is important is Milo Gailo and his vision for a better Aarde."*

"K-Kevin...? Kevin, please... please stop," whispers Jasnee.

"Guilt is a menace," continues Kevin. *"It is nothing but pain that rots you from the inside out and holds the future hostage. If you kill Jasnee, it will be another event in my life that I will get over relatively quickly and wastes your time. But it will also make Milo Gailo's vision that much easier to obtain. You and the Revivalists will be the barbarians, and the GSAU will be the defenders of all that is good. I will be your victim, and you will be the psychopaths. Killing Jasnee will ensure our total victory for the GSAU in the end. So, kill her if you're suicidal."*

Jasnee's knees give out, and she falls to the floor sobbing while Balik stands over her, keeping his pistol at his side. He stares at Jasnee, and his finger twitches, all while distant gunfire inches closer.

After some seconds of silence, with Jasnee's sobbing being the only voice, Nesschter steps forward.

"Balik, let her go," says Nesschter. "You heard Kevin Asven. Killing her will only do him favors. You need to walk away and disappear. I won't stop you. None of us will."

"I will," says Aki.

Nesschter snarls and points his claw at her. "You will not touch him!"

Aki growls, fur bristling and lips twisted from her snarl, and Balik checks his watch. He closes it eleven seconds later, and looks at Nesschter out of the corner of his eye.

"I am tired, Nesschter," says Balik. "I'm tired of all of it. And I know you are, too. I know you hear the screaming and the ticking. The memories that haunt us... They won't stop. Disappearing won't save me. I'll end it tonight. For you, for the Norkits, for Gacerae, for Vagsten."

Balik aims his pistol at Jasnee's head.

"*Wait, what are you doing?*" asks Kevin.

Jasnee looks at the camera, sniffling and blinking tears out of her eyes, her fists are clenched and her body trembles.

"I forgive you," whispers Jasnee.

"Balik, don't do it! I am giving you a way out! Take it!" says Nesschter.

"*Don't you dare do it!*" yells Kevin.

"Drop the gun, right now!" yells Don.

"There is no way out," says Balik.

Aki screams and shoots Balik. The shield generator flares, briefly blinding the group, and Balik stumbles and reflexively squeezes the trigger. The bullet rips through Jasnee's heart. She crumbles to the floor, and Aki roars and charges while shooting Balik. He is still disoriented from the shots hitting him, and when Aki reaches him, she slams her rifle against his head.

Balik drops to the floor, and when Aki goes for another hit, he lunges at her, snarling. He rams her into the drink cabinet, shattering glass and wood. Bottles roll out and shatter, spilling their contents on the floor.

"Aki!" yells Nesschter.

He and Don rush towards her, and Balik grabs Aki by the throat, lifts her, and slams her on the workstation. The desk and computers break, and Aki goes limp on the floor.

Then Balik is pushed back by Don shooting him. The shield still holds, and the distraction of Don's shots is enough for Nesschter to get close and wail on him. Punch after punch after punch. Balik's head and chest are struck repeatedly, and every strike prompts Balik's fingers to twitch. First one finger, then two, then three, and up it goes.

Once Nesschter reaches eleven strikes, Balik deflects the twelfth punch, throws Nesschter to the floor, slams his head down a few times, and then draws his knife. Don shoots him again, the shield flickers, and Balik turns to Don, snarling.

"You bald alien bastard!" yells Balik,

Nesschter rolls to his hands and knees, disoriented and ears ringing, and he sees Balik rushing towards Don.

Don ducks and weaves from Balik's slashes, and Nesschter gets up on wobbly legs and runs towards Balik.

Balik goes for another swing, but Nesschter grabs his arm, kicks out his leg, and puts him in a choke hold.

"Enough! You've done enough damage!" says Nesschter.

Balik roars and gives his body a sharp twist, throwing Nesschter off balance. He continues thrashing and twisting and turning until Nesschter disconnects, and he swiftly follows with stomping on Nesschter's gut.

Nesschter yelps and curls, clutching his gut and coughing sharply, and Balik throws a chair at Don. Don blocks the chair with his arm, and Balik charges him and punches his heart. There is a loud crack, and Don flies off his feet and hits the wall. He falls to the floor limp, eyes wide open and blood pouring from his mouth. Nesschter extends his hand with wide eyes.

"No!" cries Nesschter.

"It's almost over, Nesschter. I promise," says Balik, rubbing his fist and walking towards Aki.

Nesschter jumps to his feet, fangs bared, and claws extended, and a fiery glare locked on Balik.

"I'll kill you!" snarls Nesschter.

Balik grabs Aki by her mane and pulls her to her knees, his knife in hand.

"Good! Do it! The perfect son killing the failed experiment is the best way to end this!" yells Balik.

Then Aki bites Balik's arm. He howls and kicks Aki away and paces with heavy steps as he clutches his bleeding arm, laughing.

"Oh! Damn it! You got some teeth on you!" says Balik.

With that distraction, Nesschter picks up his knife and rushes Balik. He takes a swipe at him, and Balik uses his arm to block the blade, and he kicks Nesschter back.

Aki leaps on Balik and bites down on Balik's shoulder. He stumbles and falls, and Aki growls and shakes her head and digs her claws in him. He punches Aki in the nose, and she yelps and falls off, clutching her crooked, bleeding snout.

When Nesschter goes for a stab, Balik grabs Nesschter's wrist with both hands, deflects with enough force to unbalance Nesschter, and he headbutts him. Then does it again, and again, and again. Each time brings Nesschter lower, and each headbutt leads to him punching Balik in the side, but he is unfazed by the attacks.

Balik snaps Nesschter's arm down, twists him, and punches him on the side of the head. Nesschter drops, his bleeding ear ringing and head swimming. Nesscter's vision is distorted, and bile builds in his throat as he watches Balik pick up his knife and stab Aki in the gut. Nesschter screams furiously and strains his limbs to push himself to his hands and knees as Balik pushes Aki against the wall. He yanks the knife out and–

Nesschter's knife suddenly slices Balik's wrist, and his hand goes limp. The knife drops, and Aki slides to the floor, whimpering and clutching her gut. Balik lifts his arm to look at his defunct hand, and then he looks at Nesschter and smiles.

"There we go," says Balik.

Nesschter swipes at Balik, and he uses Nesschter's momentum to throw him down. Nesschter rolls to his feet, but Balik rams him down and presses his hand against his chest. He lunges with his mouth open and gleaming fangs aimed for Nesschter's throat.

Nesschter puts his hand in the way. He screams and howls, and he stabs Balik's shoulder while wildly kicking him. Balik's sharp fangs rip his flesh and break the bones of his hand. Tears and blood stream down Nesschter's face and arm.

As Nesschter hammers his fist against Balik's skull and kicks against his body, Balik keeps a tight hold, and sinks his teeth further in.

The bones shatter and snap, and with a sharp tug, a chunk of Nesschter's hand is ripped off, and with it, his ring and pinkie fingers. Nesschter finally kicks Balik away, yelling and cursing, and clutching his hand to his chest while blood pumps out of the gaping wound, soaking his sleeve in the hot, crimson fluid.

Balik turns on his hands and knees and spits out the mangled chunk of hand. He watches Nesschter writhe and push himself across the floor with his feet and elbow, shaking and whimpering.

Sweat and tears soak Nesschter's face, and Balik stands up, rolls his neck, and marches towards him with unsteady steps. His eyes are distant and unfocused, blood drips from his mouth while more dribbles to the floor from the numerous wounds. Nesschter's knife is still in his shoulder, but he doesn't pull it out.

"Don't... don't... don't..." begs Aki weakly.

Nesschter falls to his side, hyperventilating, sweat and blood coating him. Balik drops to his knees next to him, and his eyes drift in circles as his body wobbles.

"Did you know my team was tortured in that house I kept you and your team in?" says Balik distantly. "Xajil and this masked human named Wraith had us stripped down, took us into separate rooms, and their men went to work with tools. The walls were thick, but they had vents, so all of us heard everything. Every day we heard our screams. My team screamed, I screamed, but we never gave the AAHU or the Federation anything. So, they continued. Scream after scream, day after day. But soon the screams got weaker, and weaker... and weaker."

Balik grabs Nesschter's neck and squeezes. Nesschter grunts and grabs Balik's wrist with his good hand, and he attempts to pry him off with no success.

"Then their voices stopped. One. By. One," continues Balik, squeezing tighter and making Nesschter gag. "Until one day, there was no more screaming. No more voices. I was the last one left, and my heart barely worked, so they dragged me out, naked and bloodied, unable to move. I barely saw anything, and they threw me in a ditch with my team's bodies, and other bodies. All decomposing. The stench was bad, the feel... The rot..."

Balik shudders and briefly looks to the ceiling, before returning to look at Nesschter. He increases the pressure. Nesschter gasps for air. His lungs burn and darkness bleeds into his vision.

"While being dropped in a ditch with the dead was terrible, and seeing my team disfigured and bloodied beyond recognition was heartbreaking, that is not what stuck out to me. You see, sometimes I forget the smells, sometimes I forget the feeling of a corpse, and sometimes I even forget my teammates. By my own choices I do this.

"But no matter how hard I try, the one thing I could never forget are the screams. Those horrible, terrible screams. The screams from my team, dying one by one. They are always in my head, in my ears, I hear them constantly. And it is not just my team. It is the screams of the dying around me. Soldiers, civilians, the executed, the miserable, the burning, the fires, the bombs. The screams of mom before she disappeared. They didn't stop! They never stopped!"

Balik pulls Nesschter up his neck, so they are eye to eye. Nesschter's claws dig into Balik's wrist, drawing blood, but Balik keeps his hold tight.

"It is constant," growls Balik, with tears streaming down his face. "But out of all that torture. That torment! *I never* sold out our people! You did that. You did this to us, Nesschter! *You did all this to us!* You brought death because *that is who you are!*"

Balik peers deep into Nesschter's eyes. Watery eyes meeting watery eyes. Haze to haze. Red to red. Amber to gray. Defeat mirroring each other.

"And yet, I understand... I do... I do..." adds Balik gently. "You thought we abandoned you, and there was a darkness that could not be stopped. All you had was your nature. I'm sorry I let them torture you. I'm sorry I couldn't save you... I'm sorry for everything. I should have protected you, but I couldn't, and now I'm going to make things right..."

Balik squeezes tighter. Nesschter gags and coughs and pushes his mangled hand against Balik's face. His vision is almost completely dark now, and his lungs feel like they are in flames.

"Stop fighting. It's the only way the torment will end," says Balik.

"Balik... stop..." grunts Nesschter.

Balik shakes his head. "No... I'm doing this for you. For us. It'll be over soon, and we'll be happy."

"Balik... Stop!"

"We'll be with Mom and Dad, together. No screaming. No pain. They will see you again and me for the first time. We. Will be. Seen."

Then Nesschter removes his grip from Balik's wrist, and with a raspy yell, he jabs his claws into Balik's neck.

Balik gurgles and falls off Nesschter, clutching his throat with blood pouring and squirting through five punctures. His mouth, throat, chest, and hands become slick with blood, and he tries bracing himself, but his hand slips on the pool of blood and he collapses to the floor.

His wet gurgling quiets, and his dim, wet eyes stare at Nesschter while the blood creeps towards him. And Nesschter gasps and scrambles towards the couch on his hand and knees, rubbing his throat while making raspy wheezes and chest heaving.

Balik lays still. Gunshots and explosions are now very close to the Division 4 building, and the rubble rattles as an aircraft flies overhead.

Nesschter looks at Don, hoping to see him move, but he is still limp with his eyes open and mouth bloody. Then he looks at Aki, and sees she is staring at him. Her breathing is shallow, her hands are slick with blood, and her eyes are glazed.

Nesschter winces and crawls to a case marked with a red cross. He opens it, finding bandages, healing foam, and syringes with brown liquid, among other things. His hands tremble and his heart beats loudly as he gathers all of them, and then he crawls to Aki.

"You first. You can't save Ara if you go in shock," says Aki weakly.

Nesschter bandages his mangled hand and then injects himself with the brown liquid. He shudders and grips his heart. It beats heavier and faster, his pupils dilate, and his mouth hangs open due to his heavy panting.

But he also feels scabs rapidly forming on his wounds. It takes a couple of minutes, but when it is done, his body is marked with dozens of dark pink, wet scabs of various sizes. During this period, Nesschter works on Aki.

He removes her vest and shirt and wraps the stab wound with a bandage after applying disinfectant. Then he injects her with a fresh syringe of the brown liquid. After that, Aki buttons her jacket and puts her vest back on, and rests her head against the wall, chuckling and barely able to keep her eyes open.

"What?" asks Nesschter.

"This is the most naked you've seen me," says Aki.

Nesschter rolls his eyes and sits next to her. The two stare at the bloody mess in the room, and Aki's smile fades. Her lips tremble, then she rests her head against Nesschter's shoulder and cries.

Nesschter is silent, but he gently rubs her head. Despite the medicine working miracles, he is still in a lot of pain. Every move is like splinters scraping his flesh, and his heart is still heavy. He can still feel Balik's hand on his throat, and his eyes have trouble staying open.

The gunshots and explosions are very close now. It will be only a few minutes before the military reaches the Division 4 Headquarters, but he can't close his eyes. He must move. And there is one thing that can do that...

Nesschter's hand sluggishly moves to his pouch and pulls out an N-Light pill. He is dreading what he is about to see, and he hears Aki tearfully protesting this, but he doesn't care. He needs to stay awake.

He needs to save Ara and make Xajil pay for what he did. So, he plops the N-Light in his mouth and lets the pill work its magic.

Chapter 19

After taking N-Light, Nesschter's eyes snap open and his heart races with a heat radiating from him. The world around him becomes overlapped with other scenery of winding trees and sprawling shrubs, and the door to the safe room closes with a loud thud that sounds like an explosion.

The branches and leaves shake, and a hidden door groans as it opens behind Nesschter and Aki. Aki moves away, keeping her weapon trained on the new opening.

Past the door is a corridor with shining tile, thin green curtains, and sunlight pouring through the clean windows. In front of the two Lupinaks are a pair of Division 4 Avus armed with shotguns. Beyond them is Hosalina Jovia Norkit, a near spitting image of Nesschter, if he was an older female.

She stares at Nesschter with her hands clamped in front of her, wearing a simple green dress with leafy brown stitch patterns and a brown sash decorated with yellow leaves.

"Agent Holden Hosenheim, Director Ojin wants to talk to you," says the first Avus.

"Nesschter, is that you?" calls Hosalina, but her voice is in his ears, as though she is in his head.

Nesschter stands up with the help of a couch, wincing from the pinches of pain.

"I'm here," says Nesschter.

Aki steps forward, but the second Avus aims his shotgun at her.

"Not you. You're staying," he says.

"Why?" asks Aki sharply.

"Orders."

Nesschter walks past the two Avus. The first one grabs his arm and walks with him, and the second one keeps his shotgun trained on Aki as he steps back.

"Where is Balik?" asks Hosalina.

Hot tears bubble in Nesschter's eyes, and he holds out his mangled hand.

"I killed him," says Nesschter, short of breath and tears mixing with the blood on his scratched face.

"Killed who?" asks the first Avus.

"Just let him be. He's tripping out. See his eyes?" says the second Avus.

Hosalina sighs sadly and shakes her head. "You two always played so rough. But boys will be boys. Call Balik back in and I'll make lunch."

The hallway windows suddenly go dark. Hosalina disappears while her bloodcurdling scream echoes in the hallway.

"Mom?" calls Nesschter.

He tries running, but the Avus tighten their grip on him. As they travel down the hallway, Hoslaina screams again, but it is much further, and an all-black vehicle zooms by the window.

"Mom!" cries Nesschter.

"Where's Mom!?" yells Balik, his voice echoing without a body.

Nesschter lunges towards the fleeing vehicle, but the Avus strike him in the back and legs with with their shotgun butts, dropping him to the floor. He reaches out, but his wrists are grabbed, and he is cuffed behind his back.

"You couldn't do this the easy way, could you!" snarls the first Avus.

"Mom!" cries Nesschter.

"Nesschter?" calls Hebediah. "Nesschter! Balik! Where are you!? Where's your mom!? Where's Hosalina!?"

Nesschter is pulled to his feet, and he is forced forward. The Avus open another door that leads to a pitch-black void. Nesschter's ears droop, his feet dig in, and he tries to back up, but another bash from a shotgun causes him to stumble, and he is shoved forward. The only reason he doesn't fall is because of the right grip one of the Avus has on his cuffs.

"We found a couple of people with information, but they don't know where they took Hosalina," says an unfamiliar voice in the darkness.

A pair of gunshots echo. Each shot is accompanied by a flash of light, partially revealing Hebediah with a pistol and a human and Avus getting executed.

"Get Diaz and Talos, and have them find the rest of these rats," says Hebediah. "Nesschter and Balik, you stay with Khal. He'll protect you."

Then comes a voice that sends a shiver down Nesschter's spine and his heart racing.

"You poor, poor boy," says Mr. Verimoor.

His voice slithers in Nesschter's ears, and a tingle runs up his spine, making his fur bristle and bringing a cold sweat to trickle down his face. Ghostly hands grab Nesschter's shoulders and the Avus keep forcing him through the void.

"Such tragedy has hindered your studies. Your father told me to help you get your grades up, so how about we make some personal time after school for some tutoring?" says Mr. Verimoor.

Nesschter is thrown in the back of a jeep, and the door slams shut, plunging him in total darkness.

"Remember, your father wanted this for you," says Mr. Verimoor.

Nesschter thrashes on the seat, his eyes snapping in circles, his chest heaving from his hyperventilating as he searches for Mr. Verimoor. But Mr. Verimoor isn't anywhere to be seen. However, ghostly fingers slide over Nesschter's body, tracing his throat, his thighs, his butt, and groin.

"Get off me!" yells Nesschter.

He bites the air, kicks the door and violently thrashes as Mr. Verimoor laughs in the dark.

The Avus get in the jeep and drive down the road, breaking the darkness. Nesschter struggles to sit up, and he looks out the window and sees Hebediah waving farewell to him while vehicles carrying other Gaceraen soldiers driving past them. All of the soldiers have a mixture of nervousness, excitement, and fear.

A hand goes on Nesschter's shoulder. He looks to the side and sees Balik smiling at him.

"It'll be fine. We'll make it home. I'll protect you until the end. Promise!"

says Balik.

Nesschter stares at Balik with misty eyes. His heart is heavy, and his throat is clogged. He reclines in his seat with his rifle between his legs and stares at the sky. The two of them watch Gaceraen air transports escorted by smaller airships soar above them, leaving trails of exhaust and shaking the air.

"Don't forget, you need to make it back. You've got Ara and a family legacy to carry, whereas I have an art set. Your mission to survive is a bit more important than mine," says Balik.

Nesschter looks ahead, now bloody and eyes heavy. Ara stands in front of him, her hand held out to him. She is bloody yet smiling, and a dark forest behind her while faint lights from burning skyscrapers in the distance.

"Come on, Nesschter. We're almost home," says Ara.

Nesschter blinks tears out of his eyes and finds himself sitting on his knees in the foyer of Xajil's house.

He is kneeling front of Xajil Ojin. The Director has Ara bound and gagged, her orange prisoner jumpsuit coated in sweat and opened at the top to expose her white furred cleavage. Scratches mark her exposed body, and her eyes are heavy and bloodshot.

Xajil has his talons wrapped around Ara's throat, his other hand grips her arm. His house is dark, with the only light coming from the moon through the glass dome above and fires from the other houses shining through the large windows.

Ara and Xajil stare at Nesschter. While Xajil is stiff, his golden eyes pulsing and crest twitching. Ara is shaking and whimpering. Tears wet the white fur on her cheeks, and her black nostrils flare from her heavy breathing.

"So nice of you to join us. Did you enjoy your daydream?" says Xajil.

Nesschter's ears flick. A shiver runs through his body as Xajil's words echo in the empty house. Xajil's normal subdued, even tone is gone. His voice is almost loud, like the Director is struggling to keep himself from screaming.

Nesschter looks around and sees the two Avus are standing behind him with their shotguns at rest. The first Avus has Nesschter's knife and watch, and he stares at the faded dove covering. Its ticking haunts Nesschter's ears, and he looks at Xajil Ojin, then at Ara.

"Are you okay?" asks Nesschter.

Ara shakes her head.

"I watched you kill Balik Norkit. You did the GSAU a great service. You have my thanks," says Xajil sardonically.

Nesschter glares at Xajil with flattened ears. "You tried to kill me."

"Because you're too broken to fix," says Xajil.

"How many others had their memories altered because of you?"

"Move," sneers Xajil, nudging Ara forward with a knee to her rump.

Ara inches forward, one shaky step at a time, and Xajil keeps a tight hold on her, keeping himself pressed against her so he can smell her. When they are in front of Nesschter, Xajil's crest and tail twitch, and his eyes focus on the former Agent.

"Your gripe is nothing special. We've corrected this entire planet's memory, and there are over one hundred thousand agents operating on corrected memories, like you before you betrayed me. You were just a number," says Xajil.

Nesschter's muzzle scrunches, and the light from the moon and fires reflect off his eyes and fangs. The same goes for Xajil's eyes, as they both refuse to blink or alter their focus.

"Tell me, who did you like more? Holden Hosenheim or Nesschter Hebediah Norkit?" asks Xajil.

Nesschter is silent. His fingers flex and his claws poke against his pads, and when Ara's legs bend, Xajil hisses and digs his talons into her neck and arm, jerking her upright and making her yell through the gag.

"Stay up!" snaps Xajil.

Ara whimpers, and Xajil shakes his head.

"Stop shaking. You won't remember any of this when I'm done with you, anyway," says Xajil. He looks at Nesschter. "As for you. Before you consumed N-Light, you were happier as Holden, were you not?"

Nesschter growls. "You tortured me. You made me betray my family and my pack!"

"That was not my question!"

"You don't deserve an answer! You deserve to die for what you did! You broke Aarde! You broke me and over one hundred thousand agents! Now you want to break Ara!"

"I'M NOT BREAKING ANYTHING!" screams Xajil, his booming voice and wild eyes making Nesschter's heart stop for a moment. "Do you know what breaking is?"

Xajil kicks Ara's leg, dropping her to her knees, and she screams as his talons slide up her muzzle, sharply tilting her head up.

"Breaking is slitting her throat. Breaking is supporting a violent mob to destroy Shio. Breaking is destroying what can be fixed. I do not break things unless I have to, unlike you violent, flea bag knuckle dragging lunatics!" yells Xajil, his furious voice echoing in his house.

Xajil shoves Ara's head down so she and Nesschter are eye to eye.

"Do you want me to slash her throat open! Do you want me to break her in front of you!" screams Xajil.

"You do that and I swear to you I will kill you before you leave this house!" yells Nesschter.

The Avus guards cock their shotguns and Xajil hisses, pointing at them and his crest flexing.

"Not yet," says Xajil.

Xajil keeps his grip on Ara's neck and arm, and drags her across the floor with him, ignoring her whimpers and muffled sobs. When they are in front of Nesschter, he holds Ara's face so she is forced to look into Nesschter's eyes. Ara's wet eyes have trouble focusing, and Nesschter's gaze hardens, a loud growl rumbling in his throat.

"Take a good long look. This is the last you'll see of each other," says Xajil. "Do you know why? Because fate rewards the good. I ended the War of Unification. I saved millions by doing it. I helped take away the pain of the past and gave Aarde a new identity that is free of pain. Free of guilt. Free from a past that fuels civilizational violence. We were on our way to giving my species a paradise, fixing the broken culture of Lupinaks, and making Aarde a home for all. But like you and those hooligans out there, you are ungrateful for the world the GSAU was building. Fate will punish you, but reward me with her."

Xajil tugs Ara against his chest and traces her jaw with his talon, glaring at Nesschter.

"And you dead," concludes Xajil.

Ara's breathing quickens, and she looks at Xajil out of the corner of her eye, but he doesn't look at her. He keeps his attention on Nesschter.

"If you want to kill me. Then do it now," says Nesschter.

Ara's eyes bulge, and she shakes her head frantically, whimpering and sobbing garbled words.

Xajil frowns. "Fine." He looks at the two Avus. "Kill him."

Ara screams and thrashes, and Xajil drags drags her away while the Division 4 Avus raise their shotguns. Then a window shatters and the first Avus' head pops while the second one is knocked off his feet from bullets striking the back of his vest.

Nesschter instantly lunges at the downed Agent, despite his hands still being cuffed. His teeth rip open his target's throat.

The Avus gurgles and clutches their pouring wound, and Nesschter backs away from his target and looks around. Xajil and Ara are nowhere to be seen. Aki breaks the jagged glass off the window with her rifle's stock and gingerly climbs through, using her jacket as a covering for her hands. Then she approaches Nesschter, with her rifle in one hand and her other hand holding her gut.

"You're crazy. I don't even know how you're standing," says Aki.

"It's my stubbornness," says Nesschter.

Aki grabs Nesschter's collar and tugs him close, muzzle to muzzle, annoyed and worried glare to a tired yet bloodthirsty stare.

"Well your stubbornness almost got you killed. If I was a second later you'd be dead," says Aki.

"I'll buy you a coffee as a thanks," says Nesschter.

Aki pushes him away and goes to the Avus he bit. "You don't even like coffee."

"That's why I said I would buy you one. I'd buy myself hot chocolate."

Aki rolls her eyes, fishes out keys from the corpse, and uncuffs Nesschter. After that is done, Nesschter grabs his knife, his watch, and the guard's shotgun.

Then he checks the time. It is quarter after nine. He stuffs his watch in his pouch, and the two walk down to the mansion's lobby, keeping their weapons up and their ears swiveled. Their steps also mix with the ticking, and there are rattles and thuds of gunfire and explosions from the nearby carnage.

"Why are you helping me, anyway?" whispers Nesschter.

"I felt bad for you," replies Aki, also whispering.

"You do realize that they'll come after you, right?"

"I guess I'll just have to sneak off Aarde or join the Revivalists."

Nesschter grunts and cautiously opens a door. It turns out to be the door to the dining room, which is now empty with the tables folded and chairs stacked. All that is left in the bare room are chandeliers and a small table with one chair.

The only reason they can see these things is because the house down the street is on fire, so there is a little bit of a flickering glow giving some illumination. But since the glow isn't enough for good lighting, Nesschter sniffs the air, and he and Aki's ears swivel around, listening for any signs of movement. Nesschter can't hear anything, but he can smell a lot of dirt...

Nesschter looks at another door, taps Aki's shoulder, and points at it. The distant fire reflects off the metal door, and the two Lupinaks creep forward. Their breathing is steady, but their hearts are racing, and their muscles are tense.

Aki press her ear on the door. She grabs the doorknob and looks at Nesschter. He goes off to the side, adjusts his grip on the shotgun, and nods. Aki opens the door and Nesschter slips in.

The room is completely dark. What little light shines through is barely enough to outline the edges of metal counters and cabinets. Off in the corner is a humming fridge with the temperatures displayed, and a clock above a camera with a red dot ticks loudly.

Nesschter sniffs the air again and steps carefully into the darkness. He smells peanut oil, various spices, fruits, vegetables, meats, poultry, fish, and more dirt. Lots of dirt...

There is a sudden *whoosh* and Aki screams in pain and falls over, clenching the trigger and attempting to grab the counter. Her weapon's muzzle flashes briefly light up small areas around her, and sparks fly as the bullets rip into the ceiling, breaking tile and lightbulbs.

As this happens, a second knife zips through the dark and strikes Nesschter's shoulder. He curses and trips over himself, also setting off his shotgun.

Bullet casings roll, and Nesschter's ears snap to the patter of footsteps. His nose picks up the scent of dirt getting closer.

Nesschter fires blindly in the dark, destroying a counter and spilling ingredients on the floor. He breathes heavily, and Aki groans in a mixture of pain and anger. He can see her faint outline in the dark, hunched over and grabbing her shoulder.

"Shit, that hurt!" says Aki.

"Quiet!" snaps Nesschter.

Almost immediately after, Xajil lands next to Nesschter with a knife in hand, and he curses as the Avus brings it down. He swats the knife out of Xajil's hand with his shotgun.

When he attempts to shoot Xajil, Xajil forces the weapon down and elbows Nesschter in the jaw. The shotgun goes off, almost striking Aki, and Nesschter yelps while broken teeth scatter on the floor.

Aki scrambles up, just to fall again when Xajil throws another knife into her. Nesschter roars and brings the shotgun up again, but he is quickly disarmed and leaps away from a knife going for his neck.

Nesschter tackles Xajil, but he is easily thrown into a cabinet, breaking its door and shelves, and covering him with spices. The flood of dozens of scents makes him sneeze uncontrollably and causes his eyes to water.

His nose is blinded by all the scents, but it is made worse when he hears an aerosol can breaking. What follows is a broken scent masking can rolling towards him and Aki. The heavy scent of dirt and the moisture of the aerosol cloud rolling across the floor touches the two Lupinaks, irritating their noses and eyes, blurring their vision and dampening their sense of smell.

Aki lays next to Nesschter, whimpering and breathing heavily. Her hands tremble as she pulls the knives out, and Nesschter grabs her rifle and sharply sweeps the area.

No Xajil.

The knives that were in Aki clatter to the floor, and Nesschter passes the rifle off to her, removing the blades in him after she takes it. Each knife tugs on his flesh, and each time he seethes as they slowly come out.

A door creaks and clicks, and Nesschter's whiskers and lips twitch when he crawls on the floor to grab his shotgun. He uses it help him stand and he and Aki slowly move across the kitchen until they reach the door. After a brief pause, Aki opens the door and Nesschter peeks out, and then limps out with heavy steps, teeth bared, and a loud growl rumbling from him. His vision is blurry, but he can make out the fuzzy bodies.

Standing not too far from him is Director Xajil Ojin and Ara. Ara is still gagged, and now she is chained to a stair railing. Xajil is not too far from her. His hands are clamped in front of him, and his coat is removed.

Nesschter can only guess that Xajil has a knife in his hand and has more on his straps, due to his watery vision making everything a mess. His nose also stings and his whiskers are weighed down by the aerosol dew.

The new area is open with a line of windows that show the burning houses and the full moon. Their light reflects off the clean tile, Xajil's manic golden eyes, and Nesschter's furious gray eyes, which are now red and puffy.

Aki follows quickly behind Nesschter. Like him, she is also limping and has her rifle aimed at Xajil, and her eyes are also irritated. Her whiskers and nose are constantly twitching.

"Let her go," says Nesschter.

Xajil walks forward, and Nesschter raises his shotgun.

"Let her go, now!" yells Nesschter.

Xajil's hands snap, revealing two knives. He throws them at the Lupinaks. They dodge the knives, and when they bring their weapons up, Xajil attacks them with a vicious display of swipes, punches, and kicks.

Their weapons go off, flashing in the dark and raining bits of broken ceiling on them. During the altercation, Aki has her footing kicked out. Nesschter's shotgun is twisted out of his hand and used as a club against his side.

Nesschter yelps and slides across the floor, and Xajil dismantles the shotgun in seconds as Aki gets back up. She brings her pistol up, and Xajil grabs it and snaps her hand at a sharp angle. As she curses, he punches her in the face, and throws the pistol away after removing its ammunition.

Ara tugs and kicks at the stair's railing, loosening it ever so slightly, and Nesschter snarls and runs towards Xajil with his knife out. Xajil swiftly draws a new knife, blocks Nesschter's attack, forces it down, and slices his arm. And in a second's time, he draws a second knife, slides behind Nesschter, and stabs the back of his leg.

Nesschter screams in pain and drops, and Xajil raises his second knife, but is forced to dive away due to Aki shooting at him with her rifle. The bullets barely miss him, but they shatter his window.

Xajil rolls to a crouch and throws a knife at Aki. It strikes her, and she swears and stumbles back.

Nesschter then springs towards Xajil and rams him to the floor and delivers a few hard punches before being kicked off. Xajil quickly gets to his feet, and Nesschter brings his knife up, right as Xajil throws one at him.

This maneuver allows Nesschter to narrowly deflect Xajil's knife, but in a blink, another hits his shoulder. As he screams, another one flies into his gut. Nesschter collapses, and Aki yells and shoots at Xajil.

Xajil avoids her shots. The bullets shred the tile and shatter more windows, and he flicks a knife at Aki's leg. It pierces easily, and she screams and buckles. This gives Xajil enough time to rush her. She brings her rifle up, but Xajil slices her arm while drawing another knife, and he plunges it at an angle below her neck.

Aki's eyes widen and water, and blood pours out of her mouth and her wound. Xajil hisses as he pushes the knife in, forcing her to fall backwards and taking him with her. Her glazed eyes stare at the ceiling, and more blood bubbles out of her open mouth.

"No!" cries Nesschter.

With the knives still in him and his hazy vision blood red, Nesschter swipes his knife off the floor and charges Xajil, despite the hot, throbbing pain in his leg.

Xajil dodges Nesschter's stab and uses the momentum to throw him away.

Nesschter lands on his back with a loud thud but ignores the pain as he rolls away while yanking out one of the knives.

He sloppily throws it at Xajil, who easily deflects it, and he jumps away when Xajil goes for a kill. Xajil's knife sticks in the floor and he swipes at Nesschter with his talons.

Nesschter scrambles back and yanks out the other knife in him. He throws it, but Xajil dodges it. This moment of brief distraction allows Nesschter to go for an attack that is quickly parried, and Xajil counters by trying to stab Nesschter with his talons.

Nesschter deflects and goes for a bite. Xajil slams his hand up, whacking his jaw shut. Shock surges through Nesschter's jaw and he stumbles back, and Xajil strikes Nesschter's chest with his talons.

Nesschter falls to the floor, panting heavily with sweat and blood dribbling to the floor. Aki's blood creeps towards him, and Xajil grabs the back of his head and slams him into the floor.

The tile breaks, and Nesschter's snout crunches. Xajil hisses and digs his talons into Nesschter's head, ripping the flesh and digging against his skull. Nesschter growls and his muscles go taut as he pushes himself up on his hands and knees.

Xajil sharply jerks his head back, slams him back into the tile, and pulls him back up, with his talons gripping his throat.

Nesschter's arms are weak at this point, and he can barely see anything. His ears are plagued with a ringing and ticking, and his face stings, but through the blinding haze, he sees Ara is missing, and the stair rail she was chained to is broken.

"I fixed you," snarls Xajil. "I gave the Avus a home, I saved Aarde from its past and gave your species a future beyond savagery, but all of you are ungrateful rats!"

Xajil slams Nesschter's head into the tile again, flicking blood and broken teeth across the floor. He pulls Nesschter up again, hissing in his ear while Nesschter's bloody eye glares at him, his lips twisted in a snarl to expose the damaged teeth and crimson coating pooling and dripping past his lips.

"When I am done with you, I will raze Shio and remake it into something unbreakable. And don't worry about Ara. Once you are dead, I will fix her. I already chose her new name. Dora." Xajil grabs Nesschter's neck and tilts his head back, putting his back at a painful bend, his crest quivering and his beak open for a loud hiss. "Does that sound nice to you, Nesschter?"

Suddenly, Xajil is knocked off Nesschter by Ara's flying tackle. Xajil's talons leave scratches in Nesschter's neck. Nesschter clamps his hands around the wounds and watches the scene, heart racing and breathing raspy.

Ara and Xajil are rolling over each other like rabid animals. Ara is snarling and Xajil is clawing at her.

Ara sinks her teeth in Xajil's shoulder. Xajil squawks and stumbles, and quickly grabs a knife off the floor and stabs Ara in the side. Ara yelps, and Nesschter screams as Xajil yanks the knife out. Ara rolls to the floor and clutches her wound, whimpering, with her hands becoming slick with blood.

Xajil wobbles as he stands up, while clutching his wound. Bits of ripped flesh and broken bone dangle from his shoulder. His feathers and suit are soaked in blood, and he breathes heavily, crest and tail flicking and his manic golden eyes burning. Ara's blood drips from his knife, and he hisses and glares at her as she backs up on the floor, still holding her wound.

Xajil adjusts his grip on his knife and takes a heavy step to position himself. "I'm going to love fixing you."

Suddenly Nesschter's knife is impaled between Xajil's eye and ear, right at the temporal lobe. Xajil instantly crumbles to the floor. His body impacting the tile leads to his empty container of anti-anxiety pills and his watch to roll out, and Nesschter stands up on shaky legs, panting and clutching one of his many wounds.

Ara breathes heavily as she looks at Nesschter, and he looks at Ara's blurry form. Moonlight and firelight reflect off Xajil's blood, and Nesschter removes his pocket watch and weakly tosses it to Xajil's corpse. Then he falls to his hands and knees.

"A-Ara?" calls Nesschter.

Ara whimpers and holds out her bloody hand. Tears roll down her cheeks, and Nesschter crawls forward, collapses, then blacks out.

Ti-Tick. Tick. Tock.

Nesschter's eyes crack open. His vision is still weak and hazy, but he can make out Aki and Xajil's corpse. He is also slowly being dragged away. Ara's hands are wrapped around him, and his feet drag against the tile. His eyes close, and-

Ti-Tick. Tick. Tock.

When they open, Ara is putting him in the back of a jeep with two dead Division 4 Avus outside. She lays him flat and closes the door. He also realizes that he is wrapped in bedsheets and tape, just like Ara. His eyes drift shut and-

Ti-Tick. Tick. Tock.

A heavy rumble shakes him awake with a start. A tank rolls by them, with GSAU Avus and human soldiers holding on to its shell. A humvee is also passing them and honking, and the turret operator is waving them off frantically.

"Get off the road, you stupid cop!" shouts the Avus operating the turret.

Nesschter's eyes close once more.

Ti-Tick. Tick. Tock.

His eyes snap open from rocks and bricks hitting the Division 4 jeep, and Ara speeds up, honking and swerving, and her voice blaring through the speaker.

"Stop throwing crap at me! I stole this!" shouts Ara.

A few more bricks hit, and Nesschter winces and pulls himself up, just for Ara to suddenly jerk and throw him off the seat. His head hits the jeep's interior barrier, and everything goes dark.

Ti-Tick. Tick. Tock.

The jeep rattles and Ara mutters to herself. Winding trees arch over the road now, and Nesschter is back on the seat. He briefly wonders when he got back on, but that thought disappears and he drifts off again.

Ti-Tick. Tick. Tock.

The jeep door opens, and Nesschter's eyes crack open. He winces and props himself on his elbow, and sees Ara in the doorway, holding two thick sticks and smiling nervously.

"I know you're not in a good... healthy position, but we ran out of battery juice and need to walk," says Ara.

"Walk?" says Nesschter, his voice raspy and his lips parched.

Ara nods. "I got walking sticks! The bigger one is for you, since you'll be leaning on it more."

Ara sets the walking sticks against the jeep and helps Nesschter out of it. He grips the vehicle's frame and stumbles a bit, and Ara positions Nesschter so he is leaning against her. After he grabs his walking stick, the two begin their trek with slow, painful steps.

As they walk, Nesschter looks over his shoulder and sees the flames from Shio's skyscrapers rising into the night sky. He flinches when Ara grabs his mangled hand. He looks at her. Her eyes are glazed, her face is bloody and dirty, but she manages to smile.

"Come on, Nesschter. We're almost home," says Ara.

Nesschter swallows and nods, and every step is a sharp, painful jab in his leg. He wants to say something to Ara, but his mind is drawing up a blank. So he remains quiet, and the two walk in silence. He is almost home, and right now, being home is all he really wants.

Chapter 20

Kevin's hands grip his sink tight. His head is bowed, and his shoulders are stiff. The light above him is bright and the bathroom is spotless and stocked with the finest towels and toiletries, and yet he can't feel anything but emptiness.

Outside the bathroom is a room with soft linens, high quality pillows, comfortable chairs and couches, and a coffee table, plus a television set playing the GSAU approved morale booster videos on loop. Yet, there is no comfort out there, either.

Really, he feels more like what is beyond the walls of the political elite's airship. Cold winds with wet clouds and not enough air to breath.

"I have no guilt. Guilt holds us back. Guilt is poison," mutters Kevin. His hands tighten on the sink and his breathing becomes heavier and more erratic, and he keeps his head down. "There is no guilt. I will not have it."

Kevin tilts his head. "Why not?"

Kevin looks at the sink again. "What do you mean why not?"

He tilts his head again. "You know what I mean."

Kevin clenches his fist and brings it to his muzzle, and he tilts his head in the other direction.

"You know you messed up, don't you?" says Kevin. "You'll never see her again, even when you die, because she will be far away from a wretched rat like you. How will your son feel, knowing you let his mother die?"

"Do not guilt me. It will not work," says Kevin, looking down again. "Her death will bring us victory in the end. She's a martyr for the GSAU! Milo Gailo will understand!"

"She was the only one who saw what you were afraid to show the public, who gave you a chance, and you repaid her by letting Balik kill her."

"It was an arranged marriage."

"And yet you still loved her. Was it worth it?" Kevin looks in the mirror. Red veins have slithered in his wet eyes, the fur on his cheeks is matted with tears, and his body quivers. As his lips and whiskers twitch, he leans closer to the mirror, snarling. "Was it worth it, Kevin?"

Kevin is silent and tilts his head.

"What light Jasnee saw is gone. You're a dark void. Removing guilt has killed you, but maybe you should try bringing it back. Just a little bit. At least enough to mourn for her," says Kevin.

Kevin points at his reflection. "Don't you dare manipulate me! I will not be guilted into anything by anybody, including myself!"

Then there is a knock on the door. Kevin turns the faucet on at full blast. Hot water rushes out and splatters on the porcelain bowl as he splashes his face. The knocking returns and he exits the bathroom.

The knocking returns yet again, with a stern voice calling him, and Kevin opens the door. A colorful Iselean Lupinak guard is there, and with him is a scrawny Avus intern. No doubt fresh from college and not at all prepared for reality.

"Sir, the press conference is about to begin," says the intern.

"Cancel it," says Kevin.

"Sorry, what was that?"

"CANCEL IT!"

The intern jumps,he guard ushers the Avus away, and Kevin slams the door shut. He sighs heavily, goes to the bed, and stares at the spot Jasnee would be sleeping in if Balik hadn't executed her.

Kevin's breathing gets heavier and his fists clench. He drops to a chair and continues staring at the bed. He can hear the chatter outside but ignores the words. Eavesdropping is rude, after all.

Then his phone rings. He fishes it out of his pocket and stares at it. The number on its screen brings his heart to drop and his ears to droop. The phone keeps ringing, and he swallows and hesitantly pushes the green button. He takes a deep breath, gradually puts it to his ear, and forces himself to smile.

"Milo Gailo, what a surprise! I wasn't expecting you to call," says Kevin.

"*How's your wife?*" asks Milo Gailo; his voice being cold and hard like a stone in ice.

Kevin's heart stops. "She's... uh..."

"*She's dead.*"

Kevin swallows. "Yeah..."

"*And Shio is burning.*"

"We are getting it back under control."

"*Do you know how Balik Norkit got Federation weapons?*"

"I don't..."

"*Outpost Orange Glow gave them weapons and munitions in exchange for N-Light. I have a friend that will take care of that problem since you and Xajil ignored Outpost Orange Glow's relationship with the Revivalists.*"

"Oh... That's... Sir-" Kevin trembles and his eyes glaze over. "Sir, that was a delicate situation. A wrong move would be disaster for relations between Aarde and the Federation of Sol Systems."

"*I will deal with you when you land in Iselae City. And I would deal with Xajil Ojin, but he is dead. A fitting punishment for his failures.*"

Kevin's blood runs cold and sweat rolls down his head.

"We don't need to waste your precious time," says Kevin. "The military has moved in. We are retaking Shio. We **will** retake Shio very soon. But also... Also, we don't know if Xajil Ojin is dead. That's- That could be-"

"*I'm looking at his corpse right now. Just like I am looking at you right now,*" says Milo.

Kevin's eyes snap up and dart around the room, and then lock on the TV.

"*That's right. I see you,*" growls Milo Gailo. "*I have always seen you. I have always heard you. Even when you thought you were alone, I was there.*"

Kevin bites his hand, drawing blood and breathing erratically through his nose as he rocks back and forth.

"*I see and hear everything in every Connected City,*" continues Milo Gailo. "*Those cities are mine. Aarde is mine. And since you so boldly claimed that Shio's story is Aarde's story, that puts more value on it than what was necessary. If the Revivalists successfully hold Shio, then it will threaten the GSAU, which would not*" *have happened if you remembered your place. You had no right to give Shio such great value. The only reason you are not dead now is because you are the Alpha of Iselae. But if Shio is not retaken in a timely manner, then you will understand how weak you truly are. And unlike you, I will not regret my choices later."*

"O-Of course... I'll get it done," says Kevin.

"I'll see you very soon."

Click.

As soon as Milo Gailo hangs up, the light in the cabin turns off, leaving the soft glow of the TV to shine on Kevin's stiff posture. Kevin's hand drops seconds later, and the phone falls to the floor.

He stays still for another few seconds before he slowly goes to Jasnee's side of the bed. He falls on it, buries his face in the pillow, and whimpers alone in the dark.

Chapter 21

Colonel Barzee sits alone in a dim room. His eyes are focused on the monitor in front of him. On the monitor are three screens. The first is the largest, and it has aerial footage of Shio in flames, with convoys of military vehicles moving through the streets. The other two are of equal size and stacked on top of each other.

The first has a human in a dark purple uniform, with gold bands and crossing swords behind a planet pinned on his collar. The human is bald, has thick black glasses, and pale scaly skin, with tints of green on his cheeks and around his eyes. He is Systems General Draco Knight. Behind him is the Federation of Sol Systems flag: the gold Sculptor constellation nested in a green wreath on a blue background

The screen below him has a dark silhouette of a Lupinak with large ears. There are no features that can be seen, and his wall is blank. The screen has him labeled as Aarde President Milo Gailo.

"*You do realize that reports are showing the Revivalists using **our** weapons and **our** shield generators,*" says Draco.

"I have heard the reports, yes. Yes sir," says Barzee. He's hoping they aren't hearing his thumping heart or seeing the salty sweat trickling down his face.

"*How did they get those?*"

"My men are doing an audit and we're checking cameras as we speak. We will get to the bottom of this."

"*An audit of yourself? How quaint. Have you found yourself innocent yet?*"

Barzee swallows. "We've just started, sir. And we have no proof that the

Revivalists are using **our** equipment. There are other outposts in Gacerae that they could have used. Or they may have shipped them in from a farther location. We shouldn't be jumping to conclusions on where the Revivalists got those items from until we do a thorough investigation."

"I see... Milo, before you speak, I want to offer my sincerest apologies for the absolute lack of professionalism from Outpost Orange Glow. I will be more than happy to go down there personally to coordinate a response with you to resolve the Revivalist problem in Gacerae," says Draco.

"Apology accepted," says Milo flatly.

"Do you have any thoughts on this Shio matter, Mr. President?"

Milo exhales slowly through his nose, and speaks formally, as if in a business meeting. *"I recently talked to Regional Chairman Kevin Asven. He is working on retaking Shio. But this lack of coordination between Outpost Orange Glow and Shio and other governing bodies of Aarde has led to a breakdown in communications, including a blockade into the Syrikel Forest, which is a Revivalist stronghold."*

"That was–" starts Barzee.

"I'm talking," growls Milo.

Barzee falls silent, and Milo continues, his voice returning to its prim, proper business tone.

"The blockade restricted the capacity of Division 4 to carry out needed operations, which in turn led to the Revivalists being able to carry out their invasion on Shio. A change in leadership is needed at Outpost Orange Glow, and I will need to speak with Section 0 Command and the Federation President personally, so we can coordinate a counterattack against the Revivalists.

"Shio has been deemed an analogy of Aarde. So, if Shio falls, then Aarde will face another global war, and all the development of the Lyos System will collapse. It is in the Federation's best financial interests to make sure that does not happen."

Barzee grips the desk to hide his trembles.

"Now wait a minute. You have no right to demand my removal!" says Barzee, his voice quivering slightly.

"Be quiet, Barzee. We'll talk personally, very soon," says Draco.

"I want to speak with you personally, as well, General," says Milo.

"I figured. I'll be in the Lyos System in three days."

"I'll have a warm welcome waiting for you."

"Excellent! As for you, Colonel. Meeting's over. Get out and eat a cow or something. We wouldn't want you starving to death."

Then the screen flashes off, and the room's lights brighten.

Barzee slumps in his chair and rubs his sweaty face. Then his hands drop, and he stares at his reflection on the black screen for a moment before he gets up. His legs can barely hold him up and his steps are wobbly towards the door. He grips the doorknob, takes a deep breath, and opens the door, taking him to his dorm.

"Hanson. De Jong. We've got a lot of work to do," says Barzee as he passes the living room where his trusted associates are.

Barzee goes to his bedroom, removes his jacket, hangs it up neatly, and then goes to his living room.

"Get your closest associates and–"

Barzee freezes and his eyes widen.

Hanson and De Jong are laying in pools of fresh blood, with multiple bullet wounds in their chests and heads.

Barzee gasps and stumbles back. He fumbles for his pistol, but before he can draw it, a hand grabs his wrist, a gun barrel is pressed against his head, and everything goes dark.

* * *

Standing in the living room is a man in an all-black mask and dark suit with dark purple bands running the length of his limbs, collar, shoulders and spine. The lines connect to circles on his gloves, boots, and shoulders, and on his shoulder are little cylinders attached to his suit, plus a wrist-top computer.

The masked man stares at the three bodies, and Barzee's fresh blood trickles down the wall and spreads across the floor. After a few seconds of silence, he puts four more shots in Barzee's back, where the heart is. Then he uses a magnet to collect the bullet casings and he puts them in a sealed pouch on his belt.

He steps away from the bodies and types a command on his wrist-top computer. The bands on his suit glow for a few seconds before he fades from view. It will take a little bit of observation to see a slight disturbance in the atmosphere as the stranger walks out of the room.

"This is Wraith. Targets are down. Deactivate camera loops in five minutes," says the masked man.

"*Roger that,*" says a voice over the radio.

Wraith enters the hallway and walks with light steps so not to draw attention, and he waits by an entrance with automatic doors. When the door opens due to a pair of soldiers entering, he slips by them and goes outside. The dark sky is pierced by Orange Glow's numerous lights, and Wraith keeps a steady walk, even as soldiers and vehicles pass his invisible form.

"*This is Observation Team Saturn. Extraction zone is secured.*"

"*This is Observation Team Mercury. Shio is a mess, and Xajil Ojin and Balik Hebediah Norkit are confirmed dead. What are your orders?*"

"Return to orbit. We'll go over the information shipside and move from there. Over and out," says Wraith.

Wraith disconnects and climbs the wall using little hooks on his fingers, like a spider. When he hops the wall, he strolls through the forest, perfectly content with the way things turned out.

Sure, Shio is destroyed, and Xajil Ojin is dead, but so are the traitors, and soon Barzee's network of drug runners and schemers will face similar fates.

Chapter 22

3 Days Later...

Ti-Tick. Ti-Tock.

  Ti-Tick. Ti-Tock.

  Ti-Tick. Ti-Tock.

Nesschter Hebediah Norkit's ears twitch. The ticking is weak, barely a noise, but it is just loud enough to where he can hear it. It is mostly covered by the water drifting back and forth on the sand. Nearby birds chirp, and a soft breeze shakes the branches of the winding trees.

Nesschter's hands have small tremors, and he still hasn't been able to smell things well since the fight with Xajil. His mangled hand is pressed against his chest, and his other hand is tightly gripping the walking stick Ara gave him after they escaped Shio.

His face, head, and neck are covered with large scratches that meet up to his torn ear. His gray eyes see the lake and trees, the slowly dipping sun, and the orange hue that it is giving the clouds, but he barely registers them. His eyes are distant and weighed down with black bags, stained with crusted gunk and tainted with red. His legs have a hard time keeping him up. His whole body sways between throbbing pain, tingly numbness, and weak threads barely holding together.

The fingers on Nesschter's mauled hand twitch in tune to the broken ticking in his ears, but since his watch is no longer with him, he has nothing to look at. His mind wanders. The ticking turns to gunshots and screaming.

The stabbing, the burning pain, the teeth sinking into him, the blades tearing his flesh. He closes his eyes, his lips and eyelids twitch. There is darkness, but he still hears it all. Feels it all.

"Nesschter?" calls Ara.

Nesschter remains silent. His eyes remain closed, and his ears and whiskers twitch.

"Nesschter?" repeats Ara, closer this time.

Every scab and bruise pulses. His breathing is sharp and erratic, and his claws dig into his walking stick.

"Nesschter?" says Ara again, softer and right next to him.

She gently puts a hand on Nesschter's shoulder and his eyes snap open, glazed and unfocused. He sees Ara standing next to him. Her scratches all over her neck, face, and arms are fading, but she is smiling gently. She slinks her arms around his and gently leads him to her cabin, which is still a mess of patchwork and some graffiti, plus a couple of broken windows.

Ara tightens her grip on Nesschter as they walk up the path. Nesschter sees Khal and Fargo. Side to side, Nesschter can tell that Fargo is Khal's son. He is a spitting image of him, but now his cheek and neck are stitched, and he has a black eyepatch.

There are other Lupinaks with Khal and Fargo, and they are younger than Fargo and have similar shades to Khal. All of them are armed. By the road, Nesschter sees Mason and a few humans standing guard by armored vehicles.

Ara helps Nesschter up the stairs, and when they reach the guests, Khal and Nesschter stare at each other in silence.

"Do you remember me?" asks Khal several seconds later.

Nesschter wags his hand side to side.

"I am Khal Mason Jarim. I am the patriarch of the new Alpha Family of the Gacerae Pack. I am also your older cousin." Khal points at Mason. "And you met my associate at the Division 4 Headquarters. His name is also Mason, funny enough."

Nesschter looks at Mason, and Mason waves. Nesschter returns the wave with two fingers using his mangled hand.

"You also saved my son," says Khal. He lovingly squeezes Fargo's shoulder. "You have my gratitude for that."

Nesschter nods, and Khal points to the kitchen door.

"Let's talk inside," he says.

Ara helps Nesschter walk, and when they enter the kitchen, he eases himself into a chair, which has a bowl of peanuts positioned in front of it. Ara sits next to him while Khal sits across from them with his guards standing behind them.

"We know what you did, Nesschter," says Khal heavily. "We know you helped the AAHU and Federation destroy the Vagsten Tunnels. We know you worked for Division 4 and fought against us for a long time."

Nesschter's jaw and grip on the walking stick tighten, and Ara's ears droop. But while her eyes get misty, Nesschter's remain focused, despite them having difficulty doing so. It makes him a bit nauseous.

"The patriarchs want you executed for treason, despite Balik's orders," continues Khal.

"Are you serious?" says Ara, her hand clutching Nesschter's mangled hand. "Do you know what they did to him?"

"I do. And, as a reminder, Balik also wanted Nesschter spared. It is for those two reasons that I vetoed their wish," says Khal. "Nesschter also saved my son, so I owe him a lot. Fargo owes him a lot."

"A life debt," says Fargo.

Nesschter's eyes briefly flick to Fargo's before looking back at Khal.

"I know Xajil Ojin tortured you," says Khal.

Nesschter's throat tightens, and his eyes burn as they most over, but he stays quiet.

"I also know Xajil Ojin did things to your mind, and I also know that you killed him," says Khal. "We can't change the past, but you gave Fargo a chance at a future, and with you killing Xajil Ojin, you helped us in a very important way. But... You still betrayed us in the past. You still killed Balik, you still helped the GSAU and AAHU. So, while I'm not going to have you executed, you must pay for your crimes that made the GSAU's presence in Gacerae possible."

Nesschter's heart thumps loudly, despite his glare showing defiance, and his lips tremble slightly. Khal, meanwhile, keeps a stern expression.

"I will have to disown you," says Khal. "You won't have Hebediah or Norkit to your name, and you can't work for us. You will be just Nesschter and will have to find other means of survival in our territory."

"What!?" Ara slams her hands on the table and leaps up, ears flat and fangs bared. "How can you do that to him! You know what he's been through! You know what they did to get that information out of him and how they tricked him into working for them! You know what those monsters did and you're still doing this to him! What is wrong with you!?"

"Ara, it's okay," says Nesschter wearily. He grabs her wrist and gently tugs her down. "Have a seat."

Ara sits and glares at Khal, and Khal stares at the two with his hands folded on the table.

"He may have done the right thing by killing Xajil Ojin and saving Fargo, but he still killed Balik and served as a Division 4 Agent," says Khal. "I cannot just ignore that. Brainwashing or not. If I give him immunity, then I will have a revolt. The Gacerae Pack will be in a civil war, and it will be easier for the GSAU to retaliate against us for what Balik did to Shio. Gacerae is my responsibility, and I won't make it an easy target. That said..."

Khal waves Fargo over.

"Fargo, over here please," says Khal.

Fargo steps forward, and Khal looks at Nesschter and Ara.

"Despite what has happened, Fargo still has something to say to you," says Khal.

"As I said earlier, I owe you a life debt," says Fargo. "You may be disowned, but without you, I would not have survived the injury, so I pledge you my life. I will protect you until my final breath. This I swear with all these witnesses."

Nesschter nods stiffly. "Okay... Thank you."

Fargo returns the nod, and Khal stands up and hugs Fargo. Then the other Lupinaks exchange hugs and handshakes with him. When they are done, Khal goes to Nesschter's side and extends his hand. Nesschter hesitantly takes it, and he is gently pulled to his feet. Khal shakes his mangled hand and pats his arm.

"I can never thank you enough for saving my son, but unfortunately things have to be this way, for the good of the Gacerae Pack," says Kahl.

"I understand," says Nesschter.

Khal nods. "Good." He looks at Fargo. "Take care, son. And keep him alive."

"Will do, Father," says Fargo.

Then Khal and his escorts leave the cabin, and Nesschter, Ara, and Fargo watch the group go to the convoy parked up front. Khal and Mason exchange a few words, before everyone gets in their respective vehicles, and then the convoy drives away, leaving the cabin in peace.

Nesschter stares out the window in silence, and Ara grabs his hand.

"Come on, let's go back outside," says Ara.

Ara escorts Nesschter to the lake. Every step is a pinch of pain, and every step is a battle to keep the pressure in his throat from exploding.

Their walk may be a short distance, but it feels like a crawl through time for Nesschter. When the three reach the sandy banks of the lake and the hand-carved benches, Ara sits down, and Fargo goes off to the side to watch them at a better angle.

Nesschter doesn't sit, though. He remains standing with his stick and stares at nothing. Everyone is silent for a couple of minutes, until...

"Nesschter...?" calls Ara.

Nesschter looks at Ara, then at the lake, and then he looks at Ara again and hobbles next to her. She holds out her hand, and he gently takes it and winces as he eases onto the bench. He grips his walking stick tight as he lowers himself, his legs quivering from painful weakness.

After he sits down, he exhales with relief and tries to relax. The cool breeze blows against them, and the light of the setting sun reflects off the lake's ripples. Ara rests her head on Nesschter's shoulder and grabs his disfigured hand.

Several seconds later, Nesschter releases his walking stick and puts his good hand on top of Ara's hand and watches the reflecting light and the winding trees of Syrikel Forest.

"Will you stay?" asks Ara.

Despite the weight of everything crushing him, he still manages a small smile, and he pats Ara's hand.

"Yeah... I'll stay," says Nesschter.